A MOST NOVEL REVENGE

ASHLEY WEAVER

Allison & Busby Limited
12 Fitzroy Mews
London W1T 6DW
allisonandbusby.com

First published in Great Britain by Allison & Busby in 2016.
This paperback edition published by Allison & Busby in 2017.
Published by arrangement with St Martin's Press.

A CIP catalogue record for this book is available from
the British Library.

10 9 8 7 6 5 4 3 2 1

ISBN 978-0-7490-2089-7

Typeset in 10.5/15.5 pt Sabon by
Allison & Busby Ltd.

The paper used for this Allison & Busby publication
has been produced from trees that have been legally sourced
from well-managed and credibly certified forests.

Printed and bound by
CPI Group (UK) Ltd, Croydon, CR0 4YY

For Allison Dodson,
my cousin, best friend, and reader from the beginning

CHAPTER ONE

England
February 1933

'Well, darling, who do you suppose will turn up dead this time?'

This sudden and wildly inappropriate question had come from my husband, who didn't bother to take his eyes from the winding, snow-lined road as we drove along, the bright afternoon sunlight glinting off the drifts that lined it on either side.

'Milo! What a dreadful thing to say.'

He was, as usual, unapologetic. 'You must admit that people have had a habit of turning up dead in your company this past year.'

He had a point, though I didn't like to admit it. Over the course of the last several months, I had been involved in two murder investigations, both of which had ended with my confronting killers at gunpoint.

What was more, I was not altogether certain that our current jaunt to the country would prove entirely without incident. The way this trip had begun, I was worried there might indeed be more trouble.

The entire thing had started two days ago upon receipt of the morning post. I had recognised the violet envelope and scrawling penmanship at once. A letter from my cousin Laurel.

I sliced open the envelope to find a hastily penned note, the contents of which had been overtly mysterious.

I didn't want to send a wire, as that might call unwanted attention, but consider this just as urgent a summons. You must come to Lyonsgate at once. I won't tell you why. Perhaps that will entice you.

Below this she had scribbled in a more hasty hand:

Don't let my flippancy persuade you that I am not in earnest. You must come immediately.
Laurel
P.S. Bring Milo if you must.

The letter, in and of itself, was not especially unusual. Laurel had a flair for the dramatic, a trait which often manifested itself in her correspondence. This time, however, it was what the letter didn't say that intrigued me. I could think of no conceivable reason why she should have chosen to set foot at Lyonsgate again. Not after what had happened there.

Seven years before, while Laurel was staying as a guest, the manor had been the scene of a tragic accident, the result of a weekend of revelry gone awry. It had caused a scandal that had reverberated throughout the country and had affected my cousin deeply.

Suffice it to say, the letter had served its purpose. And that was how we had come to be driving towards Shropshire at reckless speeds in Milo's new Aston Martin Le Mans. The sleek, black automobile had been his Christmas gift to himself, and he had insisted on driving us to the country. Markham, our driver, had been, I think, a bit put out by this development, as he was anxiously awaiting his time at the wheel. Markham needn't have worried, however, for I was quite sure that the novelty of Milo driving himself would quickly wear off.

Luckily, he was still enamoured enough of his vehicle that the allure of long stretches of open road had enticed him into agreeing to the journey. He, initially, had not been at all keen on going to Lyonsgate. His idea had been to winter in Italy, and I was certain this weekend would prove a poor substitute, on several levels.

'I really haven't the faintest idea why I agreed to come along,' Milo said, as though following my train of thought. 'I've no desire to spend the week at a draughty house in the middle of nowhere with a lot of tiresome people.'

My husband was not much of one to spend a quiet weekend in the country. He was, in fact, rather known for his extensive social forays, a trait which had contributed to the near ruin of our marriage only last year. We had come to terms, however, and I had waited with bated breath to see if his reformation would take. Thus far I had not been disappointed.

'I'm sure we shall be back in London before the week is out,' I assured him. 'There's no reason to suppose that there is actually anything amiss. You know how Laurel is.'

'Yes,' he said flatly. 'What I don't know is why you insist on indulging her.'

Laurel's less than enthusiastic invitation to Milo in her letter's postscript was, on the whole, indicative of the relationship between my cousin and my husband. Milo and Laurel had never been exceptionally fond of one another, though they normally did their best to be civil with varying results.

'You must admit it is curious,' I said. 'What on earth could have induced her to go back to Lyonsgate?'

'It's been, what, six years now? I'm certain the horror has worn off.'

'Seven years. From the way she spoke about it at the time, I was sure she'd never even set foot in Shropshire again.'

'If she doesn't want to be there, I'm not sure why we should. Do you even know Reginald Lyons?'

'No.' While I didn't know the man who would be our host, I certainly knew *of* him. In fact, most of the country knew the name of Lyons, mainly because of what had taken place at their country home, Lyonsgate, during that fateful weekend in 1925.

It was only by happenstance that Laurel had been there. She had never run with a wild set, but she had been friends with Reggie Lyons and his sister Beatrice since they were quite young. Their father and his young wife had both succumbed to influenza while he was still in France, and Reggie had inherited the estate and the care of his sisters upon his return. I think it had been something of an adventure for my cousin to be invited to attend a weekend at Lyonsgate, which had become the unofficial headquarters of one of England's premier young social groups after Reggie had fallen in with a woman called Isobel Van Allen.

The undisputed leader of her clique, Isobel Van Allen had been something of a legend in her own time. Of humble and mysterious beginnings, she had propelled herself into fashionable society with a winning combination of startling beauty, sharp wit, and a will of iron. By the time she had come into Reggie Lyons' life she had been several years older than the others in their set, with a worldly allure none of them could resist.

She had a great many wild friends, and when Reggie Lyons had become her lover, she had introduced him to them. His estate, Lyonsgate, had begun to host fabulous parties, the details of which made their way into the gossip columns. There had been photographs of outlandish-themed revels, and rumours of drugs and other illicit conduct had surfaced. They were not, of course, the only group of well-off young people drawn into a spiral of reckless hedonism in the years following the Great War, but the tragedy at Lyonsgate had made them one of the more infamous.

The days leading up to that particular event had no doubt seemed to indicate it would be a weekend like any other, but by the time the weekend was over, a young man was dead and the lives of the others had never been the same.

Milo took the next turn entirely too quickly, bringing my attention back to the present.

'I'd rather not end up in the ditch, if it's all the same to you,' I said lightly.

'Of course not. I wouldn't put the car in jeopardy.'

'That's comforting.'

He shot a smile at me. 'Or you either, darling.'

'There must be some reason why Laurel has asked me to come so urgently,' I said, still preoccupied. 'I think it might have something to do with Edwin Green's death.'

Accounts varied of what had actually occurred that night at Lyonsgate. What was never contested was the fact that on a cold, dark morning after an evening of drunken revels, Edwin Green's body had been found, nearly naked, on the frozen ground halfway between the summer house and the manor.

The inquest had declared it heart failure brought on by hypothermia and a combination of extreme inebriation and a deadly cocktail of drugs, the remnants of which had been found scattered about the summer house.

It might always have been seen as an unfortunate accident, the tragic consequences of a life lived too recklessly, had it not been for Isobel Van Allen. While the others had done their best to keep things quiet, she had spoken frequently with the press, alluding to the fact that there was more to the tragedy than met the eye.

She had always had an affinity for sensationalism and a gift for words, and she used them to her advantage. Six months after Edwin Green's death, she had released a novel called *The Dead of Winter*. It had been touted as nothing more than fiction, but everyone knew the truth, that it was the account of what had happened at Lyonsgate.

Everyone who had been there had been drawn quite clearly, with different names, of course, all their vices and secrets brought to life in colourful prose.

It wasn't so much the way the book had been done that caused the fuss. What had caused the scandal was that she had insinuated that Edwin Green's death had not been an accidental overdose and hypothermia as the coroner's inquest had ruled. Instead, she claimed it had been murder on the part of a young man called Bradford Glenn, who had been Edwin Green's rival for the affections of Beatrice Lyons. Bradford had, the book alleged, taken advantage of Edwin Green's condition and purposefully dragged him into the cold to die.

No legal measures had ever been taken, of course. There was no proof. But Mr Glenn had been ruined, nonetheless, and had disappeared from society.

As for Isobel Van Allen, her book had had the opposite effect to what she had intended. Though she had made a great deal of money, she had been ostracised and snubbed at every turn by those who enjoyed the book in private but shunned it publicly as nothing more than vulgar exploitation. Eventually she had gone off to Kenya. That was the last I had heard of her.

Reggie Lyons had shut up Lyonsgate and had gone to live abroad, Beatrice Lyons had married shortly afterwards, and the youngest Lyons sister had been sent off to boarding school.

Laurel had been greatly troubled by it all, but eventually

the matter had gone to the back of all our minds. It was not something one much cared to remember.

So what was it that had brought the Lyonses back to Lyonsgate? And why had Laurel gone there? Why the urgent summons? I wanted to believe that it was nothing more than my cousin's overactive imagination, but my instincts told me there was something more to it than that.

'It will certainly be interesting to view the scene of such a scandal,' I remarked.

'I thought we disliked scandals,' he said.

Milo and I had had more than our share of scandals in the past. Though he had been behaving beautifully as of late, more than a few indiscretions had been linked to his name since our marriage.

'We dislike personal scandals,' I corrected. 'But the death of Edwin Green has no direct bearing on us.'

'As of yet.'

He was, as it turns out, correct. I dislike it intensely when he is right.

It was early afternoon when we reached Lyonsgate. The entrance to the estate came almost without warning, a gate appearing suddenly to break up the wall of trees that lined the road. Milo screeched nearly to a stop and pulled into the drive. I breathed a sigh of relief that we had reached our destination in one piece. This car moved entirely too quickly for my comfort.

Before us the wrought-iron gate was guarded by two huge stone lions on massive pillars, their mouths open, teeth bared, in what might have been either half-hearted roars or aggressive yawns.

'A bit obvious, perhaps, but I suppose impressive enough,' Milo noted.

I had to agree with him. At least, it must have been impressive one time. Now, with dead vines creeping up the rails as though to strangle the weary-looking beasts, it seemed a bit sad somehow. I knew that the Lyons family had not been in residence for many years, but it looked as though upkeep of the estate had not been a priority in their absence.

The gates were open wide to reveal a long drive. We pulled through and, once out of the little copse of trees, we had the first glimpse of the house. The afternoon sun shone brightly on walls of pale stone. It was impressive, beautiful in a sombre way, yet there was something haunting about it as well. Perhaps it was my imagination, knowing what I did about the history of the house, but it seemed to me that there was something forlorn in its appearance.

To the east, in the direction of the village, I could make out the lake and a distant building that was no doubt the summer house where Edwin Green had spent his last night. It looked quiet and peaceful in the light of a bright winter afternoon.

We pulled up before the house, and Milo came around to open my door. I stepped out of the car onto the gravel drive, looking up at the imposing stone facade. It was not what one would call a welcoming building. It was in the Tudor style and, if I remembered my history of English manors correctly, the main part of the house dated back to that period, with additional wings having been added by subsequent generations.

The house had clearly been neglected, and, though work had recently been done to refurbish it, an air of desertion still hung about the place. The stones were stained and scarred, at least what was visible of them beneath the tangled profusion of dried ivy. The oriel windows on the lower floors had been cleaned and gleamed brightly in the sunlight, but the higher windows were streaked with dirt and grime.

A cold gust of wind blew just then, and I felt what might be termed a foreboding chill.

I heard the sound of approaching steps behind us, and we turned to see a woman coming around the house, leading a horse. She was a pretty girl with honey-coloured hair glinting in the afternoon sunlight. She was young, perhaps twenty-two or -three, and I guessed that she must be the younger Lyons sister.

The sun was in her eyes for a moment, but when she stepped into the shadow of the building she caught sight of us and walked in our direction.

'I thought I heard a car,' she said. As her eyes adjusted from the glare she caught sight of Milo and stopped, a flush spreading over her cheeks. 'Oh. Hello.'

She looked up at him, dazzled. I had to admit that I sometimes forgot how very handsome Milo was until I observed other women's reactions to meeting him. With his black hair, bright blue eyes, and striking good looks, he always managed to create quite a favourable first impression. All this was supplemented with a winning

16

manner and excessive charm, which made my husband exceptionally popular with the ladies.

'Hello,' Milo replied. I was gratified that he seemed more interested in the horse than the pretty young woman leading it.

'I'm Lucinda Lyons,' the young woman said. 'Lindy, to my friends.' She smiled as she said it and, if I was not mistaken, batted her lashes.

'How do you do, Miss Lyons. I'm Milo Ames, and this is my wife, Amory.'

She looked at me for almost the first time, as though she had only just noticed that I was there.

'How do you do,' I said, amused. It was not the first time Milo had absorbed all the female attention in the general vicinity.

'You're Laurel's cousin, aren't you?' she said, recovering nicely. 'I've heard so much about you. I'm very pleased to meet you at last.'

'And I you. It was kind of your brother to invite us. The house is lovely,' I said, looking behind me.

'I don't like it at all,' she said without any particular emotion.

Her horse shifted its feet impatiently and she turned to speak soothingly to him. 'There, there, Romeo. You mustn't misbehave in front of our guests.'

'It's a beautiful animal,' Milo said, stepping forward to touch the shining chestnut coat. Milo loved horses. I suspected that part of the reason he had agreed to come, other than the opportunity to frighten me to death with hairpin turns, was that he had thought Reginald Lyons would have begun building up the stables at Lyonsgate now that he had returned. Milo liked to be sure that his horses were better than everyone else's.

'Oh, here's Henson,' Miss Lyons said as the door opened and the butler stepped out onto the portico. 'Mr and Mrs Ames have arrived, Henson,' she called.

'Very good, Miss Lucinda.'

She turned back to us. 'He'll see to you. I'll just bring Romeo back to the stables. Lovely meeting both of you.'

Her eyes were still on Milo as she said this, and it seemed that she had to tear them from his face to begin leading her horse away.

'A charming young woman,' Milo observed as we walked towards the house.

'I expect you say so because she was properly dazzled by you.'

'She's practically a child.'

'"Practically a child" and "a child" are two very different things,' I replied dryly.

Henson led us into the house, and a moment later Reginald Lyons came into the entrance hall to greet us. He was not quite what I had expected, not how I remembered Laurel describing him. He had a handsome, ruddy face and was quite tall and a bit heavyset. He looked the part of a country squire in his tweeds and hunting boots.

I didn't see much resemblance to his sister, and I judged him to be perhaps ten or twelve years older than she was. If I remembered correctly, Lucinda had a different mother than Reggie and Beatrice. Reggie had the same honey-coloured hair as his half-sister, but his eyes were dark brown rather than blue, and there was something troubled about them, a weariness that belied his robust facade.

'Mr and Mrs Ames. Welcome to Lyonsgate,' he said in a hearty tone.

'Thank you for having us, Mr Lyons. The house is lovely.'

'Thank you, thank you. I expect you'll be looking for Laurel, but she's out riding at the moment. Should be back soon enough.'

'Your sister Lucinda just came back from her ride,' I told him. 'She's a charming young woman.'

'I was admiring her horse,' Milo said. 'It's an excellent animal.'

Something flickered across Mr Lyons' face, and then he nodded. 'Thank you. I do enjoy horses. I'll give you a tour of the stables later, if you like.'

'I should like it very much indeed.'

'I suppose first you'd like to be shown to your rooms . . .'

Before he could finish his sentence, there was movement on the staircase behind him.

A tall, dark, and very beautiful woman descended them to meet us in the entrance hall. I had never met her before, but I recognised her well enough.

It was Isobel Van Allen.

CHAPTER TWO

I was very surprised to see her standing there, especially after the events we had been discussing only this morning. What she was doing here rather than in the wilds of Kenya, I couldn't imagine.

She didn't look any older than I remembered her being in all the society photographs, except for perhaps a bit of tightness around her eyes. She was still a stunningly beautiful woman, poised and almost regal, her flawless skin apparently untouched by the scorching rays of the African sun. She was nearly as tall as Milo in her heeled shoes, and her slim figure looked as though it had been designed for the French fashions she wore. The scent of her expensive perfume hovered in the air around her as she came towards us.

'Mrs Ames, isn't it? How good of you to come.'

It was, I thought, something of an odd thing for a woman who was not our hostess to say, but perhaps she was acting as hostess. After all, she and Reggie Lyons had been lovers at one time. It had been my understanding that things had ended badly between them after the incident, but it would not be the first time a shattered romance had been rekindled. I didn't have much time to process this thought, however, before she moved to stand before my husband.

Her gaze moved over Milo in an appraising way. 'Hello, Milo,' she said with a slow smile. 'I would say you haven't changed a bit, but that would be untrue. You're even more handsome than I remembered. Your age suits you. I find very few men more handsome at thirty than they were at twenty.'

She held out her hand and Milo took it, her fingers, tipped with blood-red nails, curling around his.

'Hello, Isobel. It's been a long time.'

Milo showed no sign of uneasiness, but he never did. I had been unaware that they had known one another. My husband was full of delightful surprises.

She smiled. 'Yes. Nine or ten years, at least. Funny how life brings people back around to you again, isn't it? I shall look forward to getting reacquainted.'

I wondered what exactly their past relationship had been. Both of them being exceptionally good-looking people, I had a fair idea. Milo would have been in his early twenties when they knew each other and Miss Van Allen perhaps thirty-five, but the rumour was that she had always preferred younger men. Reggie Lyons was, himself, at least ten years younger than she.

'And I'm delighted to get to know your charming wife.' She turned her attention to me then, her dark eyes sweeping over me in an assessing, yet not unfriendly manner.

'I'm so pleased to meet you, Mrs Ames,' she said.

'And I you,' I replied, not really meaning a word of it.

'You've married a beauty,' she said to Milo, her eyes still on me. 'Of course, it was only natural that you would.'

'Perhaps Mr and Mrs Ames would like to see their rooms,' Reginald Lyons said stiffly.

There was something odd about his interactions with Miss Van Allen, some strange sort of tension between them. It wasn't just that he seemed uncomfortable with her rather forward remarks. Nor was it jealousy. In fact, it seemed clear to me in that moment that there had not been any rekindling of their romance. It was fairly obvious that he disliked her intensely but was doing his best to hide it. Why, then, had he invited her to Lyonsgate? It was very curious indeed.

Milo and I were shown to our adjoining rooms by a maid, and we did not have a private moment to speak about the encounter with Isobel Van Allen.

I walked into my bedroom, and my maid, Winnelda, who had gone ahead early that morning with the luggage, turned from where she was hanging my dresses in the wardrobe. She smiled brightly when she saw me and came to help me off with my coat.

'Oh, hello, madam. I'm ever so glad you've arrived. This house is a bit frightening, isn't it? I feel as though I might be trapped in some sort of fairy castle, with ogres and things lurking about. I didn't much like to be alone here, without anyone I know.'

It would have been a fitting setting for Winnelda, as she reminded me of a fairy, pale and petite, with wide eyes and platinum hair. In truth, her actions reminded me a bit of a woodland sprite, the way she flittered from one thing to another. She had become my de facto lady's maid, and I had grown quite fond of her, in spite of her flightiness.

'It's a charming house, though, isn't it?' I said.

'It's old,' she replied disparagingly, wrinkling her nose. That was one way of describing the grand Tudor architecture, I supposed. Winnelda had become accustomed to the modern conveniences of our London flat, and I very much feared she was becoming a snob.

I took off my hat and gloves and looked around. The room was large and very cold, despite the fire burning in the fireplace. I thought I could even detect the whistle of the wind through the casements. The tapestries on the panelled wall were intricate and lovely, but they were not keeping much warmth in the bedroom. However, it was not the first draughty country house I had stayed in, and it would probably not be the last.

The furnishings were high-quality antiques that had seen better days. The bed was an enormous thing with intricately carved posts the size of tree trunks. It looked as though it might have dated back to the Tudors as well. The bedding, however, was modern, as was the thick rug on the floor. It seemed the Lyonses had done whatever they could to add a bit of warmth to the room.

Nevertheless, there remained something of the impression that the dust covers had been whisked away moments before our arrival. I wondered again what had brought them back to Lyonsgate. If the family had only returned here recently, I thought it strange that they should have wanted guests before the house had been properly prepared. In fact, I somehow felt that Mr Lyons did not want company at all. He had been cordial in the way of a man who is accustomed to behaving properly, but his enthusiasm had been artificial. This certainly wasn't an ordinary country weekend.

Laurel had wanted me to come for reasons that remained to be seen, and Mr Lyons had no doubt politely acquiesced to her suggestion. If we were not exactly welcome here, I wondered even more why Isobel Van Allen had been invited. After all that had happened, I thought it somewhat strange that she should be welcomed back with open arms to the scene of a tragedy she had attempted to exploit for her own personal gain.

'. . . ghosts creeping down the halls in long, trailing gowns. But I don't know if they wore trailing gowns, did they?'

I came back to the present to find Winnelda watching me expectantly.

'I'm not certain about the trains, Winnelda, but I don't think you need worry much about ghosts.'

'No, I suppose there are a good many strange people here already. I think it would be a shame to have ghosts as well.'

I was about to respond to this curious comment when there was a perfunctory tap on the door and Milo entered from the adjoining room. 'Rather a draughty old place, isn't it?' he said, casting his eyes about my room. 'Your room or mine, darling? I don't intend to sleep in a cold bed alone. I shall need you for warmth.'

'I'll just go and see to . . . something, shall I, madam?' Winnelda said, hurrying from the room.

'You shouldn't say such things in front of Winnelda,' I told Milo with a smile. 'You know she is easily shocked.'

'I don't see why she should be.' He came to me and pulled me against him. 'I should think she'd be accustomed to my wanton behaviour at this point.'

I looked up at him, taking the opportunity to address what was really on my mind. 'While we're on the subject of wanton behaviour, I wasn't aware you knew Isobel Van Allen.'

'Oh, didn't I mention it?' His face was the picture of perfect ease, and his arms around my waist didn't loosen in the slightest.

'No,' I said. 'You didn't.'

'Well, I didn't know her very well.'

'How well?' I questioned pointedly, looking up at him. I might as well know the worst of it.

He met my gaze without reservation. 'I was not among her coterie of young lovers, if that's what you mean.'

Well, that was direct enough. 'She seemed to harbour quite fond memories of you,' I said.

'She is, perhaps, remembering things differently from the way they were.'

I felt certain he was telling the truth. After all, we had not known one another at the time. There would be no reason for him to conceal it; I was perfectly aware that there had been women before me.

'She's very beautiful,' I said.

'I suppose, though her type has never appealed to me. Beneath her affected elegance, I found her a bit gauche.'

'You surprise me. Whatever else she may be, I think she's a very elegant woman.'

He shrugged. 'It's a very well-maintained façade, I'll grant you. But veneers wear thin. In any event, you needn't be concerned. I'm too old for her.'

I laughed. 'I'm not concerned.'

He dropped a kiss on my lips, and then I stepped back from his embrace.

'It's very odd, though, isn't it?' I said. 'Her being here, I mean. After what happened, I should have thought she would be the last person that Reginald Lyons would have invited to Lyonsgate.'

'They're not fond of one another,' Milo said. So he had noticed it, too.

'No,' I said vaguely. 'I wonder if anyone else has been invited.'

There was a sharp rapping on the door, and a moment later it was flung open and my cousin Laurel came into the room.

She wore her riding clothes, her face still flushed from the cold, her golden hair windblown. 'Amory, darling! I knew you'd come!' She brushed a kiss across my cheek and spared a glance at my husband. 'Hello, Milo.'

'Laurel,' he acknowledged, with an equal lack of enthusiasm.

'How was your trip?' she asked me. 'Did you take the train?'

'No, Milo drove us in his new car.'

Her brows rose, a hint of mockery glinting in her brown eyes. 'Did he? How very bourgeois of him.'

'I'll just give the two of you time to catch up, shall I?' Milo said. 'Lyons said he'd show me the stables.'

'Yes, of course.' I knew Milo would much prefer to spend his afternoon with the horses than with Laurel and me.

He left, and I turned to my cousin. There was so much I wanted to ask her, I was not even sure where to start. She spared me the trouble by bursting at once into a somewhat confusing speech.

'The rooms are a bit draughty, aren't they? Mine is just down the hall. All the guest rooms are in this wing, I think. Oh, Amory, I'm so glad you've come. I should have hated to come back here without you.'

'But how did you come to be here, Laurel?' I asked. 'You said you were going to visit your parents.'

'Oh, I did,' she said. 'Mother sends her love and says you are to come and see her. In any event, Reggie had happened to send me a letter. It was quite a coincidence that I happened to be at home when he sent it. He didn't have my address, of course, and sent it to Pearmont.'

Pearmont was the home of Laurel's parents, and I had spent many happy summers there as a child. Laurel's mother was the sister of my father. We had grown up very much like sisters, neither of us having any siblings.

'What did the letter say?' I asked.

'That's just it. It didn't say much of anything. Reggie asked me to come to Lyonsgate as soon as possible. I haven't seen or heard from him in years, but there was something about the letter that gave me pause.' She hesitated, a worried expression crossing her normally cheerful face. 'There's something wrong in all of this, but I don't know what.'

'Perhaps you had better start from the beginning,' I said patiently. My cousin was my closest friend and confidante, but she did enjoy making an event out of the ordinary. I might have been inclined to believe all of this was a figment of her imagination, had I not sensed for myself that something was amiss at Lyonsgate. There was just too much that did not seem right.

She dropped down on the bed. 'It's all so strange. I knew at once that you must come and untangle it all.'

'Your confidence in me is flattering,' I said wryly. 'But I really don't know what business I have coming here. I don't even know Mr Lyons, and, after all these years away from Lyonsgate, I don't see why he should want strangers crowding up the place. I should think he would like some time to set the house in order.'

'I doubt he will remain here long,' she said. 'He's anxious and uneasy. He goes for long, solitary walks in the morning and always comes back with a troubled expression. I don't think coming back to Lyonsgate was his idea.'

'What do you mean?'

'I think it all has something to do with Isobel. I didn't like to ask him, but I've rather had the feeling that she somehow convinced him to come back.'

That explained the impression I had had that Isobel was our hostess. This weekend was, in essence, her event.

'But why should he do as she asked, after what happened?' I mused.

'That's just it,' she said solemnly. 'It doesn't make sense, and that's what worries me.'

'I didn't detect any romantic feeling between them today,' I said.

She shook her head. 'No, all that ended long ago. He

28

was mad about her at one time, of course. It seemed that all the men were. We used to say she must be a witch, the way she could put any man under her spell. That was what happened to Reggie. He was always the sweetest thing. I never would have imagined . . . Well, never mind that. Suffice it to say, he was very much in love with her. I think he would have done anything she asked.'

I couldn't help but wonder what my cousin's feelings for Reginald Lyons had been at the time. We had always confided in one another, and she had claimed that she had only viewed Mr Lyons as a friend, but it had often seemed to me that there was something more than friendship in her voice when she spoke about him.

'But something happened between them,' she went on, 'even before the incident. They were cold towards one another that weekend, and we all wondered if things were coming to an end. I thought perhaps Isobel had found someone else. She was very fickle in her affections.

'Then, when it all happened and she wrote that dreadful book, I think he might have killed her if he wasn't so broken up about all of it. And after what happened to poor Brad . . .'

'Bradford Glenn?' I asked, remembering the young man Isobel Van Allen had accused of murder through her fictional account of the incident. 'What happened to him?'

Laurel looked surprised. 'You don't know?'

'No.'

'Of course,' she said. 'I'd forgotten. It was during your wedding trip. Shortly after the book was published, insinuating those dreadful things about him . . . he killed himself.'

'How dreadful,' I whispered, truly horrified. It was clear to me now why Isobel Van Allen had been forced to leave the country in the wake of such a scandal. A life had been tragically lost at Lyonsgate, but many more had been torn apart by her exploitation of the incident.

'It was awful,' Laurel agreed. 'I almost declined to come when I received his letter, but I felt that I couldn't deny him, not if he needed me. Imagine my horror upon arriving to find that he had invited her. And that's not all. He's invited all of them.'

'All of whom?'

'All of the people who were there that cursed night.'

I felt something like a chill at the words. It was the same sense of foreboding I had had standing outside, looking up at the grey walls of Lyonsgate. I was not at all superstitious, but I did wish that the uneasiness I felt would dissipate.

'Why on earth would he do that?' Already my brain was turning over the possibilities, none of them pleasant.

'I don't know, and that's why I wanted you to come at once. When I found out she was here . . . that they would all be here . . . I don't know how to explain it, but I had a feeling. Something ghastly is going to happen, Amory.'

As much as I wanted to discount my cousin's presentiment, I could not. I felt the same way myself.

CHAPTER THREE

I had done my best to quiet my cousin's fears, but I could not shake my own unease. I tried to put my dismal thoughts aside as Laurel went along to her room to bathe and dress before dinner.

I needed to freshen up, but first I went to the wardrobe to begin choosing something to wear to dinner. I hoped Winnelda had packed an evening gown that would provide at least a modicum of warmth in what was sure to be a draughty dining room. I was engrossed in the task and barely took notice of the tap at my door.

'Hello,' said a voice behind me.

I turned to see a gentleman standing in the doorway. It was a bit startling, having been talking about ghosts, to see the pale face looking at me from the dimness of the hallway. Apparently, Laurel had not closed the door tightly and it had drifted open.

The gentleman in question, however, did not look much

like a ghost. In fact, he rather reminded me of a statue of Apollo with his classical features and golden curls. Curiously intent eyes, so pale a blue as to seem almost colourless, were looking me over in a matter-of-fact way. It was quite a thorough examination, but somehow I didn't feel as though he were being rude, even if it was unusual for this strange gentleman to introduce himself to me on the threshold of my bedroom.

'Hello,' I replied, more to break the silence than for any real desire to start up a conversation. There was something vaguely familiar about the man, but I couldn't place him. I was quite certain we had never met before, but I felt that I had definitely seen that face. It was the sort of face that one remembered.

'I'm Gareth Winters,' he said.

Of course. The artist. I had seen his paintings in the homes of some of my friends. I remembered now, too, that he had been a part of that group that had been here the night that Edwin Green had died.

There had been a period before the death of Mr Green when Mr Winters' paintings had been very much in vogue, and he was generally considered to possess a good deal of talent. His portraits had been especially sought after, and I knew women who had sat for him, all of them commenting on his golden good looks. But there had not been much art since the tragedy. Occasionally a piece had come up for auction, but his name was not often mentioned in artistic circles these days. I remembered one of my friends telling me that his paintings had lost much of their fire since the Lyonsgate scandal.

'How do you do, Mr Winters,' I said. 'I'm Amory Ames.'

'Amory Ames,' he said it slowly and quietly, almost to himself, as though contemplating it. I wondered if he was trying to recall if we had ever met. 'You're a guest of Reggie's, I suppose.'

We were all guests of Reggie's, but I didn't like to point this out.

'Yes, my husband and I came at his invitation.'

'It's going to be a very unpleasant stay, I should think,' he said, his tone giving no indication of what he meant by that remark.

I didn't quite know how to respond to this. Though I had felt very much the same way, it was interesting to hear this opinion from a stranger. 'Do you think so?' I asked lightly. 'Lyonsgate is quite prettily situated.'

'No one wants to be here, of course. But there is no telling what that woman has in store for all of us.'

I knew at once that he meant Isobel Van Allen. I was about to ask him just what he meant, but he said suddenly, 'I must be off. I trust I'll see you at dinner, Mrs Ames.'

He wandered away, and I stared for a moment at the empty doorway, thinking of what he had said. None of them wanted to return to Lyonsgate, yet they had all come. I wondered what it was that had drawn them back.

One thing was certain: if all of Reggie's guests were as interesting as Gareth Winters, this was going to be an eventful dinner party indeed.

I was glad when it was finally time to go down for dinner. It seemed the entire afternoon had been building to a climax, and I would be glad to see for myself just how things stood. Perhaps nothing would happen tonight at all, but I felt somehow that observing the others together would give me some hint as to how to proceed.

Milo came into my bedroom from his just as Winnelda finished doing up my gown. I turned to him, struck, as I always was, by how handsome he looked in his evening clothes.

'How did you find the Lyonsgate stables?' I asked.

'They've only a few horses here, but they're fine animals. Not as fine as mine, of course.'

I smiled. 'Of course.'

His eyes ran the length of me. 'You look lovely, as always.'

'Thank you.' The garnet-coloured velvet gown was one of the heaviest of the gowns I had brought with me, though I suspected the usefulness of the thick fabric and long sleeves would be offset by the low-cut back.

'Are you ready to go down?' he asked.

'Yes, nearly.' I picked up my bracelet of rubies, diamonds, and onyx, and looked over my shoulder to see that Winnelda had disappeared from the room. I wrapped the bracelet around my wrist and attempted to fasten it with my free hand.

'Shall I?' he asked.

'Yes, thank you.' I extended my wrist and looked up at him as he bent over it to fasten the clasp. 'Milo, Laurel says Mr Lyons has invited all the guests who were here on the night that Edwin Green died.'

'Has he?' he asked, straightening.

'Yes, and we believe it has something to do with Isobel's return from Africa.'

'Quite possibly,' he agreed. 'It does not have the makings of a particularly happy reunion.'

'I'm afraid something dreadful is going to occur at dinner.'

'There's only one way to find out.' He smiled and offered me his arm. 'Shall we?'

I took his arm and we went out into the hallway. There were electric lights, but it seemed that not all of them were working, for the hallway was rather dark, save for the occasional pool of dim yellow light cast by one of the properly functioning bulbs in sconces. There was also a chill breeze coming from somewhere. I shivered and pressed closer to my husband.

'It's quite a pile of a house, isn't it?' he said. 'You'd think Lyons would have had it cared for in his absence.'

Such a critical sentiment was uncommon coming from my husband, yet not exactly surprising. Milo made sure that Thornecrest, our country house, was kept in beautiful form. He had inherited it from his father, and I sometimes thought it was the one thing in life that he really took seriously.

'Laurel said she didn't think he meant to come back at all. She thinks his return has something to do with Isobel.'

We made our way down the staircase, arm in arm. It was, perhaps, not fashionable for a woman to cling to her husband, but it was so very cold that I wanted to be as near him as possible. I did relax my hold on him as we reached the drawing room.

Lucinda Lyons rose from her chair and walked towards us at once.

'Good evening, Mr and Mrs Ames,' she said, looking only at Mr Ames. He had certainly gained himself an admirer.

'Good evening, Miss Lyons,' he replied. 'You're looking very lovely this evening.'

She flushed. 'Thank you.'

Reginald Lyons came towards us, the same air of unsettled distraction hovering over him. He was not, I thought, very adept at hiding his feelings, though he was clearly making a valiant effort to try.

'Good evening, Mr and Mrs Ames,' he said, a bit too enthusiastically. 'Let me introduce you to my sister, Beatrice Kline. Her husband is out of the country on business, so he was unable to join us.'

Beatrice Lyons Kline was a pretty woman, with the same smooth features as her brother. Her hair, in contrast to Reggie's and Lucinda's, was dark brown, and she wore it very short. Like her brother, she appeared a bit uneasy, but she concealed it better than he did.

'How do you do,' she said, politely but without enthusiasm. Her gaze was cool and watchful. She appeared completely at ease, but I noticed the way her gaze moved continually to the drawing-room door.

I thought the same thing must be on all our minds. We were all wondering just what it was that Isobel Van Allen had in store for us this evening.

Reggie Lyons next introduced us to Gareth Winters, who made no mention of having introduced himself to me in my bedroom that afternoon. He, too, seemed distracted, but not at all uneasy. He gave the impression that his mind was otherwise engaged by more important things than a room full of mere mortals.

A few moments later, the curtain came up on the evening's entertainment.

'I do hope I'm not late,' came the voice from the doorway. It was Isobel Van Allen. She stood for a moment outlined against the shadowy darkness of the hall behind her, until she had all of our attention. Then she made her entrance into the room, wearing an evening gown of black satin with a dangerously plunging neckline.

'Not at all,' Reggie said with a tight smile. 'I've been introducing Mr and Mrs Ames to everyone.'

'Charming group, isn't it,' she said, walking slowly towards us. I couldn't help but think she looked rather like a cat on the prowl. 'But, of course, not everyone's here yet.'

'Oh, will there be others joining us?' I questioned casually.

'One more couple,' Reginald Lyons said. 'Phillip and Freida Collins. They meant to arrive today, but their child was taken ill and Mrs Collins didn't want to leave her. They'll arrive sometime tomorrow.'

'Splendid. Then our little party will be complete,' Isobel said with a slow smile, her eyes on Reggie. He refused to meet her gaze, his jaw set.

There was another movement in the doorway, and we all turned to look.

'Ah, there you are, Desmond,' Isobel said. She stretched out her hand to him, and he came towards it, as if by unspoken command.

He, I was quite certain, had not been at the scene of the original tragedy. He was much too young. Strikingly handsome, with black hair and eyes the colour of warm honey, he was deeply tanned, despite the fact that it was the middle of winter. I wondered if he had come from Kenya with Miss Van Allen. Of course, Milo somehow managed to maintain his glowing complexion all year round, so this theory was not necessarily a sound one.

It turned out, however, that my guess had been correct.

'This is Desmond Roberts. My secretary,' she said with a smile that plainly announced he was much more than that. Whatever else she might be, there was no subtleness about Isobel Van Allen. 'He's been with me for over a year now.'

'How do you do,' he said, his smile revealing very white teeth.

Up close he was even younger than I had supposed. I should have been very much surprised to find that he was older than twenty-three or twenty-four, at least two decades younger than Miss Van Allen. It seemed that she was consistent in her preferences. I wondered idly if he actually did any secretarial work. I found it hard to picture him sitting at a typewriter as she dictated.

'I write romance novels under an assumed name, and Desmond has been invaluable to me in my work,' she went on, running a hand along his arm. 'He's found innumerable ways to inspire me.'

Milo's gaze caught mine, and his brows rose ever so slightly.

Dinner was announced just then, which spared us any additional awkwardness.

The dining room looked as though it had not much changed in the last five hundred years. It was a long, dark room with high wood-beamed ceilings, and a wooden table ran almost the length of the room. An enormous stone fireplace, carved with the Lyons crest and complete with a stag's head and battleaxes hanging above it, dominated one wall. I was glad to see there was a fire roaring in it and even gladder to find that my seat put my back towards the heat, for my evening gown was indeed proving it had not been designed with warmth as its primary objective.

The food was very good, and our conversation, though superficial, was pleasant enough. For all our politeness, however, I could sense something much less civilised beneath the surface. The tension was high, and nearly everyone looked vaguely ill at ease, everyone excepting Isobel Van Allen.

She looked pale and lovely in dim light. She sat beside Reggie Lyons, but I had not seen them speak a word to each other all evening. Nevertheless, I felt that, despite the fact that she was a guest here, she seemed to be holding court. There was the look in her eye, the self-satisfied countenance of a woman who was pleased to know something that no one else knew. I wondered when she would choose to let the rest of us know her secret.

As it turned out, she waited until dessert. A lovely trifle had just been set before us, but she did not give us time to enjoy it.

'I did hope to wait until we were all together,' she said suddenly, taking advantage of a momentary lull in conversation to make herself heard. 'But since Freida and

Phillip have been delayed, I suppose I shall tell you without them. I have some news.'

Her words had a startling effect. Though there was nothing inherently worrisome in her statement, I saw a shadow cross Reggie Lyons' face, and it felt as if everyone had gone completely still.

She paused for a moment, perhaps to revel in the atmosphere of palpable dismay, before she continued. 'We needn't hide the fact that there was a lot of unpleasantness when I published *The Dead of Winter*.'

'Unpleasantness,' Beatrice Kline said in a cold voice. 'Is that what you call our ruin – and Bradford's death?'

'I merely told the truth as I saw it. The consequences were not my fault.'

'Not your fault?' Beatrice spat out. She had gone pale, her eyes bright with some mixture of fury and grief. Whatever she professed about her feelings for him, she had not taken Bradford Glenn's suicide lightly. 'It was all your fault from the beginning. It should have been you who died.'

Isobel gave a low laugh, her dark eyes shining. 'And now the claws are out. You always were the honest one, Beatrice. No pretences. It's so much better that way, don't you agree?'

No one said anything. It seemed everyone but Beatrice had been stunned into silence. I glanced at Reggie Lyons. He was clenching his teeth, his face white.

A smile played on Isobel's lips as her eyes moved around the table. I could fairly feel the exhilaration emanating from her. She was enjoying this, every moment of it.

'Now, while we're being so honest with one another,

seems like the perfect time to make my announcement. There were a great many secrets revealed in that book, but there was more to the story than even I knew at the time. There has since been information that has come to light that I was saving until the time was right, and now it is.' She paused, letting her words hang in the air before delivering the coup de grace. 'I've decided to write a second volume.'

CHAPTER FOUR

There was a moment of absolute silence – even the logs on the hearth seemed to have ceased to crackle – before Reggie Lyons swore loudly and sprang from his seat, his chair crashing to the floor. 'You can't do this, Isobel.'

'But I am doing it, Reggie.'

'I won't allow it,' he said through his teeth.

Isobel laughed, a low, throaty laugh, but her eyes were suddenly hard. 'I don't think you're in any position to prevent it.'

His face went scarlet, and I feared for a moment he would suffer a fit of apoplexy.

It was then that Beatrice's cold voice rang out in the silence. 'Just what is it that you think you know?'

Isobel's eyes locked on hers. Hatred fairly crackled in the air between them. 'Are you sure you want me to speak so openly, Beatrice?'

Beatrice's gaze did not waver, but nor did she answer.

Isobel allowed the silence to fall as she took a slow bite of trifle, letting the question hang in the air for a long moment. I could hear Reggie Lyons breathing from across the table.

I wished I could see Milo, but he was seated on my side of the table, and I couldn't turn without being obvious. Laurel, too, was seated where I couldn't see her. I wondered desperately what both of them were thinking.

'Why gather us all together like this?' my cousin asked. Though I couldn't see her, I could detect the distress in her tone. 'Why not just write your book and be done with it?' It was the very thing that I had been wondering.

'Because I need you,' Isobel said.

Reggie Lyons gave a strangled laugh.

'What makes you think we're going to do anything to help you?' It was the first time Gareth Winters had spoken. There was no anger in his voice. He sounded almost as though he had no particular interest in her answer.

Isobel looked at him, a smile touching her lips. 'Beautiful Gareth, always so far removed from everything. You'd like to help me, wouldn't you? For old times' sake?'

He said nothing. Isobel's gaze left him and the softness dropped from it. 'I think you'll all come to see my point,' she said. 'In time. And now I think I've said as much as I care to for one night.'

With that, she rose gracefully from her chair, the men rising automatically with her, save Reggie Lyons, whose chair still lay on the floor at his feet. He was leaning heavily against the table, and I hoped that his legs would hold him.

'I think I'll just go back to my room now,' Isobel said, casting a sweeping glance around the table. 'I have some writing to do. I intend to finish the book within the month. I have a feeling it will be quite the sensation.'

She was halfway to the door when Reggie spoke.

'I'll kill you first.' The words were barely a whisper, but were perfectly audible in the dead stillness of the room.

In response to this threat, Isobel looked over her shoulder at him and clicked her tongue. 'Shame, Reggie. In front of your guests.'

And then she was gone, and it felt rather as though all of the air had gone out of the room with her.

We were all quiet for a moment, sitting in something of a stunned silence.

'If you'll all excuse me,' Reggie said suddenly. He turned and strode from the room.

And still no one spoke.

I think we were all in a bit of shock. I could not, in all my many years of society dinners, remember anything remotely as dramatic occurring at the dinner table.

It was Beatrice who marshalled her poise first.

'That was unpleasant,' she said, a profound understatement. Her gaze caught mine. 'Allow me to apologise, Mr and Mrs Ames. I'm sure that was terribly embarrassing for you.'

'There's no need to apologise,' I said. It was not, after all, she who had orchestrated the climactic scene.

'Nevertheless, Reggie must have known something like this was going to happen. He shouldn't have invited you if he planned to have that woman here.'

She turned to Desmond Roberts, Isobel's young secretary. I had almost forgotten that he was at the table.

'I should apologise to you as well, Mr Roberts,' she said, neatly avoiding actually doing so.

'Isobel can be quite provoking,' he said, without any great emotion. I suspected this was awkward for him as well, though it was also possible he was under orders to remain at the dinner table and observe our reactions to her grand announcement.

'Perhaps I had better go and see to Reggie,' Beatrice said, pushing aside her untouched dessert. 'Coffee will be served in the drawing room. I'll join you there shortly.'

I met Milo's gaze as we moved toward the drawing room, but it was, as usual, difficult to tell what he was thinking. I doubted he had been much moved by the scene. He was terribly difficult to shock. I thought if Reggie had stabbed Isobel with a dinner knife, it might possibly have elicited some slight surprise.

My cousin's countenance was a bit more voluble. Her eyes were wide, and she was pale as she caught my arm while the others went ahead of us into the drawing room. 'This is just the sort of thing I was afraid would happen,' she whispered. 'Reggie . . . did you see his face, Amory? I was afraid he would . . .' Her voice trailed off, leaving me wondering whether she feared for his health or what he might do to Miss Van Allen.

'What could she possibly have to put into another book?' I asked. I had never pressured my cousin for details about the tragedy at Lyonsgate. I had sensed it was something that she didn't wish to discuss. Now, however, it seemed imperative to know just what had happened at the time of Mr Green's death. Apparently, there were more secrets to be exposed. Isobel Van Allen's new book had the potential to wreak just as much social havoc as the first had done.

'I don't know,' she said. 'There were a lot of dreadful things happening that I wasn't aware of at the time. It could be anything.'

This was not encouraging, but we couldn't very well stand in the hallway all evening discussing the grim possibilities.

'We'll talk more about it later,' I told her.

She nodded, and we went into the drawing room. The mood was subdued, to say the least, but the others had begun to sip their coffee and attempt light conversation. Laurel took a seat near Gareth Winters. He had remained outwardly unmoved throughout Isobel's performance, but I wondered what his inner thoughts on the matter might be. Presumably, he was just as opposed to the idea as the rest of the guests were.

I was not surprised to see Lucinda Lyons had seated herself near Milo. She had appeared a bit shaken as we left the drawing room, but I was sure Milo would quickly set her at ease. I was glad of it. I expected the young woman felt a bit alone, her brother and sister having decamped and left her in a room full of strangers.

I thought perhaps Desmond Roberts felt the same way. He sat alone on a settee near the fire, sipping his coffee with every appearance of indifference, yet I suspected the air of confidence with which he carried himself was superficial. I had noticed that, when he thought people weren't looking, a very lost expression had flickered momentarily across his face.

I wondered how it was that he had fallen into Miss

Van Allen's clutches. There was, I supposed, something flattering to the male ego at having captured the attention of so exotic a woman as Isobel Van Allen. That she was twenty years his senior did not seem to be a consideration. She was, after all, very beautiful and, I assumed, quite rich.

But perhaps I was being cynical. Perhaps they truly cared for each other. It was not outside the realm of possibility. My instinct told me, however, that it was not a love match.

Well, whatever his reasons, it was none of my business. He was an adult, and there was absolutely no reason that he could not do just as he pleased. That didn't mean, of course, that I couldn't try to befriend him.

'It seems we are both outsiders here, Mr Roberts,' I said as I approached. He appeared to have been lost in thought and hurried to rise.

'Please don't get up.' I took a seat near him and accepted a demitasse from Henson, the butler.

'I'm afraid it's not just in this room, Mrs Ames,' Mr Roberts said as Henson moved away. 'I'm rather an outsider in this country.'

'Have you lived in Kenya long?'

'Nearly my entire life. I don't have many memories of England. Mainly cold, grey mornings and unending rain. This visit has done little to change the picture in my mind.'

I smiled. 'Yes, I can imagine it's not what you're accustomed to. Perhaps winter was not the best time to make a return.'

'I had very little say in the matter.'

He took a sip of his coffee, the glass dwarfed in his long, brown fingers. His nails were manicured, I noticed, and his

47

cufflinks were gold. It seemed that Miss Van Allen kept him well maintained. It was not a very nice thing to think, but the thought had come unbidden.

'Do you expect to stay long?' I asked, not entirely without ulterior motive. If I meant to do all I could to calm the troubled waters here at Lyonsgate, it didn't hurt to gather information in the form of polite conversation.

'I may never go back.' His answer was automatic, and he was gazing across the room with the unseeing look of a man lost in his own thoughts.

Within a moment, he seemed to recall where he was, however, and turned to me with an easy smile. 'Then again, I may be back within a fortnight. One never knows, does one?'

'No,' I replied. 'I suppose not.'

Fully self-possessed once again, he began telling me about life in Africa. He spoke with some animation of his homeland, and I found myself liking the young man and hoping that whatever troubles he was hiding beneath the surface would not distress him for long.

At last I excused myself and made my way towards Milo and his young admirer.

Lucinda was laughing delightedly at something he had said, the troubles at dinner apparently forgotten. She turned to me with a bright smile as I approached and Milo rose from the sofa.

'Oh, Mrs Ames! Your husband is so amusing.'

'Yes, isn't he?' I agreed. Milo was almost invariably charming. It came to him naturally, but when he put extra effort into it, the effect was remarkable. Lucinda was practically glowing under his attentions.

'He has been telling me about his horse Xerxes,' Lucinda said. 'Such fun! I do adore high spirits and glossy black hair.'

'Yes, he's quite a lovely thing,' I said, no longer certain if we were speaking of Milo or the horse.

'Mr Ames has told me the most delightful stories,' she said. She hesitated for a brief moment and then added, 'It's nice to laugh after that unpleasantness at dinner.'

'It does seem the mood has lifted since Miss Van Allen excused herself,' I said lightly.

'She's a dreadful woman, isn't she?' Lucinda said, without much feeling, as though she thought it was what was expected of her. 'But she's very beautiful.'

I could not disagree with either assessment.

'And her gowns are lovely. I wouldn't have thought she'd be much of one for stylish clothes, having lived in the wilderness for so long, but all her things are the height of fashion.'

'I suspect she made a stop in Paris,' I said. 'She seems to have adapted quite easily to European life. I'm not sure the same can be said for Mr Roberts. Not only is he in a strange country, but the conversation at dinner can't have been pleasant for him.'

'No, I suppose not.' Lucinda looked across the room at the young man in question. 'I don't know what they see in each other, really. He's much too young for her. I find older men *much* more interesting.' Her gaze flickered momentarily to Milo as she said this. 'In any event, perhaps I should go and speak to him, since Reggie isn't here to be host.'

'That would be nice of you.' She was young and quite

pretty, and I couldn't help but think it would be much preferable for her to lavish her attentions on an unmarried gentleman of her own age rather than my husband.

I really was being unbearably snide tonight.

She rose, smoothing out her skirt. 'I'll just go and keep him company for a while, if you'll excuse me.'

I took Lucinda's vacant seat on the sofa, and Milo sat close beside me.

'Come to rescue me, darling?'

'She's not the first of your admirers I've had to chase away,' I replied with a smile. 'Really, though, I'm glad you diverted her. I imagine all of this has been rather difficult for her.'

'I'd wager she's been a bit neglected.'

'Yes, I doubt her brother and sister have had much time for her since they returned to Lyonsgate.'

'I'm sure she shall be excessively diverted by Isobel's dashing amanuensis.'

One could hope. I hadn't come to discuss Lucinda, however. What I really wanted to do was speak to him about what had occurred at dinner, but we did not have the chance. Reggie and Beatrice came back into the room just then.

'Forgive us our absence,' said Beatrice, who appeared completely unruffled by the events of the evening. 'Has everyone had their coffee?'

Conversation resumed its normal course as everyone attempted to pretend that the night had not had any impact upon them.

I glanced at Reggie. He stood at his sister's side, looking as though he could use a drink.

I was not, apparently, the only one to think so, for Henson came almost at once with a glass upon a tray, the contents of which were not the strong coffee we had been drinking.

'Let's play a rubber of bridge, shall we?' Laurel suggested suddenly. She was looking at Reggie as she said it.

'Oh, I don't think . . .' he began.

'Oh, do partner with me, Reggie. We always play so well together.'

He hesitated for only a moment. 'Very well.'

'Beatrice?'

'No, thank you, Laurel.' She took a seat by the fire and lit a cigarette.

'Mr Roberts and I will play,' Lucinda said. She looked at Mr Roberts expectantly, and he nodded his agreement.

The players moved to a table in the corner, and Gareth Winters wandered over to where we sat.

'I'm glad to have escaped that,' he said. 'I don't care for the game.' Somehow I didn't find this surprising. Mr Winters didn't seem as though he would enjoy maintaining the concentration required to follow the bidding.

'I'm afraid my heart wouldn't be in it this evening,' I admitted. 'It seems you were right this afternoon when you said things were bound to get unpleasant.'

He smiled that vague smile of his. 'I'm afraid the worst is yet to come.'

Unfortunately, I couldn't disagree.

As soon as politely possible, I made my excuses and retreated to my room, leaving Milo and Mr Winters to have a drink together. It had certainly been an eventful evening, and I was very tired.

Winnelda was sitting in a chair, which she had dragged perilously close to the fire, and reading a book. She set it aside and sprang to her feet when I came into the room.

'Oh, madam!' she said with great enthusiasm. 'Is it true? Was there really a lot of shouting and threatening at dinner?'

I never ceased to be amazed at the rate at which news travelled through the domestic staff. Winnelda, in particular, seemed to be an absolute magnet for gossip. She must have made fast friends with some of the maids.

'There was a bit of unpleasantness,' I admitted. 'I'm afraid the people here are not the greatest of friends.'

'I do hope you'll tell me all about it,' she said, as she moved to unfasten my dress.

'It's rather a long story.'

'I don't mind, madam.' Winnelda never minded long stories. She was drawn to scandal like a bee to honey.

I stepped out of my gown and pulled on a nightdress as Winnelda moved to hang the dress in the wardrobe. I didn't particularly want to go over it all again, but I knew that she would never rest easy until I had given her the details.

'It all goes back to something that happened here several years ago. There was a death, and Miss Van Allen wrote a book about it.'

'Yes, *The Dead of Winter*.' Winnelda said over her shoulder. I turned to her, surprised. 'You know it?'

'Oh, yes, madam. It's one of my favourites. I was quite young when it was published, and I remember all the sensation it caused. My mother told me I shouldn't read such things, and so naturally I was all the more eager to read it. My friends and I all bought copies. Let me tell you, it set me to blushing more than once.'

'If only I had thought to find a copy of it,' I mused. 'It might have proven very useful.'

'Oh, you can read mine, madam,' Winnelda said.

I looked up. 'You have a copy with you?'

'Yes. Right here.' She went to where she had been sitting and picked up the book I had seen her reading when I came in.

'Your resourcefulness never ceases to amaze me, Winnelda.'

'Well, when I found out we were coming here to Lyonsgate, I made sure to bring it along. I thought perhaps I could recognise some of the settings. I think, though I'm not entirely sure, that this very bedroom was the inspiration for the scene where . . .'

'Yes, thank you, Winnelda,' I said.

She dropped a curtsey. 'I'm ever so glad to be of help to you, and I do think that you'll enjoy it. There is a scandalous scene where . . .'

I was spared the details as Milo came into my room from the hall. 'Will you be needing anything else tonight, madam?' Winnelda asked, setting the book on the table.

'No. Thank you, Winnelda. And thank you for the book.'

'You're welcome. Goodnight, madam. Mr Ames.'

She left and closed the door behind her, and I turned to my husband. 'I've been waiting to be alone with you all evening,' I said.

'Words I live for, my love,' he said, pulling me to him.

'That's not what I meant.'

'In any event, I've already told Parks I won't be needing him tonight, and now that you've rid yourself of Winnelda . . .'

'What did you make of what happened at dinner?'

'Your skin is like ice, darling,' he said, his warm hands moving up and down my arms.

'Yes, it's very cold in this house,' I said absently. 'What do you suppose Miss Van Allen means to write about?'

Milo sighed, releasing me. 'I haven't the faintest idea. Nor do I care.'

'There must be something Reggie doesn't want people to know. I thought for a moment things might come to blows.'

'And you enjoyed it immensely,' he said, removing his necktie and cufflinks. 'I could practically feel the glee coming off of you from the other side of the room.'

'What a vulgar thing to say. I was terribly uncomfortable.'

He smiled. 'But you found it interesting, nonetheless.'

I was spared having to deny it as Milo went to his room, leaving our adjoining door ajar.

'Isobel's always enjoyed causing a scandal,' he said from inside. 'I'd wager she's trying to rake things up in hopes of generating another profitable novel.'

'No, I think it's more than that. I think there's some secret she's been keeping.'

'Your instinct at work again, I suppose.'

I chose to ignore this aspersion cast upon my intuition. Milo could deny it all he liked, but my perceptions had been accurate more than once.

I thought back over the events of the evening. What

exactly was it that had made me uneasy? Of course, the entire scene at dinner had been unnerving, but that wasn't what was nagging at me. There was something else, something that had seemed unusual. Then I remembered.

'Mr Roberts said something very strange tonight,' I said. 'He told me he might never go home. What do you suppose made him say that?'

Milo came back into my room, clad in his bedclothes and dressing gown. 'Perhaps he supposes Isobel will drink his blood in the night and leave him for dead.'

I smiled. 'That's a bit unfair, isn't it?'

'Unfair to vampires, perhaps.'

'I just had the distinct impression that something wasn't right . . .'

'That may well be true, darling, but I don't see how it's any of our affair.'

I sighed. Perhaps he was right. Perhaps I was even looking for trouble where none existed. In any event, there was nothing more to be done about it tonight.

I got into the bed and instantly regretted it.

'One need be a vampire to withstand these sheets,' I said. 'They're like ice.'

'Well, then let me warm you,' he said. Discarding his dressing gown, he pulled back the blankets and slipped into bed beside me.

He pulled me against him, and I was soon very warm indeed.

CHAPTER FIVE

I awoke early and found myself unable to go back to sleep. The room was very cold, and, though I was reluctant to leave the warmth of my bed, I couldn't help feeling that there were things to be done. For one thing, I had not had a chance to discuss last night's events with Laurel. For another, I was terribly curious to see what would happen at breakfast.

I considered waking Milo, who sleeps like the dead, but decided against it. There was no reason he should have to rise early just because I did. I bathed and dressed as quickly as possible since the bathroom was frigid and chose one of my warmest ensembles, a smart grey wool suit with a fitted jacket and pleated skirt.

Then I went downstairs, prepared to meet the day.

Everything was laid out on the sideboard in the breakfast room, and I was a bit surprised to find it empty, save for Miss Van Allen.

She was seated at the table, a cup of coffee before her, making notes in a notebook. There was a strange expression on her face, a curious combination of concentrated intensity and something like wistfulness.

She looked up as I hovered in the doorway, and it was too late to retreat.

'Oh, good morning, Mrs Ames.'

I would not have taken Isobel Van Allen for an early riser. She seemed to me the type of woman who would enjoy lounging about in her negligee until noon, but perhaps it was unfair of me to assume such things. She certainly was well-turned-out this morning. She wore a black, exquisitely cut suit, and her make-up was flawless. Her hair, too, was perfectly done. Eschewing the more current short styles, she wore it in a low chignon at the back of her neck. The sleek elegance of it suited her.

'Good morning, Miss Van Allen.'

I went to the sideboard. There were a great many dishes from which to choose. I settled on eggs, toast, and fruit, and poured myself a cup of coffee from the silver pot.

'I see we have beaten the others to breakfast,' I said, taking a seat at the table.

'I developed the habit of rising early in Kenya,' she replied. 'I loved the sunrise. It was unlike anything on earth, I think, that bright orange globe setting everything it touched ablaze.'

There was a faraway expression in her eyes as she spoke and a note of tenderness in her voice. It was almost like the expression of a woman in love. Clearly, her adopted homeland had won her heart. I wondered once again what had really brought her back to England.

'You're wondering why I came back, I suppose,' she said, with somewhat uncanny accuracy.

I smiled. 'Perhaps it's true that no place compares to home.'

She laughed, though there was more bitterness than humour in it. 'Not at all, Mrs Ames. England has no great appeal for me, not any more. Especially in winter. I hate it.'

It was, at least, one thing that she and Desmond Roberts had in common.

'Then what brought you back? Surely you needn't have come to Lyonsgate to write your novel.' I was almost surprised to hear myself ask the question, but Miss Van Allen was a plain-spoken woman, and I didn't suppose there was any reason that I shouldn't be the same.

She looked as though she was about to say something, but then seemed to think better of it. Instead, she smiled. 'I would much rather have stayed away, but one can't always follow one's heart, can one? Of course,' she went on, artfully shifting the subject, 'you seem to have been lucky in that respect, Mrs Ames. Milo seems very devoted to you.'

Since she had been out of the country for years, I didn't think this was meant as a spiteful reference to Milo's less-than-sterling reputation and our well-publicised marital troubles.

'We're very happy,' I said, and I meant it. These past few months had been some of the happiest of our marriage, and, for the first time in years, I felt that I had found my footing where Milo was concerned.

'Yes, I can see that you are. I've always thought it would

take an extraordinary woman indeed to secure Milo Ames. I compliment you for having succeeded.'

It was an odd sort of accolade, but seemed to be a sincere one. I smiled. 'Thank you.'

She took a sip of her coffee. 'There was a time when I had hoped to find such happiness, but life often takes us in unexpected directions.' Her tone was not bitter, nor did it ask for pity. In fact, I was certain she would have despised the idea that she might elicit compassion.

This conversation was not going the way I had expected. Everything I had seen of her thus far had prepared me to dislike Isobel Van Allen completely. Now I felt the tug of some other emotion. It wasn't sympathy, exactly; she was not a woman who would require it. Yet I felt that she had revealed something of herself to me that was normally kept hidden beneath the flawless exterior. 'It's never too late for happiness, surely,' I said lightly.

She looked at me, her gaze curiously intense. 'Do you think it's necessary for people to pay for their sins, Mrs Ames?' she asked.

I hesitated. 'I believe redemption is possible,' I said at last.

Something flickered across her face. I might have mistaken it for contempt had I not been sure that there was a deep sadness in her eyes.

'I wish I could believe that,' she said, rising from her seat. 'Sadly, I think sometimes it is too late, and all one can do is prepare to make the payment. Good day, Mrs Ames.'

She walked from the room before I could formulate

a reply, and I was left wondering just who it was that Isobel Van Allen thought had a debt to pay.

Duly nourished, I decided to pay a visit to Laurel's room before rousting my husband from bed.

I found my cousin wrapped in a robe of marigold-coloured silk and drinking a cup of coffee near the fire, a tray of half-eaten breakfast on the table beside her.

'I couldn't bear to come down,' she said when I had seated myself across from her. 'Not after what happened last night. I hadn't the stomach for it this morning. Was it as awful as one might suppose?'

'Apparently, nearly everyone felt the same as you did. It was only Miss Van Allen and me at breakfast.'

'Poor Amory. It was cruel of us to leave you alone with her. I'll attend lunch, I promise. Was she unbearable?'

'Not at all. She's a very interesting woman,' I said thoughtfully. 'Laurel, will you tell me what happened that night?'

She didn't ask what night I meant. She was quiet for a moment, and then she set down her cup and saucer and pulled her robe more tightly around herself.

'I don't really know,' she said at last. 'That's the dreadful thing. Not really knowing what happened, how things might have been different if we had behaved differently.'

Her voice trailed off for a moment, and I waited, giving her time to gather her recollections.

'It was after one of the long weekend parties. Almost everyone had gone back to London, and there was only the small group of us remaining. It was after dinner, quite late, but we were all in high spirits and in the mood for a bit of adventure. Someone – I don't remember who – had the idea that we might go out on the lake in the boats and we all seemed to think this was a grand idea. But we found the water was too frozen along the shore, and so we went into the summer house. Someone started a fire and there was a phonograph. It was Isobel's, I believe. There was a little desk in the summer house, and she would go there to write, even then. We were dancing, laughing. There had been a great deal of drinking, and other things.'

'Drugs.'

'Yes. You know I've never been interested in that sort of thing. In truth, the weekend was rather more excessive than I had expected. I'd had only a glass or two of wine at dinner, and I decided after a while to go back to the house. I went to my room and fell asleep. It wasn't until morning that I knew anything was amiss. I had just come down for breakfast when I heard Freida outside, running up from the summer house. She was screaming. Sometimes I still have nightmares about her screams.'

So it had been Freida Collins, the final guest who would arrive tomorrow with her husband, Phillip, who had discovered the body. Freida was the only one of the group, aside from Laurel, with whom I was acquainted. We had been at school together, but I had not spoken to her since before the tragedy. I wondered absently what she had been doing walking outside early on a cold morning after a wild night.

'We all ran outside to see what had happened,' Laurel continued, 'all of us from different parts of the house, as if her shrieking was some sort of siren's song. Freida was hysterical, pointing in the direction of the summer house. We all ran down there and . . .'

She stopped, and I waited for her to collect her thoughts.

'And then we found him dead in the snow,' she said softly. 'It was dreadful, Amory. He was so very white. And his eyes were open, staring. Such a ghastly expression on his face.'

She shuddered. She was clearly still deeply affected by what had happened.

'I'm sorry, dear. If you don't want to say anything more . . .'

She shook her head. 'It's been a long time. Perhaps I should have talked about it before now.'

'What happened then?' I asked.

'It was Gareth who called the doctor. He called the police as well, I think. He was the only one of us who seemed to have any sense.'

I thought it surprising that the dreamy-eyed Mr Winters should have been the one with enough presence of mind to send for the authorities.

'Was everyone there when they found him?'

'I . . . I think so. Freida had collapsed up at the house and didn't go back with us, and Phillip went back to look after her. I remember Bradford walked away and was sick. It was Beatrice who got a blanket from the summer house and covered Edwin. The rest of us just stood there until the doctor came.'

'And he said it was the drugs and the cold?'

'Yes, that was what he thought. It's what everyone thought, until . . .'

Until Isobel Van Allen had written her book.

'Miss Van Allen accused Bradford Glenn of murder and shortly thereafter he committed suicide. Do you think he might really have killed Edwin Green?' I asked.

Laurel shook her head a bit as if to clear it, then she seemed to consider what I had said. 'I don't think so. Of course, I didn't know any of them very well. One can't really take people's measure in the space of a weekend, but I wouldn't have said I thought that he would do such a thing. He seemed very kind, in fact. Kinder than most of them.'

'In what way?'

'Oh, I don't know. It was little things that I noticed. He spoke kindly to the maids, for example. That isn't, perhaps, something that amounts to anything, but so few people speak kindly to maids. He was kind to Lindy, too, when most people ignored her. He was pleasant when he didn't have to be.'

That was an astute observation, the logic of which I had often seen to be true. I had known a great many people who fancied themselves to be philanthropists yet were absolute horrors behind closed doors when nothing was to be gained by presenting a benevolent front.

'And yet . . .' she said. 'There was something about him . . .'

I waited as she considered it.

'It's difficult to explain,' she said at last, 'but it seemed to me that there was something strange, almost insincere about the way he fawned over Beatrice.'

'What do you mean?'

She considered it. 'I don't know, exactly. It's been so long now, and I tried to put so much of that time from my

63

mind. It was just that, when no one else was around, he didn't seem exceptionally fond of Beatrice. It was as though he was doing it just to challenge Edwin Green, making a show of it. But I didn't know them very well, so perhaps I was mistaken.'

Somehow I doubted that. Laurel was an excellent judge of character.

'Who was the last one to see Edwin Green alive, do you remember?'

'I think it must have been Bradford. He and Edwin had fought that evening, and the others said later that it was just the two of them left in the summer house. I suppose that's why Isobel drew the conclusion that he had killed him. Both of the men were in love with Beatrice, you see.'

This fact was surprising to me. Though I had known about her purported entanglement with both men, having now met Beatrice Lyons Kline, I shouldn't have thought she was the type of woman over which men would kill each other. There was nothing disparaging in this assessment. I only felt that, as cool and aloof as she seemed to be, she would not be likely to draw such ardent romantic interest. Isobel Van Allen, with her simmering sensuality, seemed more likely to have incited such behaviour. Of course, the ways of the heart were not always as one would expect.

'Were Isobel and Bradford Glenn on good terms?' I asked.

She shrugged. 'As far as I saw. As I said, I didn't know either of them well. I wish I knew more, but I was an outsider at the time,' Laurel said. 'I had formed certain impressions, of course, of all of them. Some I liked better than others, but

I shouldn't have thought any of them capable of murder.'

'Perhaps Isobel didn't realise the impact the book would cause. Perhaps she didn't mean to cause any harm,' I suggested, not really believing it.

Laurel's doubts seemed to echo mine as she looked up at me, her brown eyes sombre. 'I think her visit here proves otherwise.'

She was right, of course. Isobel had admitted as much; she had come to make someone pay.

'I don't mind a scandal for myself,' Laurel said, 'but I'm dreadfully worried about Reggie. His nerves aren't at all good. He was never the same after the war, you see. Then that dreadful business happened, and I was worried that he might not recover. I had hoped that he would be able to go away and forget it all. I thought we had all left Lyonsgate behind, but it seems as though one can never escape the past.'

'Yes,' I mused. 'Isobel Van Allen said much the same thing.'

Back in my room, I was very much surprised to see that Milo was not only risen from the bed, but gone. The bedclothes were still askew, so he could not have been gone for long. I wondered if he had gone down to breakfast in search of me while I was in Laurel's room.

I heard movement in his room and went to look inside. It was Parks, Milo's valet, engaged in polishing Milo's shoes. Parks was very fastidious in his duties. Milo called him a dead bore but appreciated his contributions to Milo's sartorial perfection.

'Good morning, madam,' he said. 'May I be of assistance?'

'Good morning, Parks. Have you seen Mr Ames?'

'He went out perhaps fifteen minutes ago, madam. He was dressed for riding.'

Dressed for riding, was he? He certainly hadn't mentioned anything to me about it.

'Thank you.'

I went back into my room and closed the door. I was mildly put out with Milo for having run off, but I was perfectly capable of entertaining myself.

I would spend my morning reading *The Dead of Winter*. I settled into the chair near the fire and opened the book.

The ghosts of the dead walk among us, their breath the fog that hovers low. Their voiceless whispers are the chill along the spine, begging that their stories be told, and none breathe colder than the dead of winter.

It seemed Isobel Van Allen had a flair for the dramatic. This might prove to be entertaining as well as useful.

CHAPTER SIX

I had finished five chapters by the time I set the book aside. It was much as I had expected. The various players in the Edwin Green tragedy were all there, outlined quite clearly. Even with my very superficial knowledge of those involved, I could tell easily who was meant to be whom, for Isobel Van Allen had not bothered to disguise their identities other than giving them pseudonyms.

I could certainly not count the book a literary masterpiece, but it was definitely intriguing. I could see why it had caused a sensation, for there were enough salacious details to keep one turning the pages to see what would happen next.

As Winnelda had indicated, there were more than a few things that might raise eyebrows. However, I suspected the book might have had more of an impact at the time it had been written. Knowing the people involved as I did now, I felt that these stories somehow belonged to a different lifetime. Youthful indiscretions were not uncommon, after all. Of course, if those indiscretions included murder, it was quite another thing altogether.

I went back downstairs as the luncheon hour approached, determined not to let what I had read influence my perception of the other guests.

Isobel Van Allen and Desmond Roberts were not in the dining room when I arrived, and I was a bit relieved. I suspected dinner was likely to be a lively event, and I had been hoping for a bit of peace at luncheon.

Reginald Lyons came to me as I walked into the room. 'Mrs Ames, I owe you an apology,' he said at once. He seemed to be no worse the wear from his outburst the previous evening, and I was glad.

'There's no need to . . .' I began.

'Yes, there is. We behaved abominably last night. No matter what my feelings might be on the subject, I allowed things to get out of hand. Please rest assured there will be no repetition of such unfortunate scenes at dinner tonight.'

'I understand that emotions were high. I know it must not be the best of times for my husband and me to have come to visit. If you think it would be better, we needn't stay.'

Even as I said the words, I hoped he wouldn't agree that it would be best for us to return to London. I didn't want to leave Laurel, not now.

'No, please don't go,' he said quickly, much to my relief. 'I am happy to have you here at Lyonsgate.'

'Very well,' I said, 'if you're sure.'

'Yes, yes, quite sure,' he replied, rousing his hearty host

persona. 'Now let us eat some of this excellent lunch. Is your husband coming down?'

'I'm not certain,' I answered, taking the plate he had offered me to fill it from the sideboard. 'I haven't seen my husband since early this morning. I understand he's gone out riding.'

'Lindy must have dragged him with her,' Reggie said. 'She can be rather an annoyance, but she's hard to resist once she sets her mind to something.'

'Milo enjoys riding,' I said mildly. And he wouldn't have gone if he hadn't wanted to.

Laurel joined us, then, and Mr Winters came shortly afterwards. There was no sign of Beatrice Kline, and I assumed she had taken lunch in her room.

We sat down to eat, and our conversation was light and pleasant. I was much relieved to find that the atmosphere was considerably improved by the absence of the most polarising guest. It seemed she was not far from any of our minds, however.

'It seems she must have learnt something new, doesn't it?' Mr Winters said suddenly. We all knew at once whom he meant.

Reggie looked up sharply, as though he had been awaiting the topic of Isobel to surface.

'But what could she have learnt?' he demanded. He was becoming agitated and doing his best to tamp it down.

'Perhaps she doesn't know it herself,' Mr Winters suggested. 'Perhaps she has come back to discover something.'

Reggie said nothing to this, and an uncomfortable silence settled around us.

We were spared the necessity of finding our way back to a less volatile topic of conversation by the entrance of Henson.

'Mr and Mrs Collins have arrived, sir.'

'Excellent.' Reggie stood quickly, throwing his napkin on the table. 'I'll come at once.'

He started for the door, and Laurel rose from her seat. 'I'll just go with you.'

I think neither of us had much appetite left. We followed him, leaving Gareth Winters looking complacently at his plate.

Reggie's voice carried to us before we reached the entrance hall. I could sense that same forced cheerfulness in his voice.

'Hello, Freida. Phillip. Glad you could make it.'

We followed him into the entrance hall to greet the newest arrivals.

'Mrs Ames,' he said, 'might I introduce you to Mr and Mrs Collins?'

'We know one another already,' Freida Collins said, coming towards me. 'How are you, Amory?'

'Hello, Freida,' I said, grasping her hands warmly. 'It's so good to see you again.'

'Yes, it's been far too long.'

Freida Collins, or Freida Maulhause as she had been then, and I had been at school together. We had been fairly close friends, in fact. Both of us were the products of parents who were not exceptionally adept at parenthood, and we had formed something of a bond. Freida's closest friend had been her brother, Matthew, and she had missed him terribly. When he had been killed in the war, I had been the one to whom she had turned for comfort.

After school we had kept in touch, writing letters and seeing each other at various social affairs. When her fiancé had returned from France she had asked me to be a bridesmaid at her wedding. Tragically, that wedding had never taken place. Her fiancé had died suddenly, and she had begun to associate with a wilder set. We had grown apart by the time she met her current husband, Phillip Collins.

Mr Collins had moved to London from South Africa, and there were a great many unpleasant rumours that followed him. It was not that I objected to rumours. After all, I was not under the impression that Milo's reputation was something to cheer about. Nevertheless, there had been a certain dark undertone to the things that were whispered about Mr Collins.

Perhaps this was what influenced my perception of him, but my first glance into his hard face was enough to make me distrust him.

'Amory, allow me to introduce my husband, Phillip Collins.'

'How do you do?' I said.

He nodded in response, his face impassive. I wondered if he could sense my instant dislike for him. If so, it seemed the feeling was mutual.

Looking at him, one could almost see something sinister going on behind those cold blue eyes. He was not a physically imposing man, but there was something intimidating about him, nonetheless. I felt that one always had the impression one should step back when he came near. Of course, this might have been my imagination.

'And Laurel,' Freida said, turning to my cousin. 'How good to see you again.'

Freida was smiling, but it seemed to me that there was something not quite right in it. It seemed to me that there was barely concealed fear in her expression. I wondered if she, too, was on edge about having been summoned by Isobel Van Allen's mysterious demands. I could not blame her, for there was reason to be worried.

It was strange, I thought, how all of the original participants in that weekend had been willing to return to Lyonsgate, despite the memories the place must carry. I wondered what sort of power Isobel Van Allen had over them all, what secrets they were willing to return to in order to protect.

My thoughts were interrupted as the door opened again, and Milo and Lucinda entered in their riding clothes. Lucinda was laughing gaily, her eyes bright, her golden hair windblown. They stopped when they saw us all standing in the entrance hall.

'Oh. Hello, all. I'm sorry we've missed lunch,' she said, 'but our ride was such a lark and we lost track of the time.'

'Yes, well, our other guests have arrived,' Reggie said.

Reggie made introductions, and I did not miss the quickly concealed look of surprise on Freida's face when I explained that the handsome gentleman having such a lark with Lucinda Lyons was my husband.

Introductions concluded, the Collinses were shown to their room, Laurel and Lucinda went back to the dining room, and I turned to go upstairs. I was going to fetch my book and read it until it was time for tea.

I was halfway up the stairs when Milo caught up with me.

'What have you been doing all morning, my lovely?' he asked.

'Reading, among other things,' I answered, not breaking my stride. 'How was your ride?'

'It was very nice. The property is extensive. And the horse they gave me was a fine animal.'

'That sounds lovely. Lunch is served in the dining room. You should eat something. If you continue substituting riding for meals, you'll waste away.'

'Nonsense. The country air is excellent for my constitution.'

'So it seems. You'd think you were a young man again.'

'Well, I'm not exactly past my prime, darling,' he protested.

'But perhaps not *quite* as young as you think.'

He laughed, catching my arm before I went up another step. I turned to look at him. He stood on the step below me, and our faces were nearly level.

'You don't object to my having gone riding, surely?'

'Certainly not,' I replied mildly. And I meant it. I didn't begrudge Lucinda Lyons a bit of fun. I only hoped that Milo's attentions would not give her the wrong impression. It would not do for a lonely and very pretty young woman to fall in love with my husband.

'I'd much rather ride with you, in any event,' he said. 'Will you go out with me tomorrow?'

'If you like.'

'I would. You're a much better horsewoman than Miss Lyons. Besides, I like the way you look in your riding trousers.' He dropped a kiss on my lips then patted me most inappropriately to prod me up the stairs.

Before I could move, however, I heard the sound of voices. I realised at once that it was Isobel Van Allen and Desmond Roberts. They must have come from one of their rooms. We had stopped at the top of the stairway, and had not yet turned the corner into the corridor.

It was immediately apparent that the conversation was of a very personal nature, and it was too late to make our presence known without causing additional awkwardness.

'But I don't understand,' Mr Roberts said. 'Why must you be so secretive?'

'Oh, Desmond, don't be tiresome.'

'You always treat me as though I'm a child,' he told her in a sulky voice that did nothing to belie his accusation.

'I don't enjoy you when you're disagreeable, my pet,' she said lightly. 'You know perfectly well that no one is going to read my book until I've sent it to my publisher. That includes you.'

I looked at Milo. He raised his brows.

'I don't see why you should treat me this way, after all that we have been through together. After all we mean to one another.'

'You know how much you mean to me, but that doesn't change anything.'

'It should,' he said. 'It should change everything.'

When her next words came they had dropped all hint of the caressing tone she had used only moments before.

'Listen to me,' she said sharply. 'I am tired of your whining and your demands. Remember this: I took you out of nothing, made something of you. I owe you nothing.

'I will not have you, or anyone else, tell me what I will or will not do. Do you understand me?'

He must have indicated that he understood, for her next words held less venom.

'Don't look downcast, my sweet. You'll find out soon enough. Everyone will.'

'Yes, but please, Isobel. I . . . Don't be angry with me. I adore you. You know I do.'

'I know,' she said soothingly. 'Come back into my room, Desmond.'

He apparently obeyed, for I heard the door close and silence fell.

'"Walk into my parlour, said the spider to the fly,"' Milo quoted in a low voice.

'She's treating that boy rather cruelly,' I said.

'He's not a child. He knows what he's doing.'

'I don't know that he does,' I mused. It seemed to me that Desmond Roberts was desperately in love with a woman to whom he meant very little.

'It does seem the fight's gone out of him,' Milo admitted. 'I would suspect he doesn't like being "her pet", but she's got her claws in deep. Well, he's not the first. It's always been her specialty, you know, bending men to her will. I always found it rather repulsive.'

I could see now why Milo had never fallen sway to her charms. Even at a young age, he would not have wanted to be just another of her admirers, throwing his heart at her feet with reckless abandon. Passionate adoration wasn't in his nature. He was much too used to being the centre of attention to fall into orbit around someone else's star.

As we walked toward our rooms, I couldn't rid myself of an uneasy feeling. Something about the exchange we had overheard was bothering me, and I realised suddenly what it was. Desmond Roberts was besotted with Isobel Van Allen, but there had been more than love in his voice. There had been anger and something more: desperation.

Both emotions could prove dangerous.

CHAPTER SEVEN

I dressed for dinner feeling very much as though I was attending an execution rather than an evening meal at a country estate.

I didn't know what to make of Isobel Van Allen or of the conversation I had overheard between her and Mr Roberts. Why should she want to keep her book a secret from her secretary? Granted, he was not operating solely in a professional capacity where she was concerned, but it seemed she should have wanted to confide in him if no one else.

She had told me it was not always possible to follow the heart. What had she meant? Why had she come back seven years later to gather the members of that ill-fated party together?

I tried and failed to think of what her motive might be. Though it was perfectly apparent she didn't care what others thought of her, I didn't think that she was motivated by malice alone. If it had been only that, she could have come back long ago. Or she might have written the book from the comforts of her home in Kenya with the handsome Mr Roberts to type for her. She might have whipped up a scandal from half a world away if that had been her inclination.

No, there was some other reason she had chosen to return to Lyonsgate, to make this very public announcement. For some reason she had wanted to be back at the scene of the tragedy and to face the participants. Was it possible that she herself was searching for answers?

Perhaps tonight we would find out.

'You look positively downcast, darling,' Milo observed as he came into my room tying his necktie. 'What's troubling you?'

'I don't know,' I said. 'There's something wrong in all of this, and I can't quite decide what it is. It's just so very odd that Reggie Lyons should have called everyone here. Why should they all be willing to come? If I had been here, I don't think I could be induced to set foot on the spot again.'

Milo shrugged. 'It was unfortunate, yes, but there is no reason why everyone should wish to avoid Lyonsgate for ever. After all, I'd wager that there isn't a country house in the whole of England that hasn't been touched by death. Heaven knows how many people have died at Thornecrest.'

It was not a comforting thought, and I hoped it would not occur to me the next time we visited our country house.

'In any event,' he went on, 'it's safe to assume most of

the gentlemen were in the war, and half the women lost someone to it. It's not as though they would be strangers to death.'

'You're right,' I said, 'which only proves my point. There's something else that is going on here. If it was as simple as a dreadful accident, it wouldn't have affected everyone so deeply.'

'Why don't you ask your cousin?'

'I have. She doesn't really know much about it. She was not close to any of them, you know. She had only recently been invited into their circle. I don't think she was aware of everything that was happening at the time.'

'It's really none of our concern,' Milo said. He was, as usual, supremely uninterested in anything that did not affect him directly. 'Let them go on clawing at each other. At least the wine is good.'

'Milo, I do wish you would be serious.'

'I am being serious, darling. But you become much too invested in people who are all perfect strangers to us. In fact, I don't see why you should be concerned with it at all.'

'But I . . .'

'Yes, darling, I know,' he said. 'You can't bear to keep your pretty little nose out of things that do not concern you.'

I frowned. 'It does concern me, in a way. It concerns Laurel, and she's not only my cousin but my dearest friend.'

'But you've just said that Laurel wasn't deeply involved in any of this.'

'It doesn't matter. She was still affected by it. Another book has the potential to do a great deal of damage.'

'Perhaps it will not be as bad as you imagine,' he said.

I hoped he was right. 'I'm very cross with Miss Van Allen. There's no reason that she should make everyone miserable.'

'Well, let us see what kind of scene she creates at dinner tonight, shall we?'

I sighed. 'I suppose we have no choice.'

I could not help but feel we were in for a repeat of last night's performance as we took our seats in the dining room. With the exception of the additional two guests, Freida and Phillip Collins, everything was just as it had been the evening before.

I was uncertain how things would proceed after the volatile way in which dinner had ended last night. It appeared, however, that Reggie Lyons intended to make good his promise that things would not get out of hand. He nodded stiffly to Isobel when she came into the dining room and she gave him a bright smile in return. It seemed that they intended to maintain at least the pretence of civility.

We were all very aware, however, that there was more to come. It was only a matter of time until Isobel made another one of her announcements.

I looked around at my fellow guests. Though they were doing their best to go on as though nothing was amiss, I could sense the tension in the air. Freida Collins seemed particularly ill at ease, and I wondered if it was because, not having been present last night, she was unsure of what to expect. Or, perhaps, she had been apprised of last night's events and that was why she was uneasy. Her husband wore that same expression of vague contempt that had been on his face since his arrival. Whatever he was feeling, he did not intend for others to know it.

I knew Isobel was enjoying holding the group in thrall, keeping them all on the edge of their seats, wondering what she would reveal. The thought had occurred to me, of course, that there must be other secrets swirling beneath the surface. If not, why would they all be so concerned?

The time came after the last of the dessert plates had been cleared away. I thought it was probably more due to the fact that Isobel was enjoying making her audience wait rather than that she had decided to allow them to enjoy their dinner in peace.

'I realise it must have come as a shock to all of you, the way I made my announcement at dinner last night,' she began. 'I'm afraid the emotion of the moment caught up with me. I did not intend to make such a scene.'

None of us were fooled by her performance. She was clearly revelling in the tension that hung in the air, on the way all of us were hanging on her every word.

'I would have liked nothing more than to remain in Kenya for the rest of my days, but my conscience would not allow me to do so.'

I could practically feel Milo rolling his eyes from across the room.

'Conscience?' Beatrice scoffed. 'Since when have you ever had a conscience, Isobel?'

Isobel ignored this question and went on in the same even tone.

'It isn't easy for me to say this, believe me. But the time

has come that I speak openly. The truth of the matter is that I now believe that Bradford Glenn was innocent.'

This announcement was greeted without much surprise.

'How kind of you to say so, after he killed himself because of you,' Beatrice said bitterly.

Isobel continued to carry on as though she hadn't heard Beatrice. 'I came to believe in his innocence when I heard of his suicide note. He spoke not of guilt, but of love. He and Edwin hated one another, perhaps, but it wasn't Bradford that caused Edwin's death that night.'

'We knew all along it was an unfortunate accident,' Reggie Lyons said. Unlike his sister, his tone held no bitterness. If I had to name the emotion, I might have thought it relief.

'That's not at all what I mean, Reggie,' she said.

'What do you mean, Miss Van Allen?' It was Lindy Lyons who asked the question. She was trying, I thought, to hide the eagerness in her tone.

Isobel glanced at her, and then turned to Gareth Winters. 'You asked me last night why any of you would want to help me.'

He watched her from across the table, his face unreadable.

'It's because I think one of you knows the truth. I want you to tell me.'

'The truth?' Beatrice spat out. 'What do you mean? Since when have you ever been concerned with the truth?'

'My conclusion that Bradford killed Edwin was based on the evidence. They hated one another and had fought earlier that night and were left alone when the rest of us came back to the house. Edwin was unconscious when we left that summer house and dead in the snow the next morning. How did he get there?'

'He woke up,' Freida said. 'Woke up and tried to get to the house.'

Freida was trembling. I could see it from where I sat. Her husband, however, might have been made of stone. His face was hard and expressionless. Only his eyes burnt darkly as he watched Isobel.

'I don't think he did,' Isobel said. 'You see, in addition to his suicide note, Bradford wrote me a letter.'

There was a stunned silence. I glanced around the table. Everyone was watching Isobel, save for Mr Winters. He was looking down at his plate.

Beatrice, as usual, recovered first. 'What did the letter say?' she demanded.

'It was a kind letter, given the circumstances,' Isobel said. 'He said he had been hurting for years and was about to set himself free. He also told me that he wasn't a murderer. "Perhaps Edwin, too, was set free," he wrote, "but not by my hand."'

Silence fell as everyone waited for her to continue.

'And that is why I need your help,' she said at last. 'Someone here knows the truth, and it is only a matter of time until I discover it.'

'What the devil are you trying to say?' Reggie demanded.

Her eyes swept the table. There was nothing in them now of the soft melancholy I had seen at breakfast the previous morning. She might have been an avenging fury, so hotly were her eyes blazing in her pale face.

'I'm trying to say that Edwin Green was indeed murdered. And if Bradford was innocent, it means that one of you is the killer.'

'I believe Isobel missed her calling,' Milo said, as he removed his cufflinks in my room after dinner. 'She might have made a fine actress, with her magniloquent histrionics.'

As she had done last night, Isobel had excused herself after her grand announcement, leaving the rest of us to absorb the implications of her shocking claim.

Milo had been unimpressed by Miss Van Allen's theatrics, but the same could not be said of the others. Hot denials had issued forth from all present. Reggie and Beatrice seemed to agree that Isobel was lying, fabricating another tale for the sake of her second book, but I could sense the fear hovering heavily in the room.

'This can only lead to trouble,' Laurel had told me worriedly as we left the dining room. 'I'm terribly afraid of what is going to happen next.'

I shared my cousin's concerns, for it seemed that no good could come of the claim that one of the guests here at Lyonsgate was a killer. Was it possible? Or was Isobel merely trying to exploit a tragedy a second time?

'Do you really think that someone else is responsible for Edwin Green's murder?' I asked my husband.

'You'll recall, my dear, that Mr Green's death was ruled an accident by a coroner's jury.' He tossed his dinner jacket over the back of a chair in a careless manner that would no doubt offend Parks deeply. 'Isobel only wants to make a scene.'

'But why come back if she wasn't trying to learn something?'

'She's writing another book to add to her somewhat limited oeuvre and needs fresh fodder. What better way to get it than to come back claiming that the killer is still at large? Really, Amory, don't tell me you've been caught up in her wild tales.'

I thought of the note she said she had received from Bradford Glenn. I wondered why he would have bothered to write to her. Trying to clear his name before he died, perhaps? Why, then, had it taken Isobel six years to act on it?

There was something amiss in all of this. If there was not something wrong, no one would feel threatened by Miss Van Allen's claims, yet the fear and anger had been palpable tonight. And it was not just the menace of a fresh, if baseless, scandal that was worrying them. No, there were secrets that people didn't want revealed, and there was more to Edwin Green's death than a simple accident.

I only hoped that Laurel did not get tangled up in the web of lies the others were spinning. Perhaps there was some way that I could help. I had, after all, two other mysteries to my credit.

The problem with this one was that so much time had passed, and everyone involved was extremely reluctant to relive the past. I also realised that the various accounts of what had happened that night would be strongly influenced by both personal perception and recollections that had been impaired by the consumption of alcohol, drugs, or both. How much could they really remember of what had happened and how much of it was a story that had been concocted from their own imperfect knowledge of events and personal biases? There was, too, the possibility that one – or even several – of them were lying to protect themselves or one another. It was all very complex.

Perhaps the best thing to do would be to compare the various accounts and see what aspects of the story were corroborated by other accounts. There might also be the opportunity to ask someone else who had been there, the servants perhaps. I would leave that aspect to Winnelda. I might even be able to find some excuse to question the local doctor. Perhaps he would be able to tell me more about Edwin Green's death.

I looked up to see Milo watching me. I raised my brows and affected what I hoped was an innocent expression.

'You are brewing trouble in that brain of yours,' he said. 'I recognise that look on your face.'

'No such thing,' I protested. 'You haven't the faintest idea what I was thinking. I might have been considering ordering a new gown from Paris.'

He shook his head. 'I am also familiar with your ordering gowns from Paris face, and that is most definitely not it.'

I was annoyed by his ability to read me, for lack of a better expression, like a book. 'Well, what do you suppose I was thinking about, if you're so clever?'

'You were trying to determine the best way to gather accurate information about what really happened that night. The people there were unreliable witnesses, especially as it may be in their best interest to lie. Therefore, you were trying to determine the best way to glean the truth from the various accounts of that evening.'

I was astounded by the accuracy of this assessment, but I didn't intend to let him know that. 'I may have been thinking something along those lines,' I conceded.

He smiled knowingly. 'As you probably know, I think the entire thing incredibly ill-advised, and I would like nothing better than to cart you unceremoniously back to London.'

My brows shot upward.

'However,' he went on, 'since I know you would dislike being dragged away, I have no choice but to remain here and do what I can to minimise the risks.'

'I do appreciate your concern,' I said. After all, I could not discount the fact that I had nearly been shot twice in recent months, or that Milo had, in fact, been grazed by a killer's bullet. I didn't intend to take any unnecessary risks. After all, Edwin Green's death was a thing of the past. Seven years was a long time.

We finished preparing for bed and slipped beneath the icy sheets, glad to have each other for warmth.

As I drifted off to sleep, I had no inkling that murder was much closer at hand than I had believed.

CHAPTER EIGHT

I roused Milo for breakfast the next morning, but Parks seemed to be dissatisfied with the press of Milo's tweeds and so I went down alone while they worked to rectify the problem.

I had crossed the entrance hall and was nearly to the breakfast room when I heard voices issuing from within. I might have entered anyway, had the conversation not appeared to be somewhat private in nature.

'She can't know anything,' I heard Reggie Lyons saying. 'She's making all of it up. She must be.'

'Reggie, get hold of yourself.' This stern command came from Beatrice. I could picture her looking coldly at him over her coffee cup.

'But the murder . . .'

'There was no murder,' Beatrice said firmly. 'Edwin's death was a tragic misfortune, nothing more.'

'But in her letter, she said . . .'

'I know what she said,' Beatrice replied, cutting him off once again. 'You let her frighten you with veiled threats into hosting this wretched house party, when it's not possible that she has learnt anything else.'

So that was why Reggie had invited everyone back to Lyonsgate at Isobel's command. He had been afraid that she knew something and would expose it. His next words confirmed this.

'Do you suppose she knows about . . . ?'

'That will do, Reggie,' she said, cutting him off.

I heard someone coming down the stairs then, so I silently retreated a few steps, and then made sure that they heard me approaching the breakfast room. As I had expected, their conversation stopped at once.

'Pass me the honey, will you, Reggie?' Beatrice asked.

She looked up at me when I entered. 'Good morning, Mrs Ames. We've just been discussing the weather. It looks as though it may snow again.'

The lie was told effortlessly. There was no doubt in my mind that Beatrice Lyons Kline was a woman to be reckoned with. Nevertheless, I thought again how surprising it was that both Edwin Green and Bradford Glenn had been rumoured to be in love with her. There was something very careful and calculated about her, a sternness which I would not have supposed would inspire passion.

'I wouldn't mind a bit of snow,' I replied, going to the sideboard to fill my plate.

'Then again, I shouldn't be surprised if it warms up suddenly,' Reggie said.

The footsteps that I had heard on the stairs had

apparently belonged to Mr Winters, for he came into the dining room then, his pale grey eyes flickering around the room as though he were seeing something other than the occupants in it. 'Good morning,' he said, looking at no one in particular.

We greeted him, and I was prepared to return to the topic of the weather when Reggie broached the subject that was foremost on everyone's minds.

'I feel I must apologise again for what happened at dinner last night,' he said. 'I hope you understand that Miss Van Allen is . . .'

'Grasping at straws,' Beatrice interjected. 'She wants nothing more than to rake up another scandal at our expense. The whole matter is bound to die down once she realises that we will not play her games.'

'I'm sure you're right,' I assured her, though I didn't feel at all certain. I did not know Isobel Van Allen at all well, but I had the feeling that she was not one to abandon her cause.

Milo, at last presentable enough for Parks' satisfaction, joined us at the breakfast table and was shortly followed by Mr and Mrs Collins, Laurel, and Lucinda Lyons, who took a seat next to Milo. Tensions were still high, but we all went on as though everything was quite normal. I was immensely relieved that Isobel had not made an appearance. Perhaps she had taken her breakfast quite early.

We did not comment on her absence and spoke no further about her announcement at dinner the night before. I was a bit disappointed, but I thought it was probably for the best. I knew that Reggie's nerves were on edge, and

Freida looked pale and drawn as though she had not slept and kept glancing anxiously at her husband.

The meal finished, I excused myself. Lucinda Lyons had engaged Milo in another conversation, and I supposed it would be a while before she would return him to me. In the meantime, I thought that I might spend my time reading a few more chapters of *The Dead of Winter.*

Though I pretended to myself that it was research, I could not deny that I was very much caught up in the drama of the story. Isobel Van Allen was certainly capable of weaving a compelling tale. How much of it was fiction and how much was reality remained to be seen. I hoped that at some point I would be able to make the distinction.

Freida Collins and her husband had gone out of the dining room before me, and as I came into the entrance hall I saw them standing in the door of the drawing room talking to one another in low voices.

They looked up at the sound of my footsteps. He glanced back at her and said something in a voice too low for me to hear. It seemed as though she grew slightly paler as he spoke. Then he turned and walked up the stairs, leaving her standing alone in the entrance hall, her eyes on his retreating form.

For some reason her expression brought to mind another day when she had stood, looking pale and uncertain. She had held a letter in her hand, a letter that she had been afraid to open. We had stood looking at each other until, at last, she had broken the seal and found that her worst fears had been realised.

That was my sharpest memory of Freida, how devastated

she had been upon the death of her brother. Matthew Maulhause had been the first person that I knew who had died in the war. There would be more, of course. Many more. But that day it had been a terrible shock, the first jarring tragedy in a young life relatively untouched by troubles.

I had comforted her in that moment, but I had not been able to comfort her when her fiancé had died. It was not comfort she had wanted but the ability to forget. It was his death that had been the blow that had sent her whirling recklessly into Isobel Van Allen's path.

I hoped the sad memories were not replaying themselves on my face, but Freida appeared too preoccupied to have even noticed that I was still standing there. She turned and went towards the drawing room. After a moment, I followed her.

She had taken a seat near the fire and was staring into it, unseeing, when I came into the room.

'Hello, Freida,' I said softly.

She looked up. 'Oh, hello, Amory. I'm sorry. I'm a bit distracted this morning.'

'I think we all are,' I said, still hovering in the doorway. 'Am I disturbing you?'

'No, not at all. I've been hoping for the chance to talk to you. Come sit with me, won't you?' She smiled and the sincerity of it recalled the Freida I had known. She had been a beautiful young woman, and she was still extremely lovely. Her hair was still a glossy shade of chestnut brown and she had very large brown eyes. I remembered when those eyes had sparkled with laughter, but there was no laughter in them now. I wondered how much of it had to do with what was happening here at Lyonsgate and how much of it might be attributed to her marriage to Phillip Collins.

I took a seat across from her. With the fire cracking cheerily in the hearth, I could almost imagine we were back at school, sharing our secrets with one another. How much times had changed since then. I suddenly felt very old.

'It's good to see you again, Freida, though I suppose the circumstances are less than ideal.'

'Yes,' she said. 'There are many times I've thought I should write to you, but you know how life sometimes interferes in one's plans.'

'It certainly does,' I agreed. 'I hope you've been well.'

I hadn't heard much about Freida since her marriage, and I didn't think she was often in London. There was a house somewhere in France and, now I knew, the country house not far from Lyonsgate. I wondered if there was a reason her husband kept them away from town.

'Oh, yes,' she said. 'My life has been . . . rather lovely. How have you been?'

'Very well, thank you.'

A vaguely uncomfortable silence fell between us. Things were, I think, complicated by the fact that neither of us wanted to ask the other about her marriage. I had my own opinions of Phillip Collins, and I was certain Freida must have seen Milo's name bandied about in the gossip columns. It was not the sort of thing one discussed with an old acquaintance.

She brightened suddenly. 'We've two lovely children. Our son, William, is nearly seven, and I have a daughter, Alice, who's just over a year old. Perhaps you might come to tea one day so that I can show her off to you.' There was a genuine warmth in her eyes when she spoke of her children, and I could tell at once how much they meant to her.

'That sounds lovely. I shall look forward to seeing her.' I was glad that Freida had children. I remembered her telling me once that the only thing she really wanted in life was a family of her own. That was before her fiancé had been killed. I wondered, too, if that was why she had married Mr Collins. I would not have chosen him for her partner, but she clearly loved her children and I was glad for her.

'Have you any children?' she asked me.

'No,' I said lightly. 'We have not been so fortunate as of yet.' I was sure she would pity me now, thinking that I was incapable of having them. The truth of it, however, was that I had not reached a point in the last five years where I felt secure enough in my marriage to want to become pregnant.

However, things were much better between Milo and me now, and I had faith that they would continue to improve. Perhaps it would be something to be considered in the near future. We weren't getting any younger, after all. My mother had been eighteen when she'd married and barely twenty when I was born. By her standards, I was very much behind schedule.

'It does tend to happen suddenly,' she said.

'Yes, I suppose it does.'

Silence fell again, and I decided to press onward. 'I was very shocked by Isobel's announcement last night.'

'Yes,' she said, her voice suddenly strained. 'Ridiculous, wasn't it?'

'Do you think so?' I asked.

'Yes, of course.' Her eyes darted about the room before coming back to my face. 'Don't you?'

'I really couldn't say.' Again there was a silence that I took the opportunity to fill. 'I imagine it must have been terrible. You found Edwin Green's body, I understand.'

It was terribly blunt of me, but it had become clear that the conversation was not going to proceed unless I pushed it along a bit.

'I went for a walk that morning,' she said. 'I . . . I thought I left my handbag at the summer house.'

I had not asked her for her reasons for being out that morning, and it was curious that she should have presented them to me.

'And you found him in the snow?' I prompted her.

'Yes. It was dreadful.'

She had gone pale, and I felt a bit bad for having pressed her into reliving what had obviously been a traumatic experience. I did, however, have one more question. 'Did you think it was an accident?'

'Yes,' she said at once. 'It must have been an accident. No one else would have killed Edwin. Everyone but Bradford got on perfectly well with him.'

'You're certain of that?'

Her eyes met mine unwaveringly. 'Absolutely.'

There was something almost defiant in her gaze, and I could not help but feel that she was lying.

Freida excused herself a few moments later, and I sat alone in the drawing room, pondering our conversation. There had been something strange in her manner, and I wondered if she had something to hide. How I would discover what it was, however, I didn't know. It had been a long time since we had been confidantes.

Reluctantly leaving the warm seat by the fire, I went back out into the entrance hall just as Mr Roberts came down the stairs.

'Good morning, Mr Roberts,' I greeted him. I knew how hard it must be for him to be so out of place at Lyonsgate, especially since Isobel had done everything in her power to make them unwelcome.

'Good morning,' he replied absently. He reached the bottom step, and I noticed at once that something was amiss. He looked worried, almost pale beneath his bronzed skin.

'Is there something wrong?' I asked.

'I . . . I'm not certain. Isobel is in her room, but the door is locked and she won't answer.'

I felt a strange sense of foreboding that I tried to fight back.

'Perhaps she's still sleeping,' I suggested, and even as I said it I realised that it was not likely to be true. I had seen for myself that she was an early riser. I did not think she would be so deep in sleep as not to hear a knock at her door.

'I don't think so. She always rises early,' he said, echoing my thoughts.

'Perhaps she is writing and doesn't wish to be disturbed.'

He shook his head. 'I don't think so,' he said again. 'You see, she was quite ill all night. I thought perhaps she had taken poorly to something that she had eaten and that she would be well again this morning, but now I wonder if there is something seriously wrong.'

That did not sound at all encouraging.

I walked to the steps beside him, trying to fight my growing unease. 'I'm sure there's no reason to be alarmed. Perhaps she's still feeling ill.'

'I think there's something wrong,' he insisted. 'I wonder if I should ring for the doctor?'

'Perhaps we should look in on her first,' I suggested. 'She may answer the door if you try again.'

We reached the landing, and I followed him down the hall to Miss Van Allen's door. He knocked, almost pounded, against the wood, and I thought there was something like desperation in it. There was no answer at first, and he tried in vain to turn the knob. The door was locked. I began to wonder if I should ask Mr Lyons if he had a spare key.

A moment later, however, I heard the bolt being slid back. Then the door opened and Isobel Van Allen looked out at us from the dark room, a black velvet robe wrapped tightly around her. She was a bit paler than usual, but her dark eyes were sharp.

'What is it?' she asked, her tone lined with impatience. The question was directed at Mr Roberts, and I wasn't sure at first that she even noticed me standing there.

'I . . . I was worried,' Desmond stammered. 'You wouldn't answer the door.'

'I was trying to sleep. You know I was ill last night. I took some sleeping tablets.'

'Are you . . . are you feeling better?'

'Yes, Desmond,' she answered with a sigh. 'It was likely only something I ate. I'm much better now.'

'Can I get you anything?'

'Thank you, no.'

'Well, let me come in and sit with you.'

'No,' she said sharply. Then her tone softened. 'Don't worry about me. Run along and enjoy your morning. I'll need you to type for me later.'

She looked at me then, and I was caught by something in her gaze. 'You'll take care of dear Desmond, won't you?'

'I . . . Certainly,' I replied.

'Thank you for looking in on me,' she said. She reached out and patted his cheek.

'You're such a dear, my sweet Desmond,' she said.

Then she leant in to kiss him on the mouth. I turned away at once, embarrassed to be privy to so intimate a scene.

Then she closed the door.

Mr Roberts let out a breath, as though he had been holding it. I thought at first that he had forgotten me, but at last he turned from the door. He gave me a shaky and somewhat rueful smile.

'I . . . I'm sorry I made a scene, Mrs Ames,' he said. 'It was just so unlike her not to answer her door.'

'Well, I'm very glad to see she's all right.'

'Yes,' he replied vaguely, his thoughts obviously elsewhere.

We parted ways then as he went into his room. I couldn't help but think as I walked away, however, that there was something amiss in the scene I had just witnessed. Isobel had been acting strangely. It could, of course, be nothing more than that she was still feeling unwell. Sickness often made people peevish.

However, there was something in her behaviour that struck me as odd. Desmond hadn't looked satisfied with their encounter. Despite Isobel's display of affection, he had stiffened when she'd kissed him, and he had seemed distracted as he went into his room. I didn't know if it was embarrassment at her kiss or annoyance at her dismissal, but it seemed that all still was not well in paradise.

It was perhaps an hour later when Milo came into my room.

Winnelda was following Parks' example and mercilessly polishing my riding boots while I read in the chair near the fire.

'Still reading that dreadful thing, are you?' Milo asked, indicating the copy of *The Dead of Winter* in my hand. 'Well, I've come to rescue you from it. I've just been out to the stables and asked the groom to saddle horses for us. Are you ready for the ride you promised me?'

'I suppose so,' I answered absently. To be honest, I had not been reading for some time. Try as I might, I had not been able to concentrate much on the novel. My thoughts were still on Isobel Van Allen. Something about the scene at her doorway nagged at me, but I could not determine what it was.

'I am flattered by your enthusiasm,' he remarked dryly.

I smiled and turned my attention to him. 'I'm sorry. I was thinking about something else.'

He looked at me warily, but said nothing.

'A ride sounds lovely,' I told him, rising from my seat.

'Good.' He went across to the door to his room. 'It shall only take me a few moments to be ready.'

'Very well.' I set the book aside and moved to change into my riding costume, a white blouse and tan trousers tucked into my now gleaming black boots. Winnelda insisted upon brushing my dark jacket before I could put it on, so I sat back down to wait.

Normally, I would have been pleased at the prospect of a ride with my husband, but I could not seem to get my mind off of Isobel Van Allen. Perhaps she really had been ill and hadn't wanted Desmond to know.

I glanced at our connecting doorway. Milo was not finished dressing, and Winnelda was not ready to relinquish my jacket. Perhaps I should look in on Miss Van Allen again before we left. I was sure she wouldn't be pleased to be bothered again, but it would set my mind at ease to know that she was all right.

'I'll be right back, Winnelda.'

'All right, madam. I'm nearly finished.'

I left my room and went down the hall.

'Miss Van Allen?' I called, knocking lightly on the door to her room. It had apparently not been securely closed after she had spoken with us, for it opened beneath my fist.

I could see inside, but not very well. The heavy curtains were still drawn, and the room was dark. Perhaps she was still sleeping, after all. If so, I didn't want to disturb her. She had not seemed at all pleased with Mr Roberts for doing so this morning.

I hesitated on the threshold, something within in me both urging me to go in and warning me to retreat.

It occurred to me that she might be worse. Perhaps I

should check on her and call for a doctor if her condition had not improved.

'Miss Van Allen?' I called softly.

I stepped into the room, and stepped immediately into a puddle of wine, the glass lying empty on its side not far from the door.

My eyes followed the puddle and it was then I saw Isobel Van Allen lying on the floor, still in her black robe, arm outstretched, her head turned away from the door.

I was glad that I had followed my instincts. We would need to summon a doctor at once.

I went down to my knees beside her, the wine soaking into my trousers.

'Miss Van Allen? Isobel?' I reached out and touched her outstretched hand. It was cool to the touch, but not cold.

I tried to gather her into my arms to see if I could rouse her, but as she fell heavily against me, her head fell back, her dark, unseeing eyes staring up at me.

I gasped, too horrified to scream, and, gently laying her back on the floor, stumbled to my feet and out into the hallway just as Milo came around the corner.

He stopped when he saw me, an expression I had never seen crossing his face. 'Oh, God,' he breathed.

I looked down and realised that it was not wine in which I was covered. It was blood.

CHAPTER NINE

Milo was at my side in two long strides, his eyes moving over me, his hands running over my arms and then my torso. 'Where is it coming from?'

'I . . . I . . .' I couldn't seem to speak; to form the words seemed an impossible task. I felt incredibly light-headed, and my legs felt as though they wouldn't hold me much longer. *She's dead. She's dead.* The words kept playing over and over in my mind, but I couldn't seem to make myself say them.

He grasped my shoulders, his voice firm but very gentle. 'Amory, look at me.'

I blinked then forced myself to focus, to meet his gaze. The intensity in his bright blue eyes captured my attention, as did his next words. 'Where are you bleeding, darling?'

It was only then I realised that he thought the blood was mine. I had stumbled into the hallway, soaked in blood. Of course, he had thought I was injured. I hastened to reassure him, but the words were slow in coming.

'No, it's not mine. She . . . she's . . .' I pointed to Miss Van Allen's room, my hand shaking.

His hand still gripping my arm, Milo stepped into the threshold and looked into the room. One short glance was apparently all it took.

Then he moved back to my side. 'Are you hurt, darling?'

'No. I . . . We . . .' I wanted to explain what had happened. I wanted to know what he was going to do about Isobel Van Allen and to tell him that we should call for help, but I could not seem to find the words. It was as though I knew what I wanted to say, but my mind was not completely connected to my body. My thoughts were racing too quickly for me to catch hold of one enough to speak it. It was a maddening sensation.

'You're certain you're all right?'

'Yes, but . . .'

I drew in a deep breath, trying to calm myself. It was just so awful. But perhaps there was still hope. She hadn't been cold . . .

I started to step towards the room, but he slipped his hand around my waist and blocked me from the doorway.

'There's nothing you can do, darling,' he said. 'Come away.'

He was right, of course. That much was perfectly obvious, though I hadn't wanted to believe it. There was nothing anyone would be able to do for Isobel Van Allen.

Half supporting me, Milo led me down the hall and back to my room.

As he ushered me into the bedroom, Winnelda turned from where she was brushing my riding jacket. She took one look at me and screamed. Very loudly. It was enough to rouse me somewhat from my stupor.

'I'm all right,' I said. 'It . . . it isn't mine.' My voice was steady, if a bit faint.

'Winnelda, draw Mrs Ames a bath.'

She stood staring at us.

'Winnelda, please do as I ask,' Milo said impatiently.

She gave a little sob and fairly ran into the bathroom.

Milo sat me down in a chair and knelt before me, deftly unbuttoning my bloodstained blouse. 'It's going to be all right, darling. You've had a shock. We'll get you cleaned up and you'll feel much better.'

'You should send for a doctor,' I said.

He hesitated for only an instant. 'There's no need for a doctor.'

I had known it from the moment I saw her, but I hadn't wanted to believe it. 'She's dead,' I whispered.

'Yes.'

'There was so much blood.'

'I know, darling.' He stripped off the bloody blouse I was wearing and tossed it aside. I hugged myself against the cold of the room and the deeper cold I felt inside, but Milo swiftly removed his jacket and put it over my shoulders. Then he leant down to pull off my riding boots. The brightly polished boots were now stained with blood.

I looked down at my trousers, the fawn-coloured fabric bright red, and felt a wave of dizziness.

Milo looked up and must have noticed that I had paled, for he cupped my face in his hand, drawing my eyes from my bloodied trousers to his face. 'It's all right, darling.'

I nodded. It wasn't all right, but I loved him for trying to convince me that it was.

Winnelda came out of the bathroom, wringing her hands. 'Oh, madam,' she said, her voice breaking. 'Oh, madam.'

'Winnelda, you must get hold of yourself,' Milo said firmly. 'I need you to tend to Mrs Ames.'

She did a very poor job of stifling another sob, and it was apparent that I was going to have to collect myself before she went into hysterics. I wished for the first time in my life that I had been inclined to carry smelling salts. Instead, I drew in a deep, steadying breath.

'It's all right,' I said calmly. 'There's . . . there's been a . . . an accident, I'm afraid. Miss Van Allen is dead.'

'Oh!' Winnelda's hand went to her mouth.

Milo took both my hands in his. The warmth of his grip was reassuring. 'Will you be all right if I leave for a moment?'

'Yes. Yes, I'll be fine. I'm much better now.' He studied me for a moment, as though to be sure I meant it, then rose and turned to Winnelda.

'Can I trust you to look after her?'

She nodded. 'Yes, Mr Ames. I'll look after her.'

'Good. Help her off with the rest of her clothes and get her into the bath,' Milo said. He pulled a handkerchief from his pocket and, though he turned his back to me, I could see that he was wiping the blood from his hands.

He turned to me as he reached the door. 'I'd better notify Lyons and ring for the police.'

I looked up at him and our eyes met. We were both

thinking the same thing. Isobel Van Allen was dead and, despite what I had told Winnelda, it most definitely had not been an accident.

By the time I had washed the blood away in the bath and Winnelda had helped me into a dark tweed suit, I was again fully in possession of my faculties. I felt incredibly tired, drained of energy, but my thoughts were clear. I almost wished that they weren't, for I could still remember the sensation of the blood seeping into my clothes, though I hadn't been aware of what it was at the time.

Even worse, I kept picturing Isobel's dark eyes staring blankly up at the ceiling, the brightness that had flashed in them completely gone. A chill swept through me.

'Are you all right, madam? Can I get you anything? Perhaps some tea?'

Winnelda seemed to have calmed herself, and I was glad that we had both escaped the throes of full-blown hysteria.

'Thank you, Winnelda, no. I need to go down to the drawing room. I shall have to go down and speak to the police shortly.'

In truth I would have liked nothing better than to drink a hot cup of tea and lie down for the rest of the day. My head was beginning to ache, and I did not relish spending the next hours answering pressing questions. Unfortunately, I knew from experience what would be required of me.

Milo had come back shortly after leaving me to ascertain that I was all right and then had gone away again to speak with the doctor and the local coroner, who had apparently arrived together. I supposed they were examining the body –

so sad and strange to think of Isobel Van Allen in that way – but they would no doubt wish to see me soon.

'I can't believe it's happened again, madam,' Winnelda said mournfully. 'Bodies turning up wherever you go.'

'Yes, it's dreadful,' I answered. As dreadful as it was, however, I could not say that I was completely surprised. It had been shocking, of course, to find Isobel dead, but I had been uneasy since I had arrived at Lyonsgate. With emotions running high and so many secrets running deep, it had almost seemed only a matter of time before something awful happened. Not that I had expected murder. But I had seen first-hand the lengths to which people would go when they were crossed, and Isobel Van Allen had crossed a great many people.

As I went out into the hallway, I glanced in the direction of Miss Van Allen's door. It was closed. I wondered if the doctor and the police were still inside.

It appeared they were, for the drawing room was empty, save for Reggie Lyons. He was pacing the room, his face white. He held a cigarette between his fingers, but he seemed to have forgotten it was there, for the ash had built up on the tip and crumbled, unnoticed, to the rug as he paced.

He stopped for a moment when he saw me. 'This is a rotten business, Mrs Ames,' he said. His voice sounded as tired as I felt.

'Yes,' I replied. I could think of nothing better to say. 'Are the police upstairs?'

'Yes. Your husband was kind enough to show them to . . . to Isobel's room. I . . . I have an aversion to blood, you see.' If possible, he had grown even paler as he said this.

'Perhaps you should sit down, Mr Lyons,' I said gently.

He seemed too weary to protest and sank into a chair by the fire, rubbing his face with his hand.

I remembered that Laurel had once spoken of the difficult time Reggie had had upon returning home from the war. He had seen some very bad things, she said. Things he vowed never to speak of, but that had apparently replayed before his eyes at odd moments as he stared off into the distance.

I was glad he had not come across me when I had stumbled from Isobel's room. Milo had been surprised and, I thought, momentarily shocked, but it was not the sort of thing that would trouble him for long. It would have had a much worse impact upon Reggie Lyons.

Hurried footsteps echoed along the entrance hall, and Laurel came running to the drawing room. 'Is it true?' she asked. 'Is Isobel dead?'

'Yes. I . . . I found her,' I said.

'Oh, no,' she whispered, coming to my side and clutching my arm. 'All you all right, Amory?'

'Yes, I'm fine now.'

'But what's happened? I know she was ill. Was it a heart attack or some such thing?'

I shook my head. 'No. I'm afraid she was murdered.'

Laurel's hand flew to her mouth. 'No. Are you certain?'

I glanced at Reggie Lyons and lowered my voice. 'There was . . . a great deal of blood.'

'Good heavens,' she whispered.

A log popped loudly in the fireplace just then and Reggie flinched.

'Perhaps you had better talk to him,' I told her quietly. 'He's having a time of it.'

She nodded and moved to where he sat, talking to him in a low, soothing voice.

Milo came into the room then and came at once to my side. 'How are you feeling, darling?' he asked in a low voice. 'Holding up?'

'Yes, I'm fine.' I offered him an unsteady smile. 'Thank you.'

'Let me get you a drink.'

I shook my head. 'I don't need one, thank you. I'm quite well.' He studied my face, as though trying to determine if I was telling the truth.

'You don't look well,' he said at last.

'It was certainly a shock, but I assure you I am quite composed.' I didn't, of course, feel well, but I did not intend to have him fussing over me. I was not accustomed to it.

He didn't have time to argue the point, for two more gentlemen entered the room.

I had had few dealings with policemen in my life, but my involvement in two other mysteries over the course of the last year had given me a good idea of what to expect, and I might have picked these men out as policemen if I had passed them on Regent Street. The first gentleman was tall and thin with dark hair and even darker eyes. He was obviously the superior officer, for the second man stood a bit behind him.

Reggie stood wordlessly, as though waiting for them to pass sentence.

'Who found the body?' the first man asked.

'I did,' I said, stepping forward.

His dark eyes came to rest on my face, and I felt that he was taking my measure in the space of a moment.

'You are Mrs Ames,' he said.

'Yes.'

'Detective Inspector Laszlo,' he said. 'This is Sergeant Hanes. I would like to speak with you privately for a few moments.'

'Certainly.' I was not surprised by this request. In fact, I had suspected as much. Well, the sooner we began, the sooner it would be over.

The inspector glanced first at Reggie and Laurel and then at Milo, as though waiting for them to leave so we could begin our conversation.

Milo's gaze caught mine, and I nodded reassuringly.

'If you will all come with me for a moment,' Sergeant Hanes said, and they followed him from the room. Laurel looked back over her shoulder at me on her way out the door, and I could feel her silent encouragement.

'Have a seat, Mrs Ames.' The inspector indicated a chair and I sat. He did the same.

'Now, tell me what happened. In as much detail as possible, if you please.' He spoke in a low voice, curiously devoid of any emotion. There was no solicitousness in it, and certainly no sympathy. I wondered if it was his way of inducing calm in witnesses, or perhaps fear in the guilty.

I recounted the morning leading up to the incident in what I hoped was a calm, clear manner. However, I found myself hesitating a bit when I came to describing the scene I had quite literally stumbled upon in Isobel's room. It was so ghastly, I hated to even think of it, let alone speak about it. He continued to watch me with those piercing eyes, however, and I did not intend to retreat.

'. . . I realised that she must be dead, but some part of me hoped that there might be something left that we could do.' I stopped, feeling a bit ill.

'And then what?' he asked, completely unmoved by my tale.

'I went back out into the hall. I was somewhat in shock. Mr Ames had just come looking for me, and he took me back to my room to . . . change from my bloody clothes, and then he went at once to notify you.'

'Where are those clothes now?'

I refused to show any hint of alarm at this question. He was trying to set me on edge, to make me feel as though I had something to hide, but I did not and it wasn't going to work.

'Still in my room, I suppose,' I answered without hesitation. 'My maid can fetch them for you if you'd like.'

'How was she killed, do you think?' he asked suddenly.

I wondered if this was meant to be a trick question. If so, it was a clumsy attempt on his part, and he would be disappointed in my answer. I did not intend to make guesses that might lead him to conclude that I had some sort of first-hand knowledge of the cause of death.

'I expect the coroner could give you a better answer to that than I,' I told him.

His brows rose ever so slightly and he continued to watch me expectantly; I interpreted this to mean my answer would not suffice.

I could not blame him for attempting to trip me up, if that was indeed what he was attempting to do. After all, I had found the body and had emerged from the room doused in the victim's blood. I would be the first to admit that, to an outside observer, it would seem that I could very potentially be the murderer. I did not let this worry me, however. I was guiltless and therefore impervious to his veiled accusations.

I sighed. 'I don't know how she was killed, Inspector. I only know that she was covered in blood. As soon as I found her, I went back out into the hallway to find help.' I had told him as much already, but I was aware that policemen liked to repeat questions to see if the answers would be the same.

I assumed she had been stabbed, of course. That would be the most logical explanation for all that blood. I wondered if they had found the murder weapon. I didn't recall seeing a knife or any such thing lying about, but my wits had not been at their sharpest at that particular moment.

He seemed to have decided that I would not be baited into making some sort of self-incriminating remark, and decided to change the topic.

'Did you know Miss Van Allen well?' he asked casually, looking down at the notes he had written in his notebook.

'No, not at all. We only met this week.'

'And who invited you to come to Lyonsgate?' he asked.

'Mr Lyons, naturally,' I answered. 'It's his house.'

His eyes came up from his notebook, and I could tell that he had taken exception to my tone. I was, admittedly, not being a very agreeable witness, but his manner was offensive, and I felt disinclined to be pleasant.

'And have you known Mr Lyons long?'

'Not exactly, no. My cousin Laurel is an old friend of the Lyons family. She was invited, and my husband and I were also extended an invitation.'

'I see. Does your cousin often secure invitations for you and your husband?'

'My cousin and I are very close friends and enjoy spending time together,' I told him, suppressing a great many things I would rather have said.

'And there was no other reason?'

I hesitated, wondering if I should relate some of what had happened here. I supposed it was only a matter of time before someone mentioned *The Dead of Winter* and Isobel's troubled past with most of the other guests at Lyonsgate. Then again, I very much doubted he would appreciate my input on the matter.

He was still watching my face as all of this crossed my mind, and it seemed that he sensed my inner struggle.

'Is there anything else you wish to tell me, Mrs Ames? Now would be the ideal time.'

As much as I was beginning to detest this man, I could not deny that he was, in his official capacity, entitled to any relevant information I could give him. We were, after all, on the same side.

I put aside, for the moment, my growing antagonism, and told him the truth. 'Laurel thought there was the possibility of unpleasantness. There was some lingering resentment, you see, about a novel Miss Van Allen wrote some years ago.'

'*The Dead of Winter,* you mean.' It was not a question. He appeared to already know something about the book. I wondered if he remembered when it had been published or if someone had mentioned it to him today, but I was sure he would not be receptive to such a question coming from me.

'Yes,' I answered. 'It was an account of a death here at Lyonsgate seven years ago, an account very thinly veiled as fiction. It caused quite a scandal at the time, and the young man she indicated was guilty of murder, Bradford Glenn, killed himself not long afterwards.'

'I'm familiar with the book. Is there anything more?'

I was severely annoyed at his dismissive tone, but went on anyway. 'Miss Van Allen announced at dinner last night that Bradford Glenn was innocent and that she intended to write a second volume, one which would reveal the true identity of Edwin Green's killer.'

'Yes, Mr Lyons told me as much when I arrived.'

'Then I'm afraid I don't know anything else that will be useful to you.' I couldn't resist adding, 'I hope my answers have been satisfactory.'

'I was curious to see how much you would divulge,' he said, his dark eyes once again resting on my face. 'Your husband seemed remarkably unforthcoming.'

'Yes, he's always that way. It's one of his less endearing traits.' I smiled coldly. 'But neither of us has anything to hide.'

'In that case, Mrs Ames, you have nothing to be concerned about.'

'Is there anything more, Inspector?' I said, rising from my seat.

He rose with me. 'Not at the moment.'

'Very well. Good day.'

As much as I longed to be gone from the room, I couldn't resist turning at the door. 'It seems the most useful thing to do would be to read Miss Van Allen's manuscript. Whoever she planned to accuse of murder this time might be a good person with whom to start.'

'Yes, thank you, Mrs Ames, for that most valuable tip,' he said, smiling coldly in return. 'Unfortunately, the manuscript appears to have been burnt in the fireplace of Miss Van Allen's room.'

CHAPTER TEN

By the time the body had been taken away and the detestable Inspector Laszlo had at last departed, it was nearly dinner time. Beatrice had had the foresight to ask the kitchen staff to lay out a cold supper that the guests could eat at their convenience. The entire house had been in an uproar all day, and no one wanted to go through the rigors of a formal dinner.

We ate half-heartedly. I had not been very hungry, but I had known I would need to eat something in order to please Milo. He had been uncharacteristically solicitous all afternoon. I might almost have accused him of hovering had he displayed any sign of concern, but he treated me with a casual courtesy that gave no outward hint of alarm. Nevertheless, I caught him looking at me more than once, as though he were trying to make sure I was not suffering from shock or going to swoon at an inopportune moment.

Granted, I had been very near swooning this afternoon. I almost felt a bit silly now for my reaction. The experience had been horrifying, of course, but I had always supposed myself to be very level-headed. I felt somehow that I should have been more composed when I had found Isobel Van Allen lying on the floor, that I should have been able to do something more than stumble from the room in a daze. It was just that there had been something paralysing about the way her eyes had stared up at me. And then to look down and realise that I was covered in her blood.

I shivered.

'Shall I get you a wrap, darling?' Milo asked, drawing my attention back to the present. We sat in the drawing room with Reggie Lyons, Lucinda, and Laurel. We were absently drinking coffee, none of us saying much.

I shook my head. 'Thank you, no. I think I'll go back to my room now.'

I rose and the gentlemen rose with me.

Milo leant towards me and spoke quietly. 'I need to have a few words with Lyons. You'll be all right until I come up?'

'Of course,' I said lightly. 'I'm not a china doll, after all.'

He looked at me searchingly, and I smiled to reassure him. 'Don't rush on my account.'

'I'll walk up with you, Amory,' Laurel said, rising from her seat. I would be glad for a few moments alone with her, for we had not yet had the opportunity to talk in private about the events of the day.

After my infuriating interview with Inspector Laszlo, Sergeant Hanes had politely herded everyone into the drawing room while our rooms were searched. The endeavour had proved fruitless; the murder weapon had not been found.

Inspector Laszlo had then questioned everyone individually in one of the smaller sitting rooms. We had all been too much in shock, I think, for much discussion amongst ourselves, but I had been alert enough to note that no one had been with someone else in the hour leading up to the discovery of the body. This meant that anyone might have murdered Isobel Van Allen.

After the police had gone and we had eaten our light supper, Milo, Laurel, and I had found our way back to the drawing room. Apparently, Reggie Lyons had been in the drawing room all evening, and I rather had the impression that he lacked the energy to go upstairs. Lucinda had been, no doubt, interested in the proceedings, or perhaps the chance to spend more time with my husband. The others had gone back to their rooms, and I couldn't blame them. I would never have thought I would be so glad to ensconce myself in that draughty chamber.

Laurel and I excused ourselves and made our way up the stairs.

'What did you make of that inspector?' I asked her, hoping we might commiserate on his ill manners.

Her answer was the last thing I expected.

'He's very handsome,' she said.

'Is he?' I asked evasively. 'I hadn't noticed.'

'I should have thought you might have noticed, as you have an affinity for tall, dark men.'

'I assure you, the thought never crossed my mind.'

'He's not nearly as handsome as Milo, of course,' she said flatly, 'but, then, most men aren't.'

Since Laurel had always claimed that Milo's good looks were at the root of his bad behaviour, I knew it was not meant to be a compliment.

'Good-looking or not, his manners were abominable,' I answered.

She laughed. 'He's not that bad, Amory, surely. In fact, I thought him rather pleasant.'

I was not surprised that Inspector Laszlo had treated my cousin with courtesy. Not only was she a striking woman, she possessed a knack for making people feel at ease. With the exception of Milo, I had never met anyone who hadn't taken to her at once.

'I think he suspects me of killing Isobel,' I said.

At this her smile faded. 'Surely not!'

'I came from the room, covered in blood. I suppose it was only natural to wonder if it was me.'

'Well, it's all very preposterous. I assume you told him as much.'

'I did.'

Her smile returned. 'In no uncertain terms, I imagine. Then it's no wonder you didn't get along with him.'

I couldn't argue with her. The inspector had set my teeth on edge, and I had lost all desire to attempt to charm him.

'Well, I hope you gave him a good set-to. It should be immediately apparent to anyone that you wouldn't do such a thing.'

We had reached Isobel's room then and passed the door in respectful silence, as one might pass a tombstone.

When we reached the door to Laurel's room, she looked back. 'My room is nearest Isobel's, you know. Inspector Laszlo asked if I had heard a scream, or sounds of a struggle.'

I felt rather idiotic that I hadn't thought of it before now. 'Did you hear anything?'

'No. It seems I should have done, doesn't it? She . . . she must have cried out.'

'The doors are solid oak,' I said. 'Incredibly thick. Even if she had cried out, we might not have heard it.'

'It seemed strange, though, that no one should have heard anything in a room where a life and death struggle had occurred. To think I was so close when it happened . . .' She looked at me, her expression troubled. 'Who might have done it, Amory?'

'I was going to ask you the same question,' I said. 'You know these people better than I do. Who might have committed murder?'

She shook her head. 'I can't imagine it. It seems as though Isobel must have been right, doesn't it? She said that the murderer was still at large and then she was killed. Someone must have done it to silence her.'

'Be careful, Laurel,' I said.

She looked up at me, her eyes dark. 'I was going to say the same to you.'

The day had been a dreadful one, and I was extremely tired, but I felt that I could not rest, not just yet. I had told Milo I was going to my room, and I intended to, but it had occurred to me that I had not seen Desmond Roberts since the incident had occurred. I knew that he must have spoken to the inspector, for none of us could have escaped his probing. I assumed he had retreated to his room afterwards, however, for I had not seen him since.

I wondered how he was faring. Not well, I suspected. He seemed to me a sensitive young man, and I knew he had no doubt taken Isobel's death very hard. He and Isobel had been friendless among the group at Lyonsgate, and he would feel even more alone now that his lover, the last link to his home in Africa, was dead.

I went to the door of his room and, after a moment's hesitation, I knocked on it.

There was no answer at first, and I felt a wave of unease recalling what had happened earlier this afternoon.

'Mr Roberts?' I called, despite the fact that he likely couldn't hear me through the thick wood. 'It's Mrs Ames. May I talk to you for a moment?'

There was no answer from within, but a moment later the door opened. Mr Roberts stood in the doorway. He looked even worse than I had expected. His dark hair was tousled, his shirt rumpled and half unbuttoned, and he smelt very strongly of alcohol. He didn't say anything, just glanced at me with red-rimmed eyes and then slumped slightly against the doorway.

He looked so young and distraught that I fought the urge to soothe him and tuck him into bed. Given the circumstances, however, I didn't think it was a good idea to be alone with him. I didn't think he was a killer, but I had been wrong before.

'I'm so sorry, Mr Roberts,' I said gently. 'Is there anything I can do?'

'No,' he said, looking past me into the empty hallway. 'There's nothing to be done now. It's all over. Poor, poor Isobel.' He rubbed a trembling hand across his eyes. 'I never wanted it to end this way.'

'Please, Mr Roberts, Desmond, you mustn't think about that now.'

'We were the last ones to see her alive,' he said, his gaze becoming suddenly intense. 'If only she had said something. She knew something was wrong. I'm certain of it. But why didn't she say so? Why didn't she let me know?'

His voice had risen. He was clearly very distraught, and I hoped that he wouldn't do harm to himself, intentionally or otherwise. Grief and alcohol had proven a poor combination, and I wondered if I should call for Mr Lyons or one of the other gentlemen to attend to him.

'She knew something was about to happen,' he went on. 'The way she spoke to me, the words she said to you. Do you remember? "Look after my dear Desmond." That's what she said. She knew that something was going to happen.'

I hesitated as I considered the words. I had felt unaccountably uneasy about our final conversation with Miss Van Allen this afternoon. It was what had caused me to look in on her before my ride with Milo. Had there been something else in what she had said, something unspoken that had unsettled me?

'What do you think it was?' I asked carefully. Mr Roberts was undoubtedly in a troubled emotional state, but there might be something in what he said, some important detail that he might remember.

'I don't know. I've tried to think, but I just don't know.' He ran a hand through his dark hair, and the dark lock that fell across his forehead made him look even younger than he was. I felt another little pang of pity for him.

'Don't think about it now,' I said gently. 'You must try to keep up your strength. Will you eat something? Or at least have some tea?'

He shook his head. 'I couldn't.'

I had suspected as much, but it hadn't hurt to try. I only wished there was something I could do for him. It wouldn't do well for him to sit mourning alone in his room all night.

'The police will think I did it,' he said suddenly.

I looked up at him, unsure at first of how to respond. The police would look very carefully at Isobel Van Allen's lover. He was, after all, the one who had travelled with her from Africa, the one who, presumably, knew her secrets.

I didn't know Desmond Roberts at all. It was quite possible that he *had* done it. I didn't like to think so, but it had been very clear that his relationship with Isobel Van Allen was a volatile one. Might she have finally pushed him too far?

I was very careful to let none of these thoughts cross my face as I gave him what I hoped was an optimistic expression. 'I'm sure the police will make sure the guilty party is caught.'

'Did she suffer much, I wonder?' He looked at me with haunted eyes. 'I can't bear to think how awful it must have been . . .'

I didn't like to think of it either. It could not have been a nice way to die.

I was trying to think of something to say when I heard a polite clearing of the throat. 'Mrs Ames.'

I looked up to see Parks standing a discreet distance from the doorway. 'Pardon the interruption, madam, but I wonder if I may be of some assistance?'

I felt an immense relief at the suggestion. If anyone was equipped to deal with such a situation, it was Milo's unflappable valet.

'Yes, thank you, Parks. Mr Roberts isn't feeling well. Do you think you might help him into bed?'

'Certainly, madam.'

He came at once to the door and adeptly ushered the compliant Mr Roberts back inside.

As I walked away, I heard Desmond say, his voice cracking, 'I can't believe she's dead. Oh, Isobel. Isobel. How can I live without you?'

It was not until I was back in my room that I felt the full weight of the day's events descend upon me with incredible force. I needed a few moments alone to process everything that had happened today. I dismissed Winnelda at once, despite her worried glances in my direction, and began to prepare myself for bed. I washed my face, barely noticing the frigid temperature of the water, and changed numbly into my nightgown.

Then I sat on the edge of my bed, staring into the fireplace.

I had never been one much given to emotion, but I couldn't help but feel the effects of this tragedy. Something about Mr Roberts' final anguished cry had pushed it all to the forefront. Unbidden, tears sprang to my eyes, and I allowed myself a moment to cry.

'Darling.' Milo's voice from the adjoining doorway behind me should have startled me, given the state of my nerves, but somehow it was as though I had sensed him there before he spoke.

I hurriedly wiped away my tears before rising from the bed and turning to face him. 'Yes?'

He came into the room. 'Are you all right?'

'Yes, of course, I'm fine. Just a bit overwhelmed by everything, I suppose.'

'It has been a terrible day for you.'

I shrugged. 'It's not the first such day I've had, is it?' Milo and I had discovered a body together once before. That time had been awful, but there had been something worse about seeing Isobel Van Allen lying there on the floor and holding her lifeless body in my arms.

Milo was not at all fooled by my bravado.

'You needn't always put on a brave face, you know,' he said gently.

Fresh tears sprang to my eyes. I pressed my lips together, willing myself not to cry, but then Milo came and pulled me against him, and the gesture itself caused more tears to flow.

Emotions were not something I shared easily, not even with my husband. Though it shamed me to admit it, I was unaccustomed to deriving comfort from Milo. Ours had not exactly been a traditional marriage, and his new role as protector was something new to me.

I had always made every effort to hide my vulnerability,

but there was something immensely reassuring about leaning into him, allowing him to share the burden for a moment.

'It was so awful, Milo,' I whispered against his chest. 'All that blood.'

'I know, darling,' he murmured, stroking my hair. 'Try not to think about it.'

'I can't seem to stop,' I said.

I allowed him to hold me for a moment longer and then I pulled back, sniffling, and took the handkerchief from his pocket to dab my eyes.

'I don't know why I'm taking it so hard. I didn't even know her, not really. And it wasn't as though we might ever have been friends.'

'No,' he said. 'She was not a very likeable person.'

'Oh, I know everyone hated her, but I . . . I felt sorry for her. I think she was dreadfully unhappy. And poor Mr Roberts is inconsolable. Who would do such a thing?'

'That's not for you to worry about,' he said. 'I'm going to take you back to London as soon as the police allow it.'

I frowned. 'That isn't necessary.'

'I think it is. I don't want you to stay here any longer. Once the inspector releases us, I intend to go back to our flat and forget all about this rotten mess. I've half a mind to throttle Laurel for suggesting you come in the first place.'

I stared at him as he took a cigarette from the silver case in his pocket and went to retrieve a match from a box on a table near the fireplace. It was not at all like him to order me about.

'It's been a dreadful day, of course, but that's no reason

for us to abandon Laurel and the others. I know you dislike Laurel, but . . .'

'What I dislike,' he interrupted, turning to face me, 'is the sight of my wife covered in blood.'

So that was it. He had thought the blood was mine, and it had shaken him more than I had realised. I felt a rush of love for him as I looked up into his handsome, impassive face.

'I'm fine, Milo. Really.'

He blew out a stream of smoke. 'You will be much better in London.'

It seemed he had made up his mind. Well, then, I would have to work to change it.

'Let's not discuss it now,' I said. I was in no mood for a row. Perhaps tomorrow he would be more reasonable.

He was not fooled by my attempts to put him off, however. 'I know perfectly well what you are doing, darling, and it won't work to change the subject. But you've had a long day. Perhaps you should get some rest.'

I shook my head. 'I can't sleep, not now. There are too many things on my mind.' He watched me as I stepped closer. 'I could certainly do with a distraction.'

'Are you trying to seduce me, madam?' he asked.

'Is it working?' I asked softly.

He tossed his cigarette into the fireplace and pulled me into his arms.

CHAPTER ELEVEN

We all met for breakfast as if by some tacit agreement. Everyone was there, with the exception of Mr Roberts. I made a mental note to look in on him again later in the day.

The kitchen staff appeared to have felt the need to compensate for having not prepared dinner the previous night, for it was the most lavish breakfast spread as of yet. We dutifully filled our plates, though I think most of us had very little appetite.

I still felt a bit drained, but my emotions were once again firmly in hand. For one thing, if I was going to convince Milo to remain at Lyonsgate until the matter was cleared up, I would have to show him that I was not traumatised by recent events. I was not sure that I entirely cared for his newly developed chivalrous streak; I was accustomed to doing as I pleased.

It was Reggie who at last broached the subject that was foremost in everyone's minds. 'We all spoke at one time or another yesterday, I believe,' he said in strained voice. 'But I want everyone to know that I'm dreadfully upset about all of this, and I intend to do everything in my power to see that the killer is brought to justice. Isobel's death is a tragedy . . .'

'Is it?' Beatrice interrupted coolly. 'I'd say her death has been rather a boon to all of us.'

'Beatrice!' Reggie cried, his face reddening.

'I'm only speaking the truth, Reggie. Something everyone always seems loath to do.' She looked around the table, her gaze holding something of a challenge. 'With the exception of Mr and Mrs Ames, Isobel posed a threat to all of us. Her death is unfortunate, of course, but I cannot say that it is a great personal tragedy to me. Now that she is gone, there is little chance of her lies causing any more suffering.'

No one spoke for a long moment. I think all of the other guests agreed with her, but none of them much wanted to admit to such a callous sentiment.

At last Mr Collins, Freida's husband, broke the silence. 'It may be true, Mrs Kline, that her death is inadvertently advantageous to us, but we must not forget that we are now all under suspicion for murder.'

'Mr Roberts killed her, surely,' Beatrice said dismissively.

'Oh, no,' Lucinda protested. 'Surely not. I believe he was very much in love with her. I could tell, by the way he looked at her.'

'Love, more than any other emotion, has the capacity to make people violent,' Beatrice replied. She said the words tonelessly enough, but I wondered what memories came with them. Was she thinking of whatever had transpired between Edwin Green and Bradford Glenn?

I glanced at Freida. She was looking straight ahead, her jaw tight. Perhaps she, too, was thinking back to the night that Edwin Green had died. I wondered what it was that she knew.

It seemed to me that the key to Isobel's death lay somewhere in the past. If she had been correct that Mr Green's murderer was still at large, then she had likely been killed to keep the killer's identity a secret. The only way to know the truth now would be to hear what the others had to say about Edwin Green's death. The stories, the long-suppressed memories of that night and the events leading up to it were there just below the surface. If only I could get people to reveal what they knew.

'The loss of any human life is a tragedy,' Reggie said, seeming to have found at last the energy to rebut his sister. 'I hope, however, that you all know that you are welcome to stay at Lyonsgate for as long as you wish.'

'The police won't want us to leave anyway,' Laurel replied. 'Not until the guilty person has been caught.'

Silence fell again as we all attempted to think of the proper response. One wanted the murderer to be caught, naturally, but it didn't seem in good taste to say so when it might very well be the person sitting beside one at the breakfast table.

'That Inspector fellow, Laszlo, will no doubt be back round today, asking more questions,' Reggie went on.

'What a nuisance,' Beatrice said. 'We've told him everything we know. What more does he want?'

'It's a shame that none of us were together when it

happened,' Gareth Winters said over his coffee cup. 'It would have made eliminating the innocent parties much easier.'

The artist had, I noticed, a knack for seeming to have no interest in the conversation then joining it suddenly with a salient point. I had already ascertained that none of us had alibis. It was not exactly surprising, as it had been an odd hour of the morning, but it was certainly inconvenient.

Where *had* everyone been at the time of the murder? I was just about to raise the question when Milo caught my gaze and gave me what could only have been interpreted as a warning look.

'I know it's a nuisance,' Reggie told his sister, 'but I think it would be best for us to cooperate as completely as possible. The sooner he is satisfied, the sooner our lives can go back to normal.'

'But our lives haven't been normal, have they?' asked Mr Winters. 'Nothing has been as it was before. Not since Edwin's death.'

'Our lives are what we have made them,' Beatrice said. 'We will have to be content with them.'

He smiled, and it was a strange smile. 'As you say, Beatrice.'

This curious exchange made me wonder even more about Gareth Winters. Of all the group at Lyonsgate, I found his true personality to be the hardest to gauge. He was always so silent, his pale eyes trained on something outside of the immediate. I wondered how much of his airy aloofness was affected. Was he truly so oblivious to the world around him, or did he choose this persona as a means of shielding who he truly was? If I could find a moment to speak with him alone, perhaps he would be more inclined to speak openly.

Breakfast broke up then, and we rose from the table.

Laurel came at once to my side. 'I'm just going to keep Reggie company today,' she said softly. 'I want to be certain that he is all right. But you will let me know if you need anything?'

'Yes, certainly. In any event, Milo has been quite attentive.'

'Has he?' Her brow quirked as she looked over my shoulder.

I turned to see Lucinda Lyons talking animatedly to my husband.

'You know he can't resist being adored,' I said dryly. 'Let him have his fun.'

'You've grown understanding in your old age.'

'We understand each other,' I said. 'Much better than we ever did.'

She shrugged. 'So long as you are happy, my dearest one. After all, who am I to argue with the course of true love?' There was more than a hint of sarcasm in her tone, but I knew it was meant affectionately.

Laurel and Reggie went out into the hallway and I followed suit. I intended to speak to the others if I could. The problem was how to get rid of Milo while I did it.

That problem, however, took care of itself. Emerging from the breakfast room, Lucinda Lyons followed me into the entrance hall, Milo not far behind her.

'Oh, Mrs Ames,' she said breathlessly. 'Would you mind dreadfully if your husband accompanied me on a walk? I can't bear to be in the house any longer, but I don't dare go out alone. It's so dreadful, to think of what happened . . .'

'Yes, dreadful indeed,' I said. 'But Mr Ames certainly doesn't need my permission to enjoy the fresh air.'

'Wonderful! I'll just go and get my coat and hat!'

She must have ruled out Milo as the killer if she was willing to go walking alone with him. Of course, she might very well be the killer herself, in which case anything dastardly she did to Milo would be his own fault for falling prey to her pretty blue eyes.

'I didn't intend to go out walking in the cold this morning,' he said to me when Lucinda was gone, 'but it's just as well I leave you alone for a while. Perhaps you should go back to sleep. You tossed and turned most of the night.'

'I had a good many unpleasant dreams,' I said. 'In any event, you needn't worry about me. I'm perfectly capable of amusing myself.'

'That's just what I'm afraid of. What do you mean to do?'

'To begin with, I want to talk with Mr Winters.'

'Oh? What about?'

'He's a very interesting man.' I was purposefully vague.

'Yes, enthralling,' Milo replied dryly.

'You choose your friends, and I shall choose mine,' I retorted.

He smiled, but leant closer and said, 'I know I can't stop you from wheedling information out of people, but please be careful.'

'Don't fret so.'

'I mean it, Amory. Don't do anything imprudent.'

'I'm all ready for you, Mr Ames,' Lucinda called from

the doorway, now in a red wool coat and matching beret, an eager expression on her young face.

I smiled at the appropriateness of my husband's warning. 'I might say the same to you.'

By the time Milo and Lucinda Lyons had left me, I was unsure of where Mr Winters had taken himself off to. He wasn't in the drawing room, and I thought it might look strange if I hunted about the house for him. I decided to first go to my room to reconnoiter. Perhaps I would fetch *The Dead of Winter* and read for a while beside the drawing-room fire.

As I made my way up the stairs, I turned over in my mind all that had happened. What did I know so far? Not much. Isobel Van Allen had not been much liked by anyone, and it seemed that everyone had had equal opportunity to slip into her room and kill her and destroy the manuscript on which she had been working.

I wasn't at all surprised that the manuscript for the second book had been burnt. It would have been very careless of a killer to murder Isobel and leave the incriminating manuscript lying about. Nevertheless, I had hoped that it would be left out to offer some sort of clue. I would just have to continue reading *The Dead of Winter* and see what secrets it might have to reveal.

I was so lost in thought that I nearly bumped headlong into Mr Collins.

'Oh, excuse me,' I murmured.

I moved to step around him, but his hand shot out and caught my arm. 'Wait just a moment.'

His grip was not tight, but I was unaccustomed to being grabbed by strange gentlemen. I looked pointedly down at his hand on my arm and he dropped it.

'Yes, what is it?' I asked.

'I wanted to ask you about Mrs Collins,' he said. His tone was friendly in an artificial way, as though he was unaccustomed to pleasantries.

'What about her?'

'I only wondered if she's had some time to speak to you since we've been here.'

It occurred to me that he could just as easily have asked her that question. He could only be asking me because he hadn't wanted to raise the question to his wife . . . or because he hadn't believed her answer.

'We chatted for a few moments yesterday,' I told him truthfully.

'About what?' What was, presumably, meant to be a casual question came across as a gruff demand. I could not see, in any event, how it was any of his concern.

'She told me about the children,' I said. 'It has been a long time since we've seen one another.'

He smiled. 'I'm sure she would like to renew her friendship with you.' He was making a tremendous effort to be agreeable, but the result was not at all successful. I liked him less now than ever.

'Yes,' I said. 'I should like that, too. Now, if you will excuse me . . .'

He nodded, the insincere smile still frozen on his face, and I moved past him.

That was very strange. I had the distinct impression that

135

he was uneasy about what his wife might have told me. That could only mean that he had something to hide.

One thing was certain. I had not had a chance to talk with Freida since the murder, but I certainly intended to now.

'You're looking much better today, madam,' Winnelda said cheerily as I came into the room. 'Last night you were as pale as a ghost. I was quite concerned about you.'

'I do feel better today, thank you.'

'It must have been very dreadful, finding Miss Van Allen lying dead in a great pool of blood.'

'Yes, very dreadful indeed.'

She seemed disappointed that more information was not forthcoming and chose a more direct approach. 'Was she cut all to pieces?'

I knew that Winnelda had a penchant for the macabre and thus managed to be not entirely horrified by her question. 'I did not have time to notice what kind of wounds she had,' I said, 'but I can assure you the body was all in one piece.'

I had the impression that this answer was not satisfactory. She wanted tales of gore, but I had thought quite enough about those moments in Isobel Van Allen's room and did not intend to relive them.

'Well, she was stabbed a great many times, so the police said,' she told me at last, deciding to share what she knew since I was disinclined to elaborate on my own experience. 'But they haven't found the weapon, you know.'

'Yes, I know,' I said. I wondered where the killer might have hidden it.

'They're sure the killer must have hidden it somewhere,' she went on, 'but so far they haven't been able to find it.'

'How did you learn all of this, Winnelda?' I asked.

'Oh, I just heard things here and there.'

I suspected this information had been gleaned by darting up and down the stairs all day yesterday, talking to members of the household staff, and no doubt peeking around corners. I wasn't about to quibble about her methods, however.

'Was there anything else?'

She paused to think. 'Well, most of the household staff was accounted for, so the police are fairly certain it was one of you.' She stopped. 'That is, I mean . . .'

'Yes, I understand what you mean,' I told her. 'Did you speak with that inspector?'

'Yes, but only briefly. He wasn't much interested in me, madam, though he did ask me if you were in your room all that time. I told him that you were, though I was sure you had already told him as much and your word was quite as good as mine.'

'Thank you, Winnelda.'

'And I told him that you were quite upset because you had found Miss Van Allen dead and that it was a great shock to you. And then he did the most dreadful thing. You'll never guess!'

'He asked to see the bloody clothes, I suppose.'

Her eyes widened and she nodded, duly impressed. 'I should have known you'd guess, madam, being a detective yourself and all. He took the clothes and examined them closely.'

'Did he take them away?'

She shook her head. 'No, he told me I could do as I wished with them.'

'Then dispose of them, please.'

'Yes, madam.'

I had no doubt that my clothes had borne out my story. The blood would have been thickest on the knees of my trousers where I had unwittingly knelt in Isobel's blood. My shirt had been badly stained as well, but from holding Isobel against me. I wouldn't have imagined it would have looked the same had I participated in the stabbing. I shuddered a bit at the thought.

'Did you hear anything else, Winnelda? From the police or from anyone else?'

She shook her head. 'The police were fairly careful about talking in front of the domestics, and the doors are too thick for listening through.'

I didn't ask her how she had come by this knowledge, and she did not volunteer the information.

This had all been rather enlightening, and I was glad that I had had the chance to talk to my resourceful maid. As ever, she had proven to be a font of information.

I went to where *The Dead of Winter* sat on the table near the fire and picked it up. I hadn't had the opportunity to read any more of it since I had first started, and I found that the idea was oddly distasteful now. Perhaps I would wait just a bit longer to do my research. In any event, perhaps I should keep reading the offending book on my own rather than flaunting it in the drawing room for all to see. The less interested I appeared to the others, the better.

'Oh, madam, there was one other thing I forgot,' Winnelda said. 'It might be of interest to you.'

I turned.

'When Parks was in Mr Roberts' room he noticed something. Mr Roberts wanted a picture of Isobel that was in the drawer of the bureau, so Parks went to fetch it for him. But then Parks saw that there was something else in the drawer, tucked in among Mr Roberts' things.'

I waited.

'It was . . . now, let me think . . .' She frowned, concentrating. 'He said . . . Oh! It was . . . No, that's not it. Well, I can't remember exactly what Parks said it was, but it was some kind of poison.'

CHAPTER TWELVE

Leave it to Winnelda to save the most startling of revelations for last.

'Is Parks certain it was poison?' I asked.

'Oh, yes, madam. He was very sure about it. He saw the label. Parks is very clever, you know.'

'Yes, I know. But why didn't he say something?'

She frowned. 'He did, madam. To me.' I understood what she meant. Parks was not nearly as garrulous as Winnelda. He would not have said anything to Milo. He would not have felt it his place to do so.

'Did he tell the police?' The police had searched our rooms after the murder, but presumably they had only been looking for bloody knives and had overlooked the bottle in Mr Roberts' drawer.

'No,' she said. 'Miss Van Allen wasn't poisoned, after all.'

She hadn't been poisoned, but she had been ill the night

before she died. I wondered if the poison might have had anything to do with it.

'It is curious, though, isn't it, madam?'

'Yes,' I said. 'That is very curious.'

Why would Desmond Roberts have brought poison with him to Lyonsgate? Had he been intending to murder someone? It was all so perplexing. I added the mysterious poison to my list of things that I would need to know more about.

With this newest information swirling about in my mind, I went back out into the hall. I wanted to see if I could locate either Freida or Mr Winters.

If I could find Freida, I wanted to see if I could determine what it was that her husband had been worried she would tell me. Mr Collins had come from their rooms and seemed to be going back to the drawing room. I wondered if it was possible that Freida might still be in her room.

I went to her door and knocked.

For a long moment I heard nothing. Then she opened it. I was not imagining the look of relief on her face when she saw me. Who did she think I had been?

'Hello, Freida,' I said. 'I came to look in on you. I wondered if perhaps you'd like to go out walking.'

She paused. 'I . . . I don't think so, but thank you. I'm not feeling very well.'

'I expect we're all a bit ill at ease, considering all that's happened. It was dreadful about Isobel.' I had learnt from past experience that it was often best just to address directly what I was thinking. It saved time.

'Yes, I understand you found her. I can't imagine . . .'

Her voice trailed off. She could imagine, I supposed. After all, she was the one who had found Edwin Green dead in the snow.

'Who might have done it?' I asked.

She looked at me, doing nothing to hide the worry in her expression. 'I don't know.'

'Haven't you any idea?' I asked the question conspiratorially, as though we were once again those young girls discussing the boys we fancied.

'No, I've really no idea. I was writing letters in my room after breakfast. Phillip had gone out walking. Henson saw him go out.'

I had not asked for her whereabouts, and the information was only slightly useful. It only proved that either of them might have killed Isobel. It crossed my mind to wonder if they would have provided one another with alibis had Henson not seen Mr Phillips going out. I wondered if anyone had seen him come back to the house.

My thoughtful silence appeared to have unnerved her, for she began to speak again.

'I've thought about it, and it seems to me . . .' She stopped.

'Yes?'

'I don't know. I . . . I think Beatrice was right at dinner last night. Love is a very powerful thing. Perhaps powerful enough to make one kill.'

'Mr Roberts, you mean?'

'I . . .' She shook her head, and her expression became guarded. 'I don't know. Perhaps we will never know.'

'It seems unlikely that the police will let the matter drop,' I said lightly.

'Murderers have gone unpunished before.' She stepped back slightly, her hand on the door as if to close it. 'It's been lovely talking with you, Amory, but if you'll excuse me, I have a letter I must finish writing.'

'Of course.'

She began to close the door and then halted, looking out at me, a troubled expression in her eyes. 'I know murder is wrong, and perhaps it's wicked of me, but somehow I can't help but feel that Isobel brought it on herself.'

I walked back downstairs, lost in thought. I had been a bit surprised by Freida's sentiments, but I suspected they were shared by most of the others at Lyonsgate. No one, with the exception of Mr Roberts, mourned Isobel Van Allen's passing. In fact, it had come as a relief to most of them.

Though I would not have put it exactly as Freida had, it did seem that Isobel had done her best to make people angry. She had cultivated an atmosphere of suspicion and malice, and it had been her downfall. Not, of course, that that was any excuse for murder.

What had Freida meant by murderers having gone unpunished? She might have been speaking in generalities, but it had seemed to me there was something more to her words. Perhaps I would have an opportunity to continue the conversation with her later.

I went into the drawing room hoping to find Mr Winters there and was surprised to see Desmond Roberts sitting near the window, gazing out across the sprawling lawns.

He looked up when I entered and rose at once.

'Good morning, Mrs Ames.'

He was still very pale beneath his bronzed skin and there were dark circles around his eyes. Both features were accentuated by the bright morning light shining through the window, but he appeared much more composed than he had been last night.

'Good morning. Please sit down. I didn't mean to disturb you.'

'No, no. Please. Come in, won't you?' he asked. 'I . . . I'd rather like the company. I came down and found that there was no one about, so I thought I would sit here for a while. I . . . I felt I needed to leave my room.'

'I agree. It's not good for you to stay there all alone.' I came in and took a seat across from him, studying his taut, handsome face. 'Have you had anything to eat?'

He shook his head. 'I . . . I can't. Not yet.'

'Perhaps some coffee?'

'Perhaps later. I . . . I am feeling rather ill this morning.'

'I'm sorry to hear it,' I said. He did look unwell. His skin was pasty in colour, almost grey, and the sheen of perspiration on it was visible from where I sat. Grief manifests itself in many different ways, and I was not at all surprised the poor boy was ill and without appetite. I did hope, however, that he didn't go on starving himself. Perhaps Parks might be able to induce him to eat something later. I would tell Milo to put him on the job.

'I'm sorry about the way I . . . the way I was last night,' he said after a moment of silence. 'I was not myself.'

'Please don't apologise,' I said. 'I know it was a terrible shock. Is there anything I can do for you?'

'No,' he said. 'No, there's nothing. Thank you.'

I felt again a pang of sympathy for him. His sense of loss and loneliness was almost tangible. I wondered if it was left to him to make the arrangements for Isobel's funeral alone.

'Is there anything you need assistance with?' I asked him gently. 'Any family I should notify or anything of that sort?'

He shook his head. 'Isobel didn't have any family left. And I . . .' His voice broke off, and he looked out the window, as though somewhere far away. 'I don't either,' he said at last.

'What about the funeral?' I was not entirely comfortable pressing him on such a private matter, but I also knew that he was likely to need support in the days ahead. When the shock had worn off, there would be a great many other matters to be attended to.

'Isobel made arrangements to be buried in Kenya,' he said.

I looked up, surprised. 'Arrangements?'

'Yes, when all of this is over, she . . . her . . . body will be sent back to Africa.'

'When did she make these arrangements?' I asked, heedless of the impoliteness of such a question.

'Several months ago,' he said. 'When she started planning to come back to England. She said that she didn't want to be laid to rest in cold ground if anything should happen.'

'I see,' I said, but I didn't, not really. It was a very strange thing for Isobel Van Allen to have done. She was still fairly young and, presumably, healthy. I could think of no reason why she should have made arrangements for her own funeral before her journey. Perhaps it had been nothing more than careful planning on her part but, if so, it was certainly an odd coincidence.

'It worried me, of course, but she only laughed and said for me to not fret, it was only a precaution. She always laughed at my worries . . .' His voice caught and he clenched his jaw for a moment before continuing. 'Now I'm glad she did it. I'm glad things will be as she wanted.'

'It will make it easier on you.'

I watched his face as he seemed to go through some interior struggle. He wanted to say something, but wasn't sure how to go about it. At last he came out with it. 'As I told you, Mrs Ames, I have spent most of my life in Africa. There is a great deal of superstition in that country, but I have always considered myself immune to it. Good English common sense, you understand. But now I wonder . . .'

'Wonder what?'

'After all that's happened, I just can't help but wonder if Isobel knew somehow that she wasn't going to leave England alive.'

CHAPTER THIRTEEN

Mr Roberts excused himself a few moments later, and I was left alone to ponder this newest piece of information. It seemed that Isobel Van Allen had suspected her visit to England might go badly. Why else would she have made arrangements to be carried out in the event of her death? If that was the case, however, why had she come back at all? It just didn't make sense.

I went out of the drawing room and into the entrance hall, still lost in thought, and I nearly ran directly into Mr Winters.

'Oh, hello, Mr Winters.'

'Hello,' he said, not in the least startled by our near collision.

I had already determined a means by which to engage him in conversation, and I put it into action at once. 'I see you are on your way to the drawing room,' I said.

'The drawing room?' he asked, as though he didn't realise

what room it was that he had been about to wander into.

'Yes, and I hate to disturb you, but there's a painting on the wall near the dining room that I'm curious about. I was wondering if perhaps you could tell me a bit about it.'

'Certainly.' He followed me without either hesitation or enthusiasm.

It was not all a ruse, for the piece had caught my eye every time I had made my way to the dining room. It was a market scene done in vivid colours and seemed to date to the Renaissance.

We went to stand before it, and Mr Winters gazed at it with a somewhat blank expression, almost as though he was looking through it.

I knew that drugs had not been uncommon among the Lyonsgate set in their heyday, and I couldn't help but wonder if Mr Winters still indulged. Somehow, however, I didn't think so. It wasn't as though he was in a stupor; it was more of a perennial aloofness, as though he was half in this world and half in some world of his own.

'It's an authentic piece,' he said, after examining it for a moment longer, 'but not worth much, I should think. There are, however, a great many pieces of value here at Lyonsgate. Reggie might have sold them off long ago if he didn't intend to return.'

Perhaps Mr Winters was more mentally present than I had assumed he was. Perhaps the vagueness was only a ruse that he used in order to protect himself from society. One thing was certain: he was more observant than I had given him credit for.

'I see. There is a similar piece at our country house, and

I only wondered if it might be something worth insuring.'

'Perhaps,' he said vaguely.

'There do seem to be a good many lovely pieces here. I don't know much about art, of course, but I do enjoy looking at it.'

'The best of the art here at Lyonsgate is in the portrait gallery. There are some fine pieces there: an Eakins, a Rubens, and an excellent portrait of Angelique Lyons, done by David before the Revolution. That one, I expect, would fetch a pretty penny if Reggie could bring himself to part with it.'

'I shall have to look at the portrait gallery,' I said.

'I'll show you now, if you like,' he said. It was the first hint of any real interest that I had seen in Mr Winters, and I hated to dampen it. Besides, it would give me an opportunity to broach the subject of Isobel's murder.

'I should like that,' I told him.

As we proceeded up the stairway, I attempted to bring the conversation around to the matter at hand. 'I'm surprised the inspector hasn't been back again today.'

'I suppose he will return soon enough,' he answered with no hint of emotion.

'I still can't believe this has happened. It's shocking.'

'Yes.'

So far our conversation was not at all encouraging. I suspected it was going to be difficult to draw any sort of information out of Mr Winters.

The long gallery, extending the length of the front of the house and panelled all in oak, was an impressive example of Tudor architecture. Though the curtains were

149

drawn and it was quite dark, I could tell at once that it was a beautiful space.

Mr Winters went with uncharacteristic quickness across the room and pulled back the red velvet drapes that hung across the wall of the windows, allowing the morning light to spill into the room. Dust motes danced in the sunbeams, and the carpets were faded, but the room was very beautiful, nonetheless.

Mr Winters, too, was shown to best advantage by the room's illumination. His curls gleamed golden and his startlingly pale eyes nearly glowed, the colour something akin to light shining on cool water. He was rather like a piece of art himself.

I turned to the wall opposite the windows, which held an impressive array of artwork, and studied it. Here were the members of the Lyons family arrayed in all their glory: dashing gentlemen in ruffled shirts and feathered hats, beautiful women bedecked in spangled gowns, solemn-faced children, and a fair share of dour-looking elderly forebears.

'That's the Rubens there,' Mr Winters said, pointing out a portrait of a stern-faced gentleman. 'And the Eakins is that lady dressed as a shepherdess.'

'Which one is the David?' I asked, but I thought I already knew. I was by no means a connoisseur of art, but I knew a fine piece when I saw one. The woman was very beautiful, dressed in a flowing blue gown.

'Do you notice anything about it?' he asked, looking at me expectantly.

I studied it. 'It's an excellent portrait. Should I recognise it?'

'She looks rather like Beatrice, don't you think?'

I looked up again at the pale, cool gaze of Angelique Lyons and could, perhaps, see the resemblance. 'Beatrice does look a bit like her.'

'Angelique Lyons killed her first husband in France,' he said casually.

My brows rose. 'Indeed?'

'It was he that had commissioned David to paint Angelique. Then they had a row not many months later, and she stabbed him. She left Paris with a box of jewels and her portrait, taking Ivo Lyons for her second husband. He must have been a very understanding man.'

I thought it likely that Angelique Lyons had been a very persuasive woman.

We walked along the room in silence, looking at the pieces. I spared the occasional glance at Mr Winters as we went along, amazed at the change that had come over him. He was more animated than I had yet seen him, his eyes bright, his expression clear. It was as though the art had acted as some sort of tonic.

We reached the far end of the gallery, and I stopped, surprised, before a painting hung on the periphery.

'This one is of Miss Van Allen,' I said, unable to hide my surprise.

A sad smile appeared on Mr Winters' lips. 'Yes,' he said. 'I painted it that summer. Isobel had me hang it at the far end of the gallery as a sort of joke. I suppose Reggie never noticed. Or perhaps he just didn't care.'

I studied the painting. It was an excellent likeness. There was something different, softer about her face, though her sharp eyes held the same mischief that I had seen in them across the dinner table. I couldn't help but wonder if it was a reflection of who Isobel had been or who the artist had wanted her to be.

'It was inevitable, I think, that Isobel would come to a bad end,' Mr Winters said reflectively. 'She lived her life recklessly.'

I hid my surprise. 'In what way?'

He looked over at me. 'In every way possible. You must have noticed how she goaded us. It was because she enjoyed the danger of it. She was always that way, always pushing people, trying to see how far she could go. It was as though . . .' His voice trailed off for a long moment before he finished. 'It was as though she was most alive when she was tempting fate.'

I felt there was no choice but to be direct with Mr Winters. We would get nowhere if we both remained vague. 'Do you think she was killed because of what she was writing in her second book?' I asked him.

He shrugged. 'It might have been. Or it might just have easily been her young man.'

'Mr Roberts seems terribly distraught.'

He shrugged again. 'I have never been good at seeing the insides of people. It is the outside that interests me.'

He studied me as he said this. I had become somewhat used to his eerily searching gaze, but I still found those pale eyes a bit unnerving, especially as they almost glowed in the bright light of the portrait gallery. I wondered if he was contemplating who might have killed Isobel, but when he at last spoke it was on a different topic entirely.

'Have you ever been painted, Mrs Ames?'

It was clear that he was trying to change the subject, but I had the feeling he would not respond well to being pressed. I would have to broach the topic another time.

'As a child,' I said in answer to his question. 'My mother had a portrait done.'

I had not enjoyed the experience at the time, sitting still for hours in a stiff gown of rose-coloured taffeta with an itchy lace collar.

'You should be painted now, as a beautiful woman.' He said these things in an offhanded way, but I was not entirely convinced he was as innocent as he appeared. It certainly contributed to his charm, the seemingly careless way he showered one with compliments as though they were flower petals. Nevertheless, I wondered if it was all part of his carefully orchestrated persona. One could never be too careful with artists, after all.

'It would be nice to have your youth memorialised, don't you think?' he asked. 'Time passes swiftly.'

It was true, if a bit morbid. Nonetheless, I had never particularly desired to have my portrait painted. Nor did now, shortly after a murder, seem an especially appropriate time to discuss such things.

'I've never thought much about it,' I said lightly.

'I should love to paint you, Mrs Ames, if you'd let me.'

I hesitated. This conversation was not going at all as I had planned it. Somehow he looked as though my answer was important to him, and I did not think it would be right to dismiss the suggestion out of hand, especially if I hoped to gain more information from him in the future.

'That's very kind of you. I shall have to think about it.'

'I won't charge you for the portrait. It has been a very long time since I've seen someone that I wanted to paint.'

'Oh, I would be happy to pay for it,' I assured him. 'Only I'm not certain that I have brought anything proper to wear.'

He shook his head. 'No need for that. I'd much rather paint you in the nude.'

My brows rose. 'I beg your pardon?'

'Nude,' he repeated without hesitation. 'I can tell from the way your clothes hang that you have beautiful lines.' There was something very earnest about him, a straightforward intensity that left me at a loss as to how to respond. I was not sure whether I should be flattered or insulted. I knew it was common for artists' models to pose in the nude, but I also knew with some certainty that it was not at all *de rigueur* among society women. However, I felt almost sure he was not attempting to make an improper advance. The entire conversation was becoming so bizarre I was not quite sure how to respond.

He seemed completely oblivious to my discomfort. He stepped closer, his eyes roaming me freely now. I felt vaguely as though I was a piece of meat in a market.

His hand came up to my face and hovered there. 'May I?'

Without waiting for my response, he took my chin gently in his hand and turned it to the side. His finger traced the line of my jaw before his hand dropped and he stepped back.

'Yes, you've lovely lines. Your facial structure is perfection.'

'Thank you,' I said, for lack of something better to say. Not only had I lost the reins on this particular conversation, they were flapping wildly in the wind where I had no hope of regaining them.

He didn't seem to notice my hesitation, and was, in fact, gaining momentum. He stepped back, continuing to look me over, and I felt somehow that I no longer had any say in this. I had gone from a person to a subject.

'Now, let me see where I could paint you. If it was summer, I would suggest in the garden. But the conservatory would be nearly as good, I think. Where the light would play off of your lovely alabaster skin. And, of course, your eyes are magnificent in bright light.'

'Thank you,' I said again, hoping to disentangle myself from this conversation. 'But I'm afraid I shall have to think it over.'

My words seemed to bring him back from some faraway realm of artistry. 'Eh? Oh, yes. Of course. But I do hope you'll let me do it. I'm sure your husband would love the portrait.'

While I was quite sure that Milo had no objection to nudes in general or a nude of me in particular, I was not about to strip naked in a deserted conservatory with a man who might possibly be a murderer.

'I . . . I will let you know,' I said, ready to escape.

'Very well, but I do hope you'll consider it.'

He turned then, back to the painting of Isobel Van Allen, and I felt that I had been dismissed.

It didn't seem to me that I would be getting any more information out of Gareth Winters at this point. Instead, he had managed to chase me away. As I moved with haste from the long gallery, I began to wonder if that had been his intention all along.

* * *

155

Having had enough of conversation to last me for the moment, I went back to my room to read. Winnelda was not there, and I intended to take advantage of the solitude. I sat in the chair closest to the fire and picked up *The Dead of Winter.*

Truth be told, I did not have very high hopes that the book would divulge any great secrets. While it made for very interesting reading thus far, I had yet to find anything that might prove useful. Subtlety, after all, had not been Isobel Van Allen's strong suit, and I could not see that there were any secrets lurking beneath the surface of her lurid prose.

It all seemed fairly straightforward to me. While Isobel likely had taken liberties with the facts, the characters she had drawn continued to accurately reflect the various personalities as I had seen them thus far.

The gentleman meant to be Reggie was restless and uneasy, scarred by his experiences in the trenches of France and still trying to regain his footing in a society that had changed while he was gone. The artist, meant to be Mr Winters, was charming and vague, lost in a fog of drugs and a world of his own making. My former schoolmate Freida was reckless and grief-stricken in the years following the death of her fiancé. Phillip Collins, the man who would eventually become her husband, pursued her with a subtle relentlessness and was just as dark and quietly menacing in fiction as he seemed to be in the flesh.

I was relieved to find that Laurel played little part in the story. I had avoided reading the book when it had been released in part because I knew it would make me angry to see my cousin's name maligned. As it was, she was usually mentioned in passing. Isobel had retracted her claws where my cousin was concerned.

The stormy romance between the character that represented Beatrice and the two gentlemen had begun to simmer by chapter seven. Beatrice's character was lovely, cold, and restrained. Which was what made it all the more curious that both Edwin Green and Bradford Glenn should have both fallen to fighting for her hand. Perhaps she had represented some sort of dream to the young men, her intangibility making her love seem like something to be attained at any cost.

In any event, Isobel had done a fine job of creating an atmosphere of thwarted passion and growing resentment. It was clear very early on that she meant to cast Bradford Glenn as the villain of the piece, for she presented him with a brooding nature that hinted things would not end well for those who crossed him.

So absorbed was I in the book, that I didn't hear Milo enter the room until he spoke.

'Hello, darling.'

I didn't bother looking up. 'Hello.'

'Reading that book again?'

'Yes.' I pulled my eyes reluctantly from the page. 'How was your walk?'

'Cold and dull.'

I glanced at the clock. 'Yes, I imagine nearly two hours out in the winter air might be.'

'Lindy is quite a tireless little thing.'

'Milo . . .' I hesitated, the words on my lips. There was a

time, not very long ago, when I would not have wanted to speak plainly, to tell him how I really felt about the matter. As things stood between us now, I thought that I should be honest.

'It won't do to make her fall in love with you, you know,' I said softly. 'It isn't fair. She doesn't know you don't mean half of what you say.'

He smiled, my concerns summarily dismissed. 'I have been the model of propriety.'

'Your idea of propriety is not the same as other people's.'

'I don't want anyone in love with me but you, darling.'

'Yes, well, it's not you I'm concerned about.'

'Let me assure you that Lucinda Lyons is perfectly aware of how mad I am about my wife.' He dropped a kiss on my lips and took the chair opposite me.

I didn't intend to press the subject, at least not at the moment. Instead, I went back to reading my book.

'You're determined to finish that thing, I suppose,' he said.

'Yes, but it's much easier to do it in silence,' I told him pointedly.

He picked up a magazine that had no doubt been left by Winnelda and began thumbing through it. I wondered if he meant to continue sitting there while I was trying to read.

'How did your chat with Mr Winters go?' he asked, his eyes on the page before him.

'Oh, famously,' I replied. 'He wants to paint me.'

'Naturally he does.'

'Quite naturally. Au naturel, in fact.'

Milo's eyes came up from the magazine. 'Does he indeed?'

'Yes,' I went on in a casual tone. 'He thinks the light in the conservatory would highlight my alabaster skin.'

'I don't doubt it,' Milo said dryly.

'He's a very unusual man,' I said, closing the book. 'I don't quite know what to make of him.'

'Don't you?' Milo replied. 'I think it's quite clear what he's about.'

'Oh, I don't think he meant anything improper by it.'

'Your naivety is quite adorable, my love. He must believe me to be a very accommodating husband.'

'Oh, yes,' I said. 'He assured me that you'd love a portrait.'

Milo smiled. 'Why would I need you on the wall when I have you in the bed?'

'I told him I'd consider it.' I was not, of course, considering posing nude for Mr Winters, but I didn't like Milo to think I was utterly predictable.

He was unimpressed with my threats. 'Well, do be careful you don't catch your death of cold. I'm sure the conservatory is very draughty this time of year.'

I frowned at him and went back to reading my book.

A moment later there was a tapping at the door, and Winnelda entered, her expression disapproving.

'Madam, that inspector is here again. He wants to see you.'

CHAPTER FOURTEEN

I found Inspector Laszlo in the drawing room I had vacated not long ago. We greeted each other with a mutual lack of enthusiasm and then, the formalities aside, he launched at once into the reason for his visit.

'Just a few more questions for you, Mrs Ames. I'm sure you won't mind?' I felt there was a challenge in the question, but I was determined to be pleasant.

'Not at all, Inspector. I'm happy to do whatever I can to bring the killer to justice.'

He studied me as though trying to determine my level of sincerity and then went on.

'The doctor says Miss Van Allen had been dead for less than an hour when you discovered her. I am trying to account for her movements, as well as the movements of others in the house, before that time.'

I rather thought this was something he might have asked me yesterday, but I supposed he knew best how to do his job.

'We, of course, did preliminary interviews with all the guests and servants yesterday,' he said, as though he had read my thoughts. 'But shock often affects the memory, and so I've come to see if recollections are a bit clearer today.'

It was, I supposed, not a bad strategy. I grudgingly admitted to myself that he might be more competent than I had assumed.

'When did you last see Miss Van Allen alive?' he asked.

'I saw her after breakfast,' I said. 'Mr Roberts was concerned because she had been ill the night before, and I went with him to her door to see if she was feeling better.'

'You're certain that she was alive at that time?'

I repressed an exasperated sigh, as I was sure he knew perfectly well that she had been. No doubt he had already heard as much from Mr Roberts. 'Quite sure, Inspector,' I said. 'She came to the door and spoke to us for several minutes.'

'What was the conversation about?'

'Nothing of consequence,' I said, though I was not entirely sure that was true. There had been something odd in Isobel's manner, but nothing about the conversation had been especially telling. 'As I said, she had been ill the previous night, but she said she was feeling much better.'

'What was the nature of her illness?' he asked, and I thought there was a sudden sharpness in his gaze.

'A stomach ailment, I believe. Gastritis, perhaps. Mr Roberts told me she had been unwell all night.'

'Indeed.' I wondered if he knew about the poison that Parks had seen in Mr Roberts' room. Did it have some connection to the case? I wanted desperately to ask him, but I felt that if I showed any sign of interest he would make a concerted effort to reveal nothing.

'Mr Roberts is her secretary, correct?' He asked this question very casually, and it seemed to me that he was testing me in some way.

'And her lover, I believe,' I said directly.

He sat back in his chair. 'And how did you come by this information?'

I smiled sweetly. 'One need not be a detective inspector to pick up on such things.'

My comment was, as I had hoped, not appreciated. Inspector Laszlo frowned.

'They made their relationship plain to you?'

'They did not, shall we say, make much effort to conceal it.' To myself, I thought that if Inspector Laszlo had not already determined as much from his conversations with Mr Roberts, he was not much of a detective. I suspected, however, that he was much cleverer than he pretended to be. Perhaps the ruse of denseness was meant to throw criminals off guard.

'You have been involved in two murders in the past year, have you not?' he asked suddenly. The question was, I thought, meant to catch me off guard, but I had been expecting it since yesterday.

'Yes.'

'Rather an unfortunate coincidence.' His tone implied it might be more than that, but I refused to be baited.

'Yes. Tragic.'

We looked at one another expectantly.

Luckily, it was at just this moment that Laurel came

charging into the room. 'Amory, I . . . Oh, excuse me.'

Inspector Laszlo turned and, seeing my cousin, rose quickly to his feet.

'Please don't let me disturb you,' she said. 'I didn't mean to interrupt. A maid told me Amory had come this way, but I didn't know that she was speaking with you, Inspector Laszlo.'

She smiled at him, and his demeanour relaxed perceptibly.

'He was just questioning me about the other murders in my past,' I said, before he could reply.

Inspector Laszlo's mouth tightened ever so slightly.

'Oh, yes,' Laurel said sadly, walking a bit farther into the room. 'Poor dear Amory. It was so very trying for her, but she solved the cases, you know. She's very clever. Of course, I'm certain that you are handling this matter admirably, Inspector.'

She smiled brightly at him. If I hadn't known better, I might have thought he flushed. The man was clearly smitten with my cousin. I began at once to determine how we might best use this to our advantage.

However, it seemed Laurel was well ahead of me on that score. 'I know it's your duty to question everyone involved. Have you any other questions for me?'

She came and took a chair beside me without being invited. Inspector Laszlo looked momentarily as though he would like to object, but then he took his seat across from us.

'I was just trying to determine Miss Van Allen's whereabouts leading up to the murder. Have you anything further to add, Miss Ellison?' he asked.

Laurel shook her head. 'Nothing more than what I told you yesterday. I hadn't seen Isobel since the night before . . . before it happened.'

'Well, then,' he said. 'I suppose that will be all for now, Mrs Ames. Miss Ellison.'

'Thank you, Inspector,' Laurel beamed at him. 'Please let us know if we can be of any further help.'

We rose then, and Laurel and I went out of the room arm in arm.

'You're rather a wonder,' I said, when we were out of earshot. 'You came to save me from that wretched man, and I am in your debt.'

She laughed. 'I know you could have managed him on your own, but there is no use in prolonging your exposure to him if he annoys you.'

'You like him,' I said, hoping it didn't sound like an accusation.

She shrugged, but a smile pulled at her lips. 'He's very earnest, very sure of himself. I find that attractive.'

'And how is Reggie holding up?' I asked pointedly.

'Dearest, you're not very subtle are you? Reggie isn't well. But he hasn't been since the war, not really. I'm afraid for him. I thought that Edwin Green's death might be too much for him. Now that Isobel is dead, too . . .' She sighed. 'His nerves are shot all to pieces.'

'Do you think he might have done it?' I asked.

I knew Laurel's instinct would be to protest at once. Reggie was, after all, one of her oldest friends, and she would feel the desire to defend him. She was also just-minded, however, and she gave the question proper consideration.

'I don't think so,' she said at last. 'I . . . I don't really know him any more. It's been so long since everything happened, but I don't *think* he would have done it.'

'He said at the dinner table that night that he would kill her before she wrote another book,' I said quietly. I wondered if anyone had mentioned as much to Inspector Laszlo.

'It was the type of thing people say when they're angry,' Laurel said. 'He shouldn't have said it, but I don't think he meant it. Oh, I've thought about it, believe me. It isn't only that I like to think he is still the sweet, caring boy I knew so many years ago. I just don't know if he's capable of it. If he had done it, I don't think that he could have stabbed her. He can't bear the sight of blood. Surely he would have chosen some other way.'

'If not Reggie, then who?' I asked.

'I feel wretched speculating,' she said, glancing around and lowering her voice. 'But I can't help but wonder if it might have been Beatrice.'

'Any particular reason?'

'I don't know,' she said thoughtfully. 'It may be nothing more than that I think she is the type of woman who would be able to do it.'

It was not a very definite theory, but I supposed it was as good as any. Although I thought that the crime seemed more one of spontaneous fury than cold calculation, I could not rule out Beatrice Kline as a suspect. She had been very quick to point the finger at Mr Roberts. Had she been trying to hide her own involvement?

'Do you think Beatrice had something to do with Edwin Green's death?'

'I've thought about that,' Laurel said, 'and I don't see why she would have wanted to. After all, she needn't have killed him to rid herself of him; she might just have rejected his suit and sent him on his way. If she did kill Isobel, I think it was not so much because of what Isobel was going to write, but because of what she already did.'

'What do you mean?'

'I think Beatrice took it very personally when Isobel wrote *The Dead of Winter*. It was, after all, insinuated that one man killed the other over her affections. Then Bradford killed himself, which seemed to confirm it.'

'What happened between Beatrice and Bradford?' I asked. This was something I had wondered about. They had obviously parted ways after the tragedy, so I assumed that Beatrice had not been in love with him.

'She never spoke with him again after it happened, so far as I know. I did wonder if she knew something about him that the rest of us didn't, for I remember that things seemed uneasy between them on the night Edwin died. It struck me that there was something in the way that she looked at him when she didn't know others were watching, warily, as though she didn't quite trust him.'

I wondered if she had been worried about what he might do to Edwin Green. Perhaps that was why she had wanted nothing further to do with him after Edwin's death.

Another possibility occurred to me. Perhaps they had parted ways because her heart had been broken by Edwin's death, and she had not wished to pursue her flirtation with Bradford any further.

'Did she love Edwin, do you think?' I asked.

'I don't think so, not deeply, at any rate. After all, she married another man not six months after the scandal. I think she enjoyed their attentions, but I don't know that it was anything serious. Of course, I could be wrong.'

It was just so difficult to tell. Laurel was right. Beatrice was cool and calculating. I thought that she might easily be the kind of woman who would wait for her revenge.

I was about to ask my cousin what she thought had become of the murder weapon, when I was suddenly interrupted by a loud scream coming from somewhere upstairs.

CHAPTER FIFTEEN

'Help! Someone help!'

Laurel and I rushed towards the stairs. As we reached the bottom, a maid appeared on the landing, wringing her hands. 'He's fainted, madam,' she said. 'He came out of his room, pale as death, and fell on the floor. Oh, is he dead? I hope he's not dead!'

I rushed up the stairs, Laurel right behind me and, reaching the first floor, was startled to see Mr Roberts lying in the hallway outside of his door. The maid was right; his face was devoid of colour and he was lying very still.

I knelt beside him, a bit afraid of what I would find. I desperately hoped the past was not repeating itself, and I was immensely relieved to see that he was breathing.

'Is he . . . ?' Laurel asked.

'He's alive,' I said. 'He's just passed out.'

I leant closer, patting his arm. 'Mr Roberts?' I said softly. 'Can you hear me?'

It seemed to me that his eyelids flickered ever so slightly, but his eyes did not open and he didn't stir.

Inspector Laszlo must have heard the scream as well, for he appeared suddenly behind us before I had even heard his footsteps on the stairs.

He knelt beside me and put a hand on Mr Roberts' wrist.

He looked up at Laurel, his expression grim. 'Someone had better ring for the doctor.'

Inspector Laszlo and his sergeant managed to get Mr Roberts back into his room and into his bed, though he had not yet regained consciousness. Having made sure the maid had done as bidden, Laurel and I went down to await the arrival of the doctor.

'I do hope he's all right,' she said. She looked at me, asking what was on both of our minds. 'You don't suppose this has anything to do with Isobel's murder?'

'I don't know. He's been terribly upset about her death. Perhaps he was merely overwrought. He's been ill and hasn't been eating, so perhaps that was it.'

'Do you really think so?'

I sighed. 'I wish I knew.'

'I just hope that another tragedy doesn't befall us,' she said. 'I suppose I had better find Reggie before he hears of this and becomes alarmed. He doesn't need anything else upsetting him.'

The doctor arrived at last and was ushered into Mr Roberts' room. I followed him upstairs, wishing there was something more I could do. I hated it when there was nothing to be done but wait.

I wondered briefly where Milo had taken himself off to this morning, but did not have long to ponder it. Inspector Laszlo came out a moment later.

'Is Mr Roberts all right?' I asked.

'He's regained consciousness,' he said. 'There doesn't seem to be any lasting damage.'

I breathed a sigh of relief. 'Did he say what happened?'

'He's been quite ill,' Inspector Laszlo said tersely. 'The doctor says he must be in need of fluids.'

I frowned. Both he and Isobel had been ill. Was it possible that it had something to do with the murder? I reminded myself not to jump to conclusions. It was much more likely that they had both merely contracted the same illness. After all, they were in close contact with one another.

Inspector Laszlo must have noticed my thoughtful silence, for he said, 'Is there something you would like to tell me, Mrs Ames?'

I looked up at him. I knew our relationship had not gotten off to the best start, but perhaps there was still time to mend it. 'I heard that there was poison discovered in Mr Roberts' room.'

His brows rose. 'Did you? Where did you hear that?'

'The servants talk,' I said. 'One of them saw it.'

His face went suddenly blank, and I thought for a moment he was not going to say anything else. Then he sighed. 'There was a vial of what was thought to be poison in Mr Roberts' room, but it was not what caused either Miss Van Allen or Mr Roberts to be ill.'

'How do you know?' I pressed.

'Because the poison in his room was cyanide. The

symptoms are not consistent. Death would have been nearly instantaneous if taken in any significant quantities, and the vial appears to be full.'

That was certainly a good reason. It raised a number of other questions, however.

'Why would he have such a thing in his possession?' I asked, forgetting in my excitement that Inspector Laszlo would likely be unreceptive to my questions.

He seemed to make note of my eagerness, but answered nonetheless. 'A very good question, and one you can be sure I asked him. He claims they used cyanide as a fumigant on the ship they took from Africa, and he obtained a vial to use for similar purposes, as he had heard Lyonsgate had long been uninhabited.'

What a ridiculous lie.

'That seems rather unlikely,' I said.

'Indeed,' he replied. 'But not something you should concern yourself with, Mrs Ames.'

'Oh, certainly not,' I replied quickly.

He looked at me as though he was not at all fooled, and I wondered again if I had underestimated Inspector Laszlo.

'I'm going to go and speak to my sergeant. Perhaps you had better have some tea and rest after your ordeal this morning.'

I managed to bite my tongue in the face of his patronising manner and offer him a tight smile as he walked away.

The encounter had left me with more questions than answers. I did not for a moment believe Mr Roberts had possessed the poison for fumigation purposes. Nevertheless, the fact remained that Isobel Van Allen had not been poisoned to death. Whatever the cyanide had really been meant for, it had not been put to use.

I found it hard to believe that Mr Roberts had possessed it for some nefarious purpose. He seemed a harmless, confused young man, and I hoped that he would be able to recover from all of this and have a happy life. I hoped the doctor was giving him a thorough examination and could help with whatever ailment he had.

Was it, I wondered suddenly, the same doctor who had been called to the scene of Edwin Green's death? If so, this might provide an ideal opportunity to speak to him.

I went to the door of Mr Roberts' room and stood outside. Unfortunately, Winnelda had been correct. The wood was much too solid to hear anything going on inside. I could not even discern the sound of voices.

It was not that I wanted to eavesdrop upon the details of Mr Roberts' ailment. Though I was concerned about him, I had no wish to invade his privacy in that matter. However, I did want a chance to talk to the doctor. I wondered when he would come out. I didn't want to miss him, but I also wondered how I could approach him without seeming overly curious.

I stepped back, wondering what I should do next. I decided to hover about in the hallway and see if he made an appearance. I would think of some plausible reason for wanting to speak with him.

I was rewarded for my patience a few moments later when the door opened and a tall, stout gentleman stepped into the hallway. I approached him at once.

'I beg your pardon. Are you the doctor?'

He turned, surveying me in a practised glance from dark eyes beneath bushy brows. 'Yes.'

'I wonder if I might have a word with you.'

'Certainly. How may I help you?' Despite his reassuring words, he looked at me a bit warily, though I couldn't quite blame him. Lyonsgate seemed to make people uneasy. Besides, I had been hovering outside the door waiting to pounce, and I was afraid I had not been very subtle about it.

'I . . . I'm not feeling very well. I wonder if I could have a moment of your time.' It was not, in fact, a lie. I wasn't feeling at all well. Though I hadn't wanted to admit it, even to myself, I did not feel entirely recovered from the ordeal of finding Miss Van Allen's body. I had not slept well since, and there was a continual dull ache in my head that I did my best to ignore.

'Certainly,' he said.

'Thank you. My room is this way.'

I led him to my bedroom and he closed the door behind us, setting his bag upon a table near the door.

'Inspector Laszlo tells me that Mr Roberts has regained consciousness,' I said. 'Will he be all right?'

'He seems to be feeling better. He needs rest and fluids. I'll come back around tomorrow to check on him. What can I help you with?'

'I'm sorry to have troubled you. I just thought that, while you were here . . .'

'No trouble at all, Mrs . . .'

'Ames.'

'Mrs Ames. My name is Dr Jarvis. What seems to be the trouble?'

173

'Oh, it's hard to say, specifically,' I said. 'I just have been feeling a trifle under the weather. I'm very tired and my head aches a bit.'

It seemed that his gaze became a bit sharper. 'Have you had any stomach trouble?'

'No,' I said. 'My stomach has been fine.'

'Dizziness?'

'No.'

He appeared to be losing interest. 'Is your throat sore?'

'No, my throat isn't troubling me.' I decided, since my time with the doctor would no doubt be limited, that I had better be direct. 'It was dreadful about Miss Van Allen.'

'Yes,' he said non-committally. 'Have you had a fever?'

'I don't think so. It was very dreadful for me because . . . you see, I . . . I was the one who found her.'

A bit of sympathy fought its way to the surface of his expressionless face. 'That must have been very difficult for you,' he said.

'Yes, I've been quite troubled by it.' This was not a lie either, though I allowed a slightly exaggerated note of distress to creep into my tone. If he thought I was a hysterical female, so be it.

'This could be the source of your difficulties. Such a thing can affect one profoundly. Very trying to the nerves, you know. The best thing for it is to get plenty of rest. Have you had trouble sleeping?'

'Yes,' I answered honestly.

'Would you like me to prescribe you a sedative?'

'No, I don't think so. But perhaps if I could just talk to you for a few moments.'

'Certainly,' he said kindly. 'Would you like to tell me about it?'

'Well, I went to her room to speak with her and found her on the floor. I didn't realise she was dead at first. I thought perhaps she had fallen and hit her head or some such thing, for there was a glass on the floor beside her. It seemed to me that she might have been taken ill while drinking her wine.'

'Indeed.' There was something guarded about this response, as though he found the information interesting but didn't want me to know, and he looked into his bag as though searching for something. It seemed that I would have to press on.

'I understand that this is not the first time that someone has died tragically at Lyonsgate,' I said sadly.

He looked up at me. 'What do you mean?'

'There was a death here several years ago.'

'Oh, yes,' he said brusquely. 'Edwin Green, I suppose you mean.'

'Yes. I suppose you were called out here at that time, too.' I wondered if my pressing for information would seem too obvious, but I could really see no other way to get the information I was searching for.

'No, I wasn't the doctor here then. That was Dr Brockhurst.'

'Oh,' I said, a bit deflated. It had been my hope that he would be able to give me a first-hand account of Edwin Green's death. Now it seemed that I had exaggerated my symptoms to no effect. There was still the off chance I might be able to learn something useful, but I was not

175

optimistic. Perhaps if I could speak to this Dr Brockhurst.

'He moved away after the scandal occurred, I suppose?' I said casually.

'No such thing. He still lives in the village. Retired, you might say, though he still sees patients from time to time. Some of his older patients haven't taken to me. Six years and I'm considered a newcomer.'

'I see. So you weren't living in the village at the time of Edwin Green's death.'

'No. I remember reading about it in the papers, of course. I was hesitant to take a job here, I don't mind telling you. I don't hold with scandal. But things have been fairly quiet . . . until now, at least. But you'd best not think too much about it, Mrs Ames. If you start to feel troubled, drink a glass of brandy.'

It seemed he would be of no further use to me at the moment. 'Thank you, doctor.'

There was a perfunctory tap at my door and Milo came into the room. 'I hear there has been some excitement. I . . . Oh, excuse me,' he said, his eyes moving from me to the doctor and back again.

'Dr Jarvis, sir,' the doctor said. 'You are Mr Ames?'

'Yes.'

'I wonder if I might have a word with you in the hallway.'

Milo's eyes came back to me, and then he nodded. 'Of course.'

Dr Jarvis turned to me. 'Make sure you get plenty of rest, Mrs Ames. And take the brandy if you feel that you need it.'

'Thank you, Doctor.'

He hesitated on the threshold. Then, seemingly afraid I might seek a second opinion, he added, 'Dr Brockhurst is in Italy just now. Must be lovely there this time of year.'

Milo shot me a significant look, refusing to let me forget that we had exchanged a holiday in Italy for this dismal trip to Lyonsgate.

Then the gentlemen went out, and I breathed a disappointed sigh. Dr Jarvis had not been at all helpful. To make matters worse, the doctor who had been called to the scene of Edwin Green's death was away on holiday. I wondered if it would be possible to find anyone else in the village who would be willing to share their recollections of the incident.

A few minutes later Milo came into the room and shut the door behind him. 'What was that about?' I asked.

'The doctor said your nerves are in a most fragile state and that I should treat you delicately,' Milo said sceptically. 'You've clearly been lying to him.'

I laughed. 'He prescribed brandy and sedatives. He seems to think I will feel much better if I am nearly unconscious.'

'Speaking of unconsciousness, I hear that there has been some trouble with Mr Roberts?'

'He lost consciousness in the hallway. It was very alarming.'

'And you were so distraught that you needed to speak to the doctor, I suppose.'

'Something of that nature.'

He raised a brow and waited for me to continue.

'I wanted to know about Edwin Green's death,' I admitted with a sigh, 'but he was not the doctor at the time, so he was of very little use to me.'

'How unfortunate. Let us hope he was at least of use to Mr Roberts, who was actually in need of his attentions.'

I made a face. 'You needn't make it sound as though I callously stole the doctor's attentions. Mr Roberts is going to be fine. I would not have called Dr Jarvis away if I felt that it would be detrimental to Mr Roberts' health.'

'Well, that's reassuring.'

'Yes,' I replied, refusing to be baited. 'I'm very glad that Mr Roberts is going to be all right, but I do wonder . . .'

'Wonder what?'

'I wonder if it's a coincidence that Isobel and Mr Roberts both became ill.'

'Amory . . .'

'Yes, yes, I know. It's none of my concern.'

As Milo had begun to assume his exasperated face, I decided it was best to let the subject drop for the present. That did not mean, however, that I intended to forget about it.

CHAPTER SIXTEEN

Dinner that night was a strained affair. We were all of us, I thought, a bit demoralised by Mr Roberts' illness. There was an atmosphere of oppression that seemed to steadily grow the longer we stayed at Lyonsgate. It seemed as though the house was closing in on us.

I was not the only one who felt it. Laurel leant towards me as we went in to dinner. 'I do wish we didn't have to stay here any longer. But I can't leave Reggie to bear all of this alone. Beatrice is not in the least sympathetic, and Lindy cares only for men and horses. Reggie needs me, as much as I should like to get away.'

I knew the feeling. Truth be told, I was sorely tempted to accept Milo's suggestion that we escape to Italy. I didn't feel, however, that I could leave now, not with everything unresolved. I certainly didn't want to leave Laurel to deal with the matter herself. As capable as she was, I knew how disheartening it was to face things alone. So Laurel would stay for Reggie, I would stay for Laurel, and we would all just wait and see what might happen next.

It was a relief when the meal was over, and I was able to go back to my room. Laurel went up with me and we talked in hushed voices as we walked along the shadowy hallways. I felt vaguely as though we were heroines in some gothic novel. If only the villain would commence twisting his moustache and laughing maniacally. It would make things so much easier.

We stopped at Laurel's door. We were anxious to discuss the murder, but also very tired. There would be plenty of time for commiserating and conspiring tomorrow.

Laurel opened the door to her room, but didn't go in at once. 'There's got to be a way to find out who's done this. Only, I worry . . .' She looked at me. 'What if the truth is worse than not knowing?'

'I suppose we must cross that bridge when we come to it,' I said.

She nodded wearily. 'Yes, you're right. One day at a time.'

'Yes, perhaps a good night's rest will give us clearer heads.'

'I hope so. I'm exhausted but I feel as though I shan't sleep a wink.'

I knew very well how she felt. I had not been sleeping at all well myself.

'Well, goodnight, Amory.'

'Goodnight.'

I went to my room and found the fire crackling brightly in the hearth. Everything was still and quiet. I had given

Winnelda the night off. I had meant for her to get rest, but I had little doubt that she was somewhere gossiping with the household staff.

I prepared for bed, changing into a pair of silk pyjamas. Even with the fire roaring in the fireplace, the cold left me wishing I had something more along the lines of thick flannel.

As quickly as possible, I ensconced myself within the bedclothes. Milo was having an after-dinner drink with the gentlemen, so I would have a few moments of peace to read.

I picked up the book again. It was certainly rife with juicy titbits, and I could see why it had caused such a furore. Nevertheless, it had not been exactly enlightening as far as containing possible motives for murder.

I flipped to the beginning of the next chapter and began to read. I had taken to substituting their real names for the pseudonyms Isobel had given them. It was much easier that way.

After a few paragraphs, I sat up. This passage was particularly interesting. I started reading quickly and then forced myself to slow down so I could absorb the details. It seemed that there was something here that might be important. I didn't know how, exactly, but something told me this was a piece of the puzzle not to be overlooked.

The torrid affair between Beatrice, Edwin, and Bradford was coming to a head. In the novel, the characters meant to be Bradford and Beatrice had arranged to meet in her room after the house was asleep. The reason for the secrecy of their rendezvous was not exactly clear to me, given the rather open nature of the relationships occurring at

Lyonsgate. I could only assume Isobel had wanted to add an additional element of tension to the novel.

It appeared to have been an effective strategy, for I was drawn into the scene at once.

It was nearly two o'clock in the morning and the house was silent, save the creaking of its ancient beams as the wind screamed and clawed at those warm and safe within its walls. Bradford slid from the bed and moved into the corridor as quickly as he dared. Already, it was very late. Beatrice might think he wasn't coming, and he couldn't bear the thought of a lonely princess waiting in her tower.

He made his way down the dark passages, careful to avoid the squeaking boards that ached to betray his secrets with each footfall. With every step he felt the beat of his heart increase and his breath quicken in anticipation.

He reached her room and tapped softly on her door, his hand trembling. There was no sound from within, only the heavy silence of the darkened passageway in which he stood. Overcome with emotion, he flung open the door and moved into her bedroom without waiting for a response. There she was, standing before the fireplace. She wore no negligee and her nightgown was thin and translucent. The light from the fire glowed through, illuminating the outline of her beautiful body. It was as though she was swathed in flame. Desire surged through him and something more: love so deep it hurt.

He stood, frozen and speechless, looking at her. She turned slowly, as though she had not been waiting for him at all, as though she barely knew that he was there. He always felt that way, as though she were some sort of mirage he could never quite touch. Whenever she was in his arms, he wondered how it was that he had come to be worthy of her.

Wordlessly, he rushed towards her, anxious to feel the warmth of her against him, to be enveloped in her flame. It was only when she resisted being pulled into his arms that he realised something was wrong.

'What is it?' he asked in a breathless whisper.

'It is never going to work between us, Bradford.' Beatrice's face was drawn and quite white, and Bradford knew at once that this was not one of the games she liked to play. He felt himself grow cold as he looked at her, as though something inside him was beginning to die, the fire withering to embers.

'What do you mean?'

'Well, we've had our fun, haven't we? We have enjoyed one another's company, but these kinds of things never last.'

He stepped back, reeling. 'Don't say such things. You mustn't say such things.'

'I'm sorry.' Her voice was cool and hard, and she didn't sound sorry. She sounded as though she couldn't wait to be rid of him. He couldn't believe it. He felt momentarily numb, dumbfounded. And then *a surge of a new kind of heat, hot fury, as another thought occurred to him. Somehow he knew. He knew exactly what it was.*

'It's Edwin, isn't it? Tell me. Tell me the truth!' He sounded like a madman to his own ears, but he didn't care. He had been sure she loved him, sure that they were going to be together. And now this.

She looked back at him, those brown eyes he had always loved, that he had seen as brimming with warmth and laughter, were suddenly flat and dark with hidden secrets. He felt in that moment that he could kill her. It was not a meaningless thought, born of anger, and sweeping quickly through him. It was like a sudden weight in his chest, bearing down on him, crushing the life from his heart. It was real, pure hatred, totally consuming the love he had felt only a moment ago, and he clenched his fists to keep himself from putting them around her long, white neck.

'You look rather as though you're enjoying that,' Milo said. I hadn't heard him come in from his room. He stood in the doorway of the bathroom in his nightclothes and dressing gown.

'It's rather tawdry stuff,' I said. 'But there's something very interesting about this.'

'Indeed?' He did not sound at all convinced.

'Yes, listen to this.'

I read aloud to Milo the passage I had just read, and then continued on.

She was saying something, but somehow he couldn't hear what it was. It was as though he were underwater, as though she was holding his head beneath the sea, and speaking to him, mocking him with her artificial platitudes. She was killing him, that's what she was doing. Killing him slowly with her heartless indifference.

He felt as though his heart would explode. He couldn't breathe.

Milo snorted, spoiling the intensity of the moment. I ignored him and continued reading.

She was everything to him, and now he realised that it had all meant nothing. He had nothing left, nothing in the whole world to live for. And he still couldn't breathe. He gasped for breath, felt as though he were going to die for lack of air.

'This is quite ridiculous.'

'Do be quiet, Milo.'

'Pure melodrama.'

'*He needed air,*' I read loudly, determined to ignore my husband's distracting commentary. He rolled his eyes, but sat down in a chair and let me go on.

If he didn't have air he would die. And it was Beatrice who was stopping him from breathing. It was her fault. This pain was all her fault. The only way to stop it was to stop her. The only way to breathe was to stop her from taking all the air.

Milo sighed heavily.

She let out a strangled cry as he put his hands around her throat and began to squeeze.

She struggled against him, her nails clawing at him, but he barely felt the sting.

'Do you mean to tell me she made money writing this drivel?' Milo asked, putting a cigarette to his lips.

'A great deal of money.'

'Astounding.'

'Be still and let me finish reading this passage.'

He took his lighter from his pocket and sat back in his chair, lighting the cigarette.

I read on.

They struggled, hitting a table, sending it crashing to the floor, the objects upon it shattering into thousands of pieces like his heart had done. The noise was tremendous, ringing in his ears, yet he did not release his grip on her throat.

Suddenly there was a blinding flash of light as pain exploded through his head. He crumpled to the floor. It was only a moment later, the air pounding in his lungs, that he came to himself.

Beatrice stood over him, gasping for breath, a heavy brass candlestick clutched in her hand.

He looked up at her, dazed. How had this happened? His hands burned and his fingers ached from what he had done. And yet he could not really

believe he had done it. Had he really tried to strangle
her? Had she really hit him? It seemed as though it
must have been a dream, but he lay on the floor and
she looked down at him, an expression of absolute
revulsion transforming her beautiful face into a mask
of horror. It was all much too real.

The door was flung open just then and Reggie and
Isobel stood in the doorway.

'What the devil's happened?' Reggie demanded.
'Beatrice, are you all right?'

Bradford didn't look at them. Instead, he lay on
the floor, looking up at Beatrice with the expression
of a suppliant.

'Beatrice,' he whispered brokenly, 'I'm sorry. I
didn't mean it. But you must believe that my love is
true. You must.'

'Get up and get out of here,' she hissed. 'Get out
of here at once.'

He staggered to his feet, dizzy and disoriented. He
rushed from the room, past Reggie and Isobel, spots
dancing before his eyes.

But the pain in his head was nothing compared
to the pain in his heart. His entire world had come
to an end.

I closed the book and looked up at Milo. He blew out a
stream of smoke, supremely unimpressed.

'What absolute rot,' he said. 'No wonder she was forced
to leave the country after its publication.'

'She's not Dickens, naturally,' I said. 'But it's fairly

compelling stuff. Bradford Glenn tried to kill her. No wonder she wanted nothing more to do with him after the murder. And Isobel witnessed it. It seems clear now why they all thought that he killed Edwin Green. He was clearly capable of violence.'

'If, that is, it happened as she said.'

'It seems very realistic to me.'

'It's fiction, my love. For all you know, she fabricated every bit of it.'

'Perhaps,' I said, unconvinced. Isobel might very well have invented the confrontation, but to what purpose? She had been very careful to portray each of the people at Lyonsgate very clearly. This confrontation between Bradford and Beatrice definitely made a case for Bradford having killed Edwin.

'She included this for a reason,' I said. I opened the book again and started the next chapter. 'Because it gave Bradford Glenn a motive to kill Edwin Green.'

'Or because she knew she would make a great deal of money exploiting and embellishing a tragedy. Who knew being a novelist was so lucrative? Perhaps I should take up writing. Would you like me with a furrowed brow and ink-stained fingers, darling?'

'I think the typewriter is customary in this day and age,' I said, turning the page.

'Then I shall have to have a secretary.'

I looked up at him. 'A young, pretty one, I suppose.'

'Naturally.'

'In that case, I forbid it.'

'And thus ends my career as a celebrated novelist, thwarted before it's begun.'

'I suppose you shall have to content yourself with being handsome and rich.'

He did not argue as I went back to reading.

The next chapter did not expound about the late night encounter between Bradford and Beatrice, saying only that Bradford 'eyed her with extreme distress and longing across the breakfast table.' Beatrice had apparently been unmoved by these silent entreaties for she left to go out walking with Edwin Green shortly thereafter.

I again wondered if it had really happened as Isobel wrote it.

I could think of only one way to set my mind at ease about the subject. I was going to have to ask Beatrice Lyons Kline.

CHAPTER SEVENTEEN

I slept fitfully and woke up just before dawn, my mind in a tumult. I knew at once that it would be useless to try to go back to sleep. It would be too early for breakfast, and I didn't feel as though I wanted much to eat at any rate.

Not that being awake at such an hour would prove of much use. I doubted anyone else would be up. In any event, it would be impolitic to discuss murder at this hour. Beatrice Kline seemed unapproachable at the best of times; I could only imagine how she would react to being questioned before breakfast.

It was then I remembered that Laurel had said Reggie Lyons often took long solitary walks about the property quite early in the morning. I wondered if there was any chance I could seek him out. We had not had a chance to talk privately, and I felt that his part of the story was something that might prove useful. He had been Isobel's lover, after all. He would likely have insight that the others did not.

I rose and dressed in my warmest wool suit as well as my cream-coloured wool coat with fur collar and cuffs. I selected a hat that was an excellent compromise between warmth and fashion and pulled on a pair of leather gloves. My sturdy walking shoes diminished the overall effect somewhat, but practicality won the day.

Properly turned out for my errand, I looked back at the bed. I had not been particularly quiet, hoping that I would wake Milo and he would be persuaded to accompany me. It was just as well that he did not wake, I supposed, for I thought that Reggie would be more likely to speak openly to me if I was alone.

I saw only one maid in passing and made my way outside into the frigid morning air. The sky was a strange silvery colour, glowing almost white as the sun rose above the horizon. I stood for a moment on the steps, deciding in what direction I should walk. I did not even know if Reggie Lyons had ventured out this morning, let alone in what direction he might have travelled.

My eyes travelled east towards the lake, glistening with the sheen of ice in the early morning light. Halfway around, near the shore, I could see the summer house, the scene of the tragedy, nestled in a copse of trees. I wondered if there might be anything useful to be gained from investigating it.

It was, I thought, probably farther away than it looked, but there was only a dusting of snow. I didn't think it would be too difficult a walk, but I wondered how I might explain my curiosity. There was really no good reason for me to go peering in the windows.

It wouldn't hurt, however, to walk in that direction. The bracing air felt as though it would be useful for clearing my head.

I walked across the gravel drive and then onto the lawn and down towards the lake, the frost on the grass crunching beneath my feet. I could see my breath in the air. It was an exceedingly cold morning, and I felt as though my breath was turning to fog in my lungs.

I was perhaps halfway to the lake when I caught sight of a figure walking from the opposite side of the lake. It was Reggie. I veered in his direction. He was walking slowly, his head down, and I didn't think he had seen me.

'Good morning, Mr Lyons,' I called when I was within shouting distance. I felt a bit silly calling out so loudly to him, but I didn't want to startle him.

He looked up, gave me a wave, and began walking in my direction.

'Good morning, Mrs Ames,' he said when he reached me. 'You're up early this morning.' His face was bright red with cold, and I wondered how long he had been out in the elements.

'Yes, I couldn't seem to sleep and thought I could do with some fresh air. It's very beautiful out here this morning.'

'Yes,' he said. He glanced around, but it seemed to me that he paid no particular attention to our surroundings.

'I thought I would walk to the lake.' I looked at him somewhat expectantly and began walking in that direction. He was too polite not to accompany me.

We walked in a not uncomfortable silence for a few moments, each of us lost in our own thoughts. When we reached the shore, we stopped, both of us gazing out at the water.

There was a stone bench sitting nearby. The sun must have warmed it, for there was no snow on it. I took a seat and looked out at the lake. The summer house was a good distance away now, almost directly across the lake.

I looked up to see Reggie standing stiffly beside me, his gaze trained on the water.

'Do you want to sit for a moment?' I asked.

He looked at me as though he had only just remembered that I was there, but he took a seat beside me.

The air was very cold and the place felt lonesome somehow, as though bad memories still lingered in the air around the lake. Reggie Lyons seemed to feel it, too, for he was rigid, his eyes dark with unspoken memories.

'It's rather tranquil here,' I said at last. This, of course, would not be perceived as a tranquil spot to anyone who had been here that day seven years ago.

He pulled his collar up a little higher around his neck and crossed his arms, as though to keep out the cold. His eyes had gone back to the lake and there was that faraway look in his eyes that I had seen so often on the faces of others since coming to Lyonsgate.

'I don't know whether I love or hate this place,' he said. 'When I was a child it seemed there was no place in the world as wonderful as Lyonsgate. Now I feel as though it's some sort of prison. A place that I will never be able to escape, no matter where I go.'

'I know it must be difficult,' I said, 'with everything that has happened.'

'It's been wretched. I wish I had never come back.'

'Do you think . . . would you like to talk about it?' Though I was interested in his account of the murder for my own reasons, it was genuine concern that motivated the question.

'That was a rotten business,' he said at last.

I didn't have to ask him what he meant. He wasn't talking about Isobel's death, but that night seven years ago. It seemed that no one who had been there at the time had been able to forget it. I suspected that, though they had not all been responsible for Edwin Green's death, each of them felt a certain responsibility for what had happened. They had revelled in the frivolity of youth, and they were still paying the price for it.

'Yes, I imagine it was awful.' I hoped my sympathy would inspire him to reminisce further, and it seemed to have worked. I wondered if any of them had ever had the opportunity to discuss it with someone who had no preconceived ideas about the incident.

'Edwin and I grew up together, perhaps you'd heard that.' He didn't wait for my answer but continued, as though he was afraid to stop himself. 'We went to war together and came home together, and I thought that perhaps he would be my brother if he married Beatrice. I would have liked that.'

'It seems that everyone was rather fond of him, excepting Mr Glenn.'

'And Collins,' he said. 'He and Collins got into more rows than I can count. Of course, they were in some sort of business together, and Collins was forever saying that Edwin had no head for it.'

This was new information. I hadn't heard of any bad blood between Edwin Green and Mr Collins. Freida had told me distinctly that everyone but Bradford had been friendly with Edwin Green. It seemed that was not the case.

'What sort of business?' I questioned casually.

'Some investment or other that Collins had been involved in in South Africa. Mines, I think. I remember Collins received a telegraph that week that made him fly into a rage. Then, of course, Edwin was killed and there was nothing else to be done about it. Collins made a good deal of money in the end, I think.'

This was a curious development. I wondered why there had been no mention in Isobel's book of volatile business dealings between Mr Collins and Edwin Green.

'Just as well for Edwin that he died, really. Might have been just as well for any of us not to have survived that night . . . I'm sorry. I shouldn't say such things. I don't mean them, you know. It's just that . . .'

He stopped, and for a moment there was no sound but the gentle rippling of the water and the melancholy call of a bird somewhere in the distance.

I ought to have felt uneasy sitting there with him, I was sure. There was something in his tone, some bitterness that I didn't like. But somehow I didn't feel as though I was in any danger. Whatever malice had been in him was in the past. It still ate at him, but there was a finality to it as well.

'I understand that he had had too much to drink,' I said hesitantly. It wasn't, perhaps, nice of me to press him in his obviously emotional state. Nevertheless, I felt I should take advantage of this moment, when he was inclined to talk.

'I don't remember much about that night. None of us do, really. We all gave our accounts to the police, of course. Couldn't very well tell them that we were too far gone to know what was happening. But it's all sort of a haze, like a dream. Or perhaps a nightmare.'

I said nothing, giving him time to collect his thoughts, to decide what he wanted to say. At last he continued.

'Edwin and Bradford had had a row that night. I'm sure you've heard about that.' He laughed bitterly. 'If you've read Isobel's book, you'll know most of what happened.'

'I've read some of it,' I conceded. I had not yet reached the part of the book that recounted Edwin Green's death. After I had read the chapter aloud to him, Milo had made it very difficult to concentrate on reading.

Reggie nodded. 'Most people read it. Rotten luck for Bradford.' He rubbed a trembling hand across his mouth, and it was almost as though he was drinking from an invisible glass. 'They came to blows, though they were both too intoxicated to do much harm to each other. I think it was Isobel who stepped in at the last and kept them from going at each other's throats.'

I found this interesting. Everything I had seen of Isobel Van Allen indicated that she enjoyed provoking confrontation, not putting a stop to it. But perhaps that was an unfair assessment of her character. I had not known her, but I had seen a glimmer of something other than cold malice beneath the mask of incendiary behaviour.

Reggie had stopped, but my silence seemed to encourage him, and he went on.

'After a while, things began to become a blur. It was

cold in the summer house. One of the servants had started a fire, but we had let it go out. Most of us decided to go back to the house, though we were not in much condition to get there. We had all had too much to drink, and some of us had had worse than liquor. I'm surprised we all made it, in fact. It was lucky only one of us was found frozen on the lawn.'

His voice trailed off and I wondered if he would continue.

'It was very cold that night?' I asked to gently prod him on.

'Yes. Very cold. I had had far too much to drink,' he said again. 'I wandered into the drawing room and passed out on the sofa.'

I wondered where Isobel Van Allen had been at the time. She and Reggie had been lovers, but I also recalled that things had not been going well between them. Perhaps she had gone to her room alone.

'I woke up hours later, very much disoriented. It was no longer dark, but it was very cold in the drawing room. I remember thinking that it must be what the dead feel like, stiff and cold. I had no idea . . .'

He was quiet again for a moment and I left him with his thoughts. I didn't want to press too much. I felt as though he needed to tell me in his own time and in his own way. It would be better for him that way. And, in all probability, the information would be more useful.

'I thought I would wander into the dining room, perhaps find something to eat for breakfast. It was then I heard the screams.'

His voice trailed off for a moment and I waited. He reached into his pocket and removed a cigarette case. He offered me one, which I declined, and then set one between his lips, shielding the flame of his lighter with his hand.

He breathed in deeply then blew out a cloud of white smoke into the cold air and then went on, his eyes on the lake.

'I didn't know what was happening at first. I went out into the entrance hall and Freida came in, still screaming and white as death. I don't know that I've ever seen anyone so pale.'

'Everyone was there? In the house, I mean?'

He nodded. 'I don't know where they all spent the night. They came running from various places and various stages of undress. We all ran out of the house and charged towards the summer house, as though there was something we could do. The cold air was refreshing. I remember that it felt good on my aching head, the cold wind.'

He took another long draw on his cigarette before continuing.

'We got nearly to the summer house, and all knew at once that it was far too late, by then. He was already stiff. And his eyes were wide open, staring.'

I resisted the urge to shudder that had nothing to do with the wind. How awful it must have been. How terrible to wake up to such a thing. I could well understand why it had been so difficult for all of them to move past it.

'I'd seen my share of bodies, of course, in France,' he said, and his voice had lost some of the haunted note that had been in it a moment before. 'Friends just as good as Edwin Green.'

'But this was so unexpected,' I said.

'Yes.'

'Did you think, at the time, that Bradford Glenn might have been in any way responsible?'

'I thought that it was just what it appeared to be. A man had taken too many drugs and had drunk too much alcohol. I never had a thought of anything else.'

I remembered what I had overheard him say to Beatrice in the breakfast room, about wondering if it was possible that Isobel Van Allen 'knew'. What was it that he thought she might know?

'It must have been a shock when Isobel Van Allen wrote that book,' I said.

He swore under his breath. 'Yes. She was always writing things. It was a great dream of hers to write a novel. She wrote often in the summer house, scribbling stories and things. I suppose she saw this as her chance. What happened here was in every paper in London.'

'And she chose to exploit it,' I said.

'I shouldn't have been surprised. She was forever having photographs taken of us, and she would stash articles from the gossip columns we were mentioned in away in her desk drawers like they were prizes we had won. It was fame she was after. She was willing to get it any way she could.' He sighed. 'Isobel always got what she wanted, one way or another.'

'That must have been difficult for you, especially since she was a woman you cared about.'

'I hated her,' he said, tossing down his cigarette and grinding it beneath his boot. 'I suppose that's a wicked thing to say, now that she's dead. But it's the truth. There was a time when I would have done anything – anything – to make her love me. Now I can't believe that there was ever a time when I didn't despise her.'

If that was the case, I wondered where exactly he had been at the time of Isobel's murder.

'It was a terrible thing for me,' I said, 'finding her body that way.'

'Yes, I can imagine. All that blood . . . Still, she earned it, didn't she? It's her own fault that she's dead.'

I said nothing, and he seemed suddenly to come to himself.

He shook his head, smiled ruefully. 'I'm sorry. I shouldn't have said such things to you.'

'Please don't apologise, Mr Lyons.'

'Reggie,' he said with a tired smile. 'We're friends now, aren't we?'

'I hope so,' I said. I certainly didn't want to be his enemy.

CHAPTER EIGHTEEN

Reggie didn't seem ready to leave the lake, so I walked back towards the house alone.

I wasn't sure if I had learnt anything new, but I felt that there was something in his story that had given me some idea I just hadn't quite been able to take hold of yet. That was how I felt about this entire thing, as though the pieces were all scattered about my feet, and I was picking them up at random, trying to make some sense of them.

Reggie Lyons was a complex gentleman, to be sure. I wasn't entirely sure what to make of his story. I didn't think that he had killed Edwin Green, if indeed Edwin Green had been murdered at all. If anyone had had a reason to murder Isobel Van Allen, however, it was Reggie. Their love had soured, and she had betrayed him, taken advantage of a personal tragedy, and cast a shadow upon the Lyons name.

No, it would not surprise me if he had wanted her dead, but by all accounts he was horrified by the sight of blood.

It seemed unlikely, then, that he would have stabbed her repeatedly. Of course, there was no predicting what one might do in the heat of passion.

I was so lost in thought that I didn't hear the voice until it called me the third time.

'Mrs Ames!' I looked up to see Gareth Winters coming from the direction of the stables.

He was not wearing a coat and his face was pink with cold. His pale eyes were bright in the morning light, his curls tousled by the wind, and I was struck again by his golden good looks.

'Good morning, Mr Winters.'

'I've just come from the stables,' he said as he reached me. What he was doing in the stables at this time of morning and, more to the point, why he had chosen to tell me this, I couldn't imagine.

'Oh, I see.'

'Have you made up your mind about the painting yet?' he asked.

His conversational shifts were dizzying. I had not thought much more about it. Part of me was hesitant to commit to the venture, but I also knew that it might be my only chance for an extended conversation with the flighty Mr Winters. Perhaps he would be more comfortable within the familiar surroundings of his milieu. It was worth a try.

'I think I would like you to paint me, after all,' I said.

He smiled. 'Excellent.'

'But I'm afraid I won't be able to disrobe,' I added quickly.

He shrugged. 'Very well. I suppose one can't have everything, can one? In evening dress, perhaps?'

'That ought to do nicely.' I thought over the garments that Winnelda had packed for our trip to Lyonsgate. 'I have a dress of silver satin that might do.'

He shook his head decisively. 'No, blue.'

He was not questioning if I had a gown of blue. It seemed a foregone conclusion that I would have one at my disposal. It turned out, however, that he was correct. Milo favoured me in blue, and, as it tended to complement my colouring, I often wore the shade.

'We should start as soon as possible,' he said. 'We don't know how long we will have, after all.'

I was certain that he must mean we would all be going home soon, but, given the events of late, his turn of phrase made me a bit uneasy.

'Very well,' I said. 'Perhaps this afternoon?'

He nodded. 'That would be excellent.'

'I shall look forward to it then.'

I was prepared to leave him then and go into the house for breakfast, but he was looking at me in that watchful way again, and I hesitated, wondering if there was something more he wished to say.

'Do you like horses, Mrs Ames?' he asked. Another strange question. I really didn't know what to make of Gareth Winters.

'Yes, I suppose I do,' I replied. 'My husband is very fond of them and keeps an excellent stable.'

'Will you come into the stables with me for a moment?' he asked at last.

I hesitated. I felt as though I could trust Mr Winters, but I didn't much want to stake my life on it. After all, someone at Lyonsgate was a murderer, and I had no reason to believe that it could not be the man standing in front of me.

He seemed to have realised that I was debating his intentions and offered an explanation for his odd request.

'An idea has just come to me. We may not need your evening gown after all.'

'Oh?'

'Yes, you see, since you said that you did not wish to be painted in the nude, I thought that perhaps I should paint you in a scene with a horse, perhaps in riding clothes? Would you come and look at the horses? There is one in the stable that would suit your colouring perfectly.'

This was very bizarre, but he seemed entirely in earnest. And surely the stables would not be completely deserted at this hour of the morning.

'Very well. Lead the way.'

He smiled and turned without further comment. I followed him into the stables and towards a stall at the end. It housed a sleek, pale grey gelding which was, admittedly, a very beautiful animal. I supposed if one was to hear that an animal complemented them, at least it was a fine specimen.

'Stand here, will you?' he asked, grasping me by the shoulders and moving me to one side to stand before the stall. His eyes raked over me, from head to toe and back again. Somehow I felt as though I had ceased to be a woman and had become simply an object to be painted.

The horse, however, seemed unimpressed by Mr Winters and his artistic visions. With a mouthful of hay, the horse came up behind me and sniffed at my hair.

I turned, laughing, spoiling, I am sure, the artistic mood of the moment.

'Hello there,' I said, patting the horse's nose. 'What a beauty you are.'

'It seems that horse would not be a good poser,' Mr Winters said.

I turned to look at him over my shoulder. 'You don't think so?'

Mr Winters shook his head. 'No, I don't think it would work. I should love to paint you on horseback, but the horse won't do. Besides, it's too cold, and the lighting wouldn't be right in here. I don't suppose we could bring the horse into the conservatory.'

'No, I don't suppose we could.'

He shrugged. 'Well, I suppose evening dress will have to do.'

He came up beside me then, very close, and reached out to pat the horse's nose. He stood so near to me that his arm brushed mine, and I wondered again how aware he was of social niceties. Was he making advances as Milo had suggested, or was he simply friendly and somewhat oblivious to the way in which he might be perceived?

There was a clearing of the throat, and we turned to see a gentleman standing behind us. Based on his dress, I assumed he must be the groom.

'Oh, good morning,' I said.

'Good morning, madam. Sir.' He was watching us with a vaguely suspicious expression on his face, as though we were intruders in his domain, which, in a way, we were.

'We were just admiring the horse,' I said.

It seemed that speaking of horses was the right thing to do, for he came a bit closer, his troubled expression easing.

'That's Miss Lucinda's horse, Romeo.'

'He's very beautiful.'

He nodded. 'He's a fine animal, if a bit skittish.'

'He seems quite calm to me,' Mr Winters observed.

The groom frowned. 'He may seem that way now, sir, but you've yet to see him when he sees a rat. Miss Lucinda said there was one ran across his stall the other day, and he was likely to kick his way out. She was worried that he might hurt himself. Miss Lucinda would never forgive me if that happened.'

'Well, I'm sure you take very good care of him,' I said.

The groom smiled proudly. 'I certainly do my best, madam.'

'My husband told me that you keep an excellent stable.' He hadn't, of course, said it exactly in those words, but a light compliment from Milo was a strong compliment indeed where horses were concerned.

The groom's expression brightened. 'Is your husband Mr Ames?'

'Yes.'

'He's a fine horseman, madam. A very fine horseman. And a good judge of horseflesh.'

'Yes, he is very fond of horses.'

'He said that you might like to ride, madam. Come out any time, and I'd be happy to saddle a horse for you.'

'Thank you. I shall.'

Having wished the groom a good day, Mr Winters and I went back into the house. He talked animatedly of his plans for our session that afternoon and seemed much more interested in preparing the tools of his trade than in eating breakfast. We parted ways in the entrance hall, and I went into the breakfast room after discarding my outdoor attire. I was surprised to see Milo sitting at the table. In an extremely unlikely turn of events, he appeared to have beaten all the others to breakfast.

'Good morning, darling,' he said, rising as I came into the room.

'Good morning,' I replied. 'You're up rather early.'

'The bed was much too cold without you. The temperature dropped at least twenty degrees when you left.'

'I couldn't sleep,' I said, as I went to the sideboard to fill my plate. I had not had much of an appetite as of late, but the fresh air and exercise seemed to have done the trick, and I was suddenly famished.

'You've been out in the stables this morning, have you?' Milo asked. I wondered if he had wandered outside and seen me. I certainly hadn't seen him.

'Yes, Mr Winters and I have been discussing my portrait.'

'Indeed. Have you agreed to pose for him?'

'Yes.' I took a seat beside him at the table, not bothering to inform my husband that I would be posing in an evening gown rather than in nothing at all.

'Should I be jealous?'

'That won't be necessary,' I said, spreading blackberry jam across my toast. 'Mr Winters behaves with perfect propriety.'

'Yes, I'm sure he does. By the by, you have straw in your hair,' Milo observed.

I turned to him, flushing at the implication.

He leant towards me, and reached up to pluck a piece of it from my hair. It must have lodged there when the horse had sniffed at me.

'Rolling in the hay with the handsome artist? Really, darling, how cliché of you.'

I was about to retort, but it was just then that Beatrice Kline came into the breakfast room. I was certain she had overheard Milo's remark, but she was too polite to act as though she had. What was worse, there had been nothing in Milo's tone to indicate that he was joking.

I shot daggers at Milo for his ill-timed bon mot, and turned to Beatrice.

'Good morning, Mrs Kline.'

'Good morning, Mrs Ames. Mr Ames.' She went to the sideboard without further comment and began to fill her plate.

'It's a lovely morning,' I said. 'Cold, but lovely.'

'Yes, the weather has continued much the same the past month,' she said, taking a seat at the opposite side of the table. 'Has my brother been down yet?'

'I saw him when I was out walking this morning. I suppose he may come in soon.'

'Perhaps. Reggie walks for hours at times.'

'Well, if you ladies will excuse me,' Milo said, rising from his seat. 'I feel as though I could do with some fresh air of my own. It seems to have worked wonders on you, darling.'

I frowned at him, still annoyed that his teasing should have been overheard by Beatrice, and was further annoyed when he winked at me as he left the room.

At last, however, I had found myself alone with Beatrice Kline. She was engrossed in buttering her toast in an extremely methodical manner, which gave me the opportunity to study her.

She really was a very striking woman. Her short, dark hair complemented the smooth lines of her face, and her eyes were large and dark, framed with thick lashes. Perhaps it was not entirely surprising that men might lose their heads over her. I wondered, however, if she had always been so cool and forbidding. Was it this trait that had drawn men to her, eager to break through the ice of her reserve? Or was it, perhaps, that the coldness had come after everything else?

I was not entirely sure how to approach the subject of Edwin Green's death with Beatrice. After all, how did one go about questioning a near stranger about past love affairs? I was certain she was bound to be reticent. It was, after all, common knowledge that she had been at the centre of the dispute between Edwin Green and Bradford Glenn. With one dead and other publicly accused, she had married a third gentleman not long afterwards.

It was all rather muddled, and I somehow thought it was not something she would like to revisit. I wondered how much of it was true and how much had been embellished for the sake of good fiction. There was, I supposed, only one way to find out.

She appeared indifferent to my presence, but I suspected the indifference would not last once I began asking impertinent questions.

I hesitated a moment, trying to determine what might

be the best approach. Beatrice Kline did not seem one to mince words. Therefore, I decided to go with the most direct approach and hope it worked in my favour.

'I've been reading *The Dead of Winter*,' I said.

This caught her attention. She looked up from her plate, her face suddenly an expressionless mask. Even her eyes seemed veiled and distant.

This was, I realised, the instinctual response whenever I mentioned the book to one of the people who had been entangled in its pages. It was as though they steeled themselves to what might be coming.

It must have been a dreadful thing to have had always to remain on one's guard, waiting for the moment when someone might mention it. I could understand why they had all hated Isobel Van Allen. She had, in essence, changed their lives for ever. The stigma would fade in time, perhaps, but it would never be completely gone.

Beatrice did not respond to my statement, but waited for me to continue. It was a strategic move on her part, holding her defence until she knew what the attack might be.

I felt suddenly a bit guilty for approaching her this way. No one liked to be reminded of past incidents they had worked hard to forget. It was too late now, however. There was nothing to be done but to plunge ahead.

'I don't believe half of it to be true,' I told her lightly.

'Most of it is true,' she replied, watching me very steadily. Her answer surprised me. I had given her the opportunity to dismiss it as rumour and blatant falsehood, but she had not taken it.

If she was going to be straightforward, then so should

I. 'Do you believe that Bradford Glenn was involved in the death of Mr Green?'

It seemed as though she paled slightly, but her expression did not change. 'At the time, it seemed as though it might be possible. They had always hated one another. He said in his suicide note that he was innocent, but he might have been lying.'

'Or perhaps it was just an unfortunate accident, after all.'

A small, humourless smile tipped up the corner of her mouth. 'I don't think you believe that any more than I do, Mrs Ames.'

'Were they both in love with you?' I asked suddenly. It was a terribly bold thing to ask, and yet I felt somehow that the answer was important.

She seemed to consider the question. When at last she spoke, there was a note of sadness in her voice.

'I don't know what we were, Mrs Ames. We were all very young and reckless. I was, for a time, fond of both of them, but it was never more than that. I wasn't thinking serious thoughts about the future. Perhaps I played them against one another when I could. Girls that age are often cruel, and I'm afraid I was no exception. It was all a game to me. Life was such a grand game.'

'Did Bradford Glenn really try to strangle you?' As soon as the words had passed my lips, I was shocked at my boldness. Beatrice, however, did not seem surprised that I had been audacious enough to bring up the events of that shocking chapter of Isobel's book.

Her eyes met mine steadily. 'Yes. In a moment of passion, he forgot himself. But that doesn't mean he killed Edwin.'

'No, of course not.'

'It was a great shock to me when Edwin died.'

'I imagine it is painful to relive it.'

She looked past me, her eyes looking out of the window and into the past. 'People usually assume that one would want to forget something like that. But that isn't the case. I only wish that I could remember. I've thought about it again and again, and I just don't know what happened that night. I remember Bradford and Edwin fought in the summer house. They had never much cared for one another. After that, I have only a hazy memory of walking back to the house.'

'I see.'

She looked up at me then, her cool eyes brimming with some sudden emotion.

'So you see, living with the memory of a tragedy is not the worst thing, Mrs Ames. It's far worse to live with only the vague outline of one, with a hazy memory of something that should be imprinted on one's brain. It feels like a betrayal, somehow, not knowing what happened that night. Edwin didn't deserve to die the way he did. Someone should have been with him. I might have prevented it.'

'I'm sorry,' I said.

She blinked, as though she was surprised to realise what she had just told me, and the veil dropped back over her eyes.

'But we all have our tragedies, I suppose. At least I was lucky enough to find my husband. He understands me,' she said with a soft smile, and for just a moment some of the sadness faded from her face. 'I think true understanding is better than a fierce passion. I know that, no matter what happens, he will be by my side. It's comforting, knowing that.'

I could sympathise with the sentiment. There had been many times during the course of my marriage when I would have much preferred steadiness to the uncertainty of passion. Now that my marriage had begun to settle into something resembling normalcy, I was very much relieved.

'I hope you will be very happy, Mrs Kline,' I said, and I meant it. I did not feel as Miss Van Allen did, that everyone must suffer for ever for what had happened in the past. I hoped that everyone here at Lyonsgate would be able to move forward, to live the lives they had always imagined.

Even as I thought this, however, I realised that it could not be that way. At least one person here would not live happily ever after, not if justice was served.

Beatrice was watching me as these thoughts crossed my face.

'I don't know if anyone's told you, Mrs Ames, but you have a way of making people feel comfortable talking to you.' I felt, somehow, that it was not entirely meant as a compliment.

In any event, I had not, in fact, realised this. Charming people was Milo's domain. I always felt a bit awkward when emotions became transparent.

'I've heard, of course, of your involvement in other such matters,' Beatrice said.

So that was it. She had heard about the Brightwell and what had happened at the Viscount Dunmore's masquerade ball. I wondered if she resented my presence here.

'Word travels,' she went on. 'I wondered that first night why it was that you had been invited here. Perhaps Reggie suspected there would be trouble. I see his instincts were correct.'

'Laurel told him to ask me,' I admitted. 'She thought things might go amiss. I had hoped that she was wrong.'

'Yes, well, I hope you will be careful, Mrs Ames,' she said, rising from her seat. 'There is a killer among us, and being a stranger here does not guarantee your safety.'

CHAPTER NINETEEN

It was not a very subtle warning, yet I did not think I detected a threat in it. I felt that Beatrice only meant I should be careful, and I agreed with her. After all, there had already been too many calamities at Lyonsgate to grow complacent.

Speaking of calamities, I wondered how Mr Roberts was faring and thought that perhaps I should check in on him. However, I encountered one of the maids in the hallway and was informed that he was still asleep. Not wanting to disturb him, I went back downstairs.

There was still information to be gleaned, but I thought perhaps I had done enough interrogating for one morning. Beatrice Kline had seen quite clearly what I was about, and I didn't mean to make a nuisance of myself, peppering people with questions.

I sighed. I didn't feel at all as though things were coming together clearly in my mind. I had anticipated that I would be able to get information from *The Dead of Winter* and from the other guests, but things were not going exactly as I had hoped. For one thing, everyone was so frightfully reticent. Not that I blamed them, of course. After all, I was perfectly aware of how difficult it was to find oneself repeatedly at the scene of a murder. Innocent or not, it could prove dreadfully awkward.

It didn't help matters that the inspector was in no way forthcoming. Of course, I couldn't blame him. He didn't know me and had no reason to trust me. I was aware that my rather cooperative relationships with police in past situations could not be considered to be the norm. I found myself wishing for the comforting presence of my old ally, Detective Inspector Jones. Not that I would ever admit to him that his presence was comforting. It was just so much more comfortable working with someone with whom one had worked before.

That gave me an idea.

'I wonder if I might use your telephone,' I asked Reggie casually when I had located him in the sitting room. 'I had an engagement with a friend, and I'm afraid I need to ring her up and reschedule.'

'Certainly. There is a telephone in the entry hall near the stairs, or one in the library, if you'd prefer.'

I went to the library, as the call I had to make would be better made in privacy. I had stretched the truth a bit to Reggie. The 'engagement' in question had not been scheduled for a precise date, but was more a perpetual invitation to tea with an old friend, a very well-informed old friend.

Mrs Yvonne Roland, a society widow with whom I had been entangled on more than one occasion in the past, always seemed to have an abundance of information at her disposal. I could think of no outsider that would be more well versed on the events of that Fatal Party.

Perhaps she might even know something about Isobel Van Allen's life in Kenya. I wondered if her web of societal intrigue extended as far as Happy Valley, but somehow I didn't doubt it.

'Oh, Mrs Ames! How delightful to hear from you!' she said when she came on the line. 'You're well, I hope? And Mr Ames? I do hope he is recovering from that sordid bullet wound.'

'Yes, Mrs Roland, thank you. We're both doing quite well.'

'Good, good. Glad to hear it. Are you in London, then?'

I hesitated for only a fraction of a second, knowing that any slip on my part could prove disastrous. I did not think, as of yet, that my name had been connected with Isobel Van Allen's death, and I hoped to keep it that way for as long as possible.

'No, I'm with friends in the country at the moment, but I had a question on a point of society history, and I knew at once that you were the authority on the matter.'

I could almost hear her preening over the telephone. 'Well, of course, I'd be only too happy to do anything that I can.'

'You've heard, of course, of the book *The Dead of Winter*.'

'Oh, certainly! Quite a sensation it caused, I can tell you that. All my friends were simply wild with curiosity about it.' She stopped suddenly, and I could almost feel her trying to read information in my voice. 'You're away from

London, did you say? Did you hear about what happened to the author, Isobel Van Allen?'

She had intuited that I was staying at Lyonsgate. I was almost certain of it.

'Yes,' I said without hesitation. 'I heard about her death, and that is what has made my friends and I so interested in the matter. I knew at once that you would be the right person to ask for information.'

'Yes,' she said, and I could tell that she was still suspicious. 'You know I am only too happy to share what I know. It's only too bad that you are not at Lyonsgate.'

She paused, as though expecting me to make some sort of confession. I was not to be so easily tricked.

'I should not relish being involved in another murder investigation,' I said truthfully. I didn't relish it at all.

'Yes, dear. It would be very unfortunate if you were subjected to such a thing.'

I was not entirely sure she believed me, but it appeared that she was no longer going to press the matter, at least for the time being. 'I understand Isobel accused a young man named Bradford Glenn, and he killed himself not long after the book's publication.'

'Yes. That was all very unfortunate. I knew a friend of the family, and it was a very difficult time for all of them.'

'There was no doubt that it was a suicide?' I asked, an idea coming to me suddenly.

'Oh, no, I don't think so. He left a note, you see. His family verified that it was in his hand.' That seemed to settle that.

'They also said that he had been very depressed ever

since the goings-on at Lyonsgate,' she went on. 'I don't wonder that they believed that he had had some part in Edwin Green's death. In fact, I think everyone accepted it as fact. One doesn't kill oneself if one has nothing to hide, does one?'

She seemed to expect a response, so I said vaguely, 'Perhaps not. But perhaps the guilt was placed upon him falsely.'

'Yes, I suppose you're right. It may be that he could not live with people believing he had done it. One never can tell who might be a sensitive soul, can one? Although, if I recall, the note left some ambiguity in the matter.'

'I don't suppose you remember anything of what was in the note?'

'Something about how he was guilty of one thing, but not another. A very troubled soul, it seems.'

'And Isobel Van Allen went off to Africa, untouched by it all,' I said, almost to myself. I wondered if she had had any idea of the devastation she would leave in her wake when she had set pen to paper. Would it have made any difference to her? Somehow I suspected she would not have changed anything.

'You've heard about the things that happened in Kenya, of course,' said Mrs Roland expectantly.

'Yes, I've heard the rumours,' I said, drawn back to our conversation. I could recall no rumours about Isobel Van Allen in particular, but a great many tales of the wanton lives of the British colonists in Kenya had trickled back to our shores. It was, I thought, exactly the sort of place in which Isobel Van Allen would have thrived.

'Oh, yes, my dear. It was all rather hushed up, I believe. But my third husband's niece was at school with a girl whose mother ran off with a man to Kenya. The mother wrote extensively of the sordid goings-on.' She lowered her voice slightly, in deference to the scandalous information she was about to impart. 'Illicit parties. Sharing spouses with one another and things of that nature. Not the sort of thing I would write to a daughter, if I had one. But the modern generation is so much less reserved than we were in my day.'

'Yes,' I said, realising that I might as well roll along with the gossip train rather than be run over by it. 'I understand she had taken up with a young man called Desmond Roberts.'

I had almost spoken this as fact, but remembered in time that I should demonstrate no first-hand knowledge of Isobel Van Allen's life.

'Roberts,' she said quickly, 'Roberts, Roberts.' It was as though she was trying to summon up any information that might come with the name. 'There was a young man named Roberts who died tragically, I believe. About a year ago. He was shot, if I recall.'

'Shot?' I repeated. That was certainly something new. I wondered if there was any connection to Desmond Roberts.

'I think that's what it was. Oh, dear me. One hears so many things that it's sometimes difficult to remember. I could find out, but it might take me a few hours to do so.'

'Oh, would you, Mrs Roland? Perhaps if I ring you back tomorrow?'

'Certainly, my dear. I should be only too happy to

investigate the matter.' She sounded positively thrilled at the prospect.

I thanked her and rang off. As I had suspected, Mrs Roland was a font of tell-tale knowledge. I wished that she had been able to be a bit more specific, but it was certainly something to think about.

'Perhaps you shouldn't be in dark rooms alone with a killer on the loose.'

I started at the voice. Turning, I saw Mr Collins standing just inside the door. I hadn't heard the steps behind me, and yet somehow he had approached within a few feet of me. It was a bit unnerving. I wondered how long he had been standing there.

'Mr Collins,' I said. 'I didn't hear you coming. Yes, I was just using the telephone. It's a bit more private here than it is in the entrance hall.'

'Yes, it is, isn't it?' he replied dryly.

'Have you come for a book?' I asked him pointedly. We were, after all, in the library. What other reason could he have had for following me here?

'Yes,' he said. 'I very much enjoy reading.' Somehow I didn't picture him as the type of gentleman to sit placidly reading a novel, but I supposed one could never really judge.

'There's quite a selection here,' I said, casting my eyes around the shelves. I was still uncertain of his motives and had thus reverted to my training from childhood, polite conversation based on stating the obvious.

'Of course, I've never much cared for novels myself,' he said, his dark eyes meeting mine. 'They seemed to me a waste of time.'

'Perhaps,' I said lightly. 'Then again, they are an entertaining way to pass the time. And one can often learn things from fiction without realising it.'

He didn't step closer, but he had not moved out of the doorway and I found myself a bit on edge. There was, after all, a good possibility that he was a killer. And being alone with a killer was an experience I would rather not repeat.

It seemed to me that he sensed my unease and enjoyed it. This annoyed me into behaving rashly.

'Perhaps you prefer books on mining. I understand that you and Edwin Green were involved in a mining venture together.'

Some unnamed emotion flickered momentarily across his face, but he covered it so quickly I could not be sure.

'That's true,' he said. 'Edwin was a terrible businessman. It was no great loss to me financially when he died, I can assure you.'

'I see.'

I wondered what was behind this sudden bravado. It seemed as though he was purposefully casting suspicion on himself. Perhaps it was meant to throw me off guard?

'Then you weren't close friends?'

'No. There was something about him that I didn't like. He was too quiet by a half, as though he was always plotting something. Even when he drank, he just sat there moodily, staring at people as though he knew exactly what was going on inside their minds. It made one uneasy.'

'I suppose it was still a shock to you when he died,' I said, giving him some opportunity to show at least a hint of human emotion.

'Not entirely,' he answered, thwarting my efforts. 'It was bound to happen to one of us, as reckless as we were.'

'It seems it had a profound effect upon Freida,' I said.

Unaccountably, it seemed as though his face softened. 'Freida has not had an easy life. I've tried to take her away from all of this, to help her forget. I didn't want to come back to Lyonsgate at all.' And yet he had. What hold had Isobel Van Allen had over him?

'Well, perhaps this will all be over soon, and we shall be able to forget it.'

He smiled an unpleasant smile. 'I don't think we'll ever be able to forget it.'

'No, I suppose you're right. I shall always remember finding Miss Van Allen's body,' I said truthfully. 'Some things one will always remember. As, I suppose, you remember where you were when Edwin Green's body was discovered.'

'I was not there when Freida found the body. I had just gone back to my bedroom a bit earlier when I heard her screams from outside.' He was implying, then, that he and Freida had spent the night together.

'I see. Well, if you'll excuse me, Mr Collins, I suppose I had better go and find my husband.'

He stepped aside, and I walked out into the hallway, one question foremost in my mind.

If Mr Collins had spent the night with Freida, why had she been walking out towards the summer house so early on that morning?

CHAPTER TWENTY

I was relieved to make it back to the relative safety of the entrance hall. There was something very untrustworthy about Mr Collins, and I had not enjoyed being alone with him. Still, there had been a moment of unexpected softness in him when he had spoken of his wife. I thought it just possible that he cared for her more than I had believed. I wondered what implications this might have on possible motives for the crime. After all, if he was willing to protect Freida, he might have been willing to kill Isobel to do it.

'Oh, there you are, darling.' I looked up to see Milo, who was halfway up the stairway. He came back down to meet me. 'I was just coming to fetch you. It's a lovely morning and the snow is melting. Will you go riding with me? It will do you well to get out of the house for a while.'

'I would like to, but . . .' I thought of my blood-soaked riding clothes and barely suppressed a shudder. 'I haven't anything to wear.'

'Certainly you do. I told Winnelda before we left the flat to be sure to include at least two changes of riding clothes. I anticipated we would be outside rather more often than we have been.' Leave it to Milo to be sure that my wardrobe was suitable for his plans. I was glad for his foresight, however, for I could certainly benefit from a change of scenery.

'Well, in that case, I should love to get out for a while.' I had tried to keep my tone bright, but Milo, as ever, was not fooled.

'How are you holding up?'

'I'm quite well.'

'Little liar,' he said, his eyes on my face. 'You're only pretending to be well so I don't whisk you off to London. In truth, you're not eating well and have barely been sleeping.'

'I'm fine,' I insisted, a bit alarmed at his astute observations. Milo had always been perceptive, but this rather assertive devotion was something new and I was a bit at a loss as to how to respond to it.

'Truly,' I said, meeting his gaze.

'Very well. I shall pretend to believe you for the time being.'

I smiled and he dropped a kiss on my lips and then started back up the stairs. I followed him up, and we went to our rooms to dress.

Winnelda was nowhere to be seen, but I located the change of riding clothes in the wardrobe and put them on. I was standing before the mirror adjusting the jacket of black velvet when Milo came back into my room. 'Before we go, I've got a present for you.'

I turned. 'A present?'

'Yes, I picked it up a while back and have been waiting for the right occasion on which to present it to you. Since you won't be persuaded to leave Lyonsgate, now seems like a good time.'

He handed me a wooden box, somewhat the worse for wear, with metal corners and a beaten brass clasp. Milo's gifts tended to be in velvet jewellers' boxes, and I was curious to see what this anomaly might hold.

I unlatched the clasp and opened it. It was, indeed, lined with velvet, and on the bed of worn scarlet fabric lay a little pistol with a pearl handle.

'Oh, Milo,' I breathed, running my finger along the smooth, glossy handle, 'it's lovely.'

He laughed. 'I've given you a lethal object and the best you can say is how lovely it is.'

'Well, you did choose me a pretty one, but if you like it better . . . Oh, Milo, how deadly it looks!'

'I take it then, that you're pleased.'

'Of course, I'm pleased. Thank you.' I leant to kiss him before turning back to my gift, lifting it gingerly from the case to examine it. 'It's much more practical than jewellery.'

'I thought, if you're going to continue to dash about the country involving yourself in affairs, you might need something with which to protect yourself.'

It was terribly sweet of him. Especially since he was continually trying to dissuade me from my detecting efforts. I hoped I would never have cause to use it, but I would enjoy carrying it in my handbag if ever I felt I might need it.

'You are to be very careful with it, of course,' he went

on. 'I should be most annoyed if you shot yourself, and I certainly don't relish the thought of being shot again myself.'

'I shall be very careful with it.'

'I'll show you later how to shoot it. Perhaps this afternoon.'

'Perhaps tomorrow.' I put the gun back in the box and set it aside. 'I have an engagement this afternoon.'

'Oh? With whom?'

'I'm sitting for Mr Winters.'

'Ah, I see. Well, perhaps I shall teach Lindy instead.'

'You know, I do believe you're right,' I reflected.

'About what?'

'It would be very unpleasant indeed if you were to get shot again,' I told him tartly, and walked from the room.

Lucinda Lyons was standing near the stables when we came out.

'Oh, are you going riding?' she asked. 'I was just preparing to go out myself.'

Some part of me wondered cynically if she had overheard part of our conversation in the entrance hall and had decided to join us at the stables. However, I had no objection to her riding with us. I had never been particularly territorial where Milo was concerned.

'Yes, we'd just planned to go out for a while, if you'd like to join us,' I said.

She smiled brightly, her eyes flicking to Milo. 'I should love to.'

The groom brought out the horses and we mounted up.

'It's nice that the sun has come out,' I said as we set off. The warmth of it felt good after so many days in the draughty house.

'Yes, much warmer than yesterday,' she answered. 'I'm glad. I don't like the cold much at all. Sometimes I dream of living in a place where it's warm all year long.'

The temperature had increased remarkably since my walk this morning, and already the snow had begun to melt, leaving the way fairly clear for the horses. Lucinda's horse, however, did not seem to like the occasional patch of snow that he encountered. He stepped in one and sidestepped, snorting. 'Romeo has a bit of a temper,' she said with a laugh. 'He likes to pretend to be a great brute, but he's really a darling.'

I noticed, however, that she had used the opportunity to guide Romeo closer to Milo.

'He certainly is a lovely horse,' I said.

'Thank you. Milo tells me you have a great many horses at Thornecrest. I would love to see them.'

If she was hoping for an invitation, she was going to be disappointed.

Since Milo and Lucinda – Lindy – were on such good terms, I thought it might be an ideal time to question her regarding her recollections of the night of Edwin Green's death. She had been young and had not been a participant in the revels at the summer house, but that didn't mean her recollections would not be valuable.

'It is nice to get out a bit,' I said, hoping to steer the conversation in that direction. 'Things have been strained in the house. Of course, I suppose it's only natural, given everything that has happened.'

'Yes,' she answered vaguely.

I glanced at my husband, knowing he would have better luck than I. Milo took my cue at once with the effortlessness of a born actor. 'It must bring back unpleasant memories of when Edwin Green died here. I imagine that was very difficult for you.'

As I had suspected, Milo's concern warmed her at once. 'Oh, it was dreadful.'

His question was, perhaps, a bit obvious, but Lucinda was not likely to notice, besotted as she was. I wished that he would lead the conversation along to the possible suspects.

'I imagine your brother has had a difficult time of it,' he said, in that unnerving way he had of knowing just what I was thinking.

'Reggie was never the same after the war,' Lindy said sadly. 'Oh, he made it through all right. Never got a scratch, not even a fever while he was there. We Lyonses have always been healthy as horses.'

She laughed a little at her joke before continuing. 'But it affected him greatly, nonetheless. He came back and, even as young as I was, I knew that he had come back a different person. He sometimes gets a sad, faraway look in his eyes, and I know he's thinking about what happened over there. That's why he was so wild, you know. He wanted to forget. It didn't work, though. And then that awful thing happened, and we were very much afraid for a time that he wouldn't be able to make it through. He was very close to Mr Green, you know. They had been best friends since they were in knee pants.'

'Did you know Edwin Green well?'

'Not very well. I wasn't allowed to spend much time with them. Reggie and Beatrice didn't much want me tagging along. They said I was a nuisance. I did sit with them sometimes, when they were outdoors. Mr Winters taught me to sketch. I was quite good at it, I think, but I lost interest.'

'But you were there on the night of the death?'

'Not at the summer house, but I was here at Lyonsgate. Home from school on holiday.'

'And were you there the next morning when Mr Green was discovered?' Milo said encouragingly. 'It must have been very trying for you.'

'Yes. That was an awful morning.' She had a faraway expression on her face now, just the kind she had described when discussing her brother's memories of the war. 'I remember the morning was cold and there was a great fog everywhere. It was pressing against the windows, as though it wanted to get inside. I was having chocolate at breakfast. Mother had never liked me drinking such rich beverages so early in the morning, but Reggie had said I could have whatever I liked.' She looked up at me and gave a little laugh. 'Funny, the inconsequential things one remembers.'

I nodded, afraid to speak and intrude upon her recollections.

'It was very quiet in the breakfast room, as though the fog was swallowing everything up. And then I heard something outside, a long cry. I thought perhaps it was a bird at first. But then it got closer, louder. I could hear it as she approached the house. I got up from the table and went out into the entrance hall to see what the noise was. Freida materialised out of the fog like a ghost. And she was screaming. "He's dead! He's dead!" She kept saying it again and again. Oh, it was dreadful. I can barely stand to think about it, even now.'

She looked away, and for a moment all was silent but the hooves of our horses on the wet earth and the gentle creaking of the saddles.

'They wouldn't let me go with them to the summer house, but I didn't want to. I knew it would be awful.'

I ventured a question. 'Was there . . . was there any suggestion that it might have been Mr Glenn at the time?' I felt somehow that her willingness to reminisce might end at any moment, and I might as well get information while she still felt like talking.

'Oh, no!' she said quickly. 'I remember how distraught Bradford was when he saw the body. It was as though he couldn't believe it. He told me later that he had hoped never to see death again, not after the war.'

She looked straight ahead, but not in time to hide the tears glistening in her eyes.

'I'm sorry. We shouldn't have brought it up,' I said, glancing at Milo. 'We didn't mean to cause you pain.'

'It's all right,' she said quickly. 'I suppose it's good, in a way, to talk about it. I wish Reggie would talk about things. I've tried to talk to him, about the war, but he won't speak of it. I suppose some things need to be let out. It can't be good, can it, keeping all that inside?'

I felt suddenly sorry for the family, sorry for the string of tragedies that had plagued them. It had been said that they had deserved what had happened to them after Edwin Green's death, but I could not feel that carelessness and the excesses of youth should have been held against them for the rest of their lives. Unless those excesses had been murder, of course.

I was about to comment, but at that moment a rat scurried across the field in front of us, and Lucinda's horse took off like a shot.

CHAPTER TWENTY-ONE

Her horse raced across the field and she clung to his back.
'Help me!' she cried out. 'Help!'

Milo nudged his horse and took off after her, swiftly
closing ground. I considered following after them, but there
was really nothing I could do. I followed along at a bit less
of a breakneck pace and hoped that Milo would be able to
catch her.

He accomplished it rather quickly. Milo was too expert a
horseman to be outrun for long, and he cut a rather dashing
figure as he brought his horse up beside hers and reached
out to grab the reins, bringing Lucinda's horse to a stop.

He quickly dismounted and reached out to soothe
Romeo.

Lucinda must have said she wanted to dismount as
well, for he reached up and helped her down, his hands
on her waist. She slid from the saddle and practically fell
into his arms.

Really, the whole thing was like watching a romance novel in action.

I rode up behind them so I wouldn't miss the dialogue.

'Oh, thank you, Milo,' she said, her hands pressed against his chest. 'I was so afraid that I was going to be thrown and break my neck.'

She looked up at him adoringly, and I felt a sinking feeling. I had warned him. He had been too free with his charm, and I was very much afraid the girl was halfway to falling in love with him.

'You're not at all hurt, are you, Lucinda?' I asked.

She looked up at me, and it seemed for the briefest of instants, an expression of displeasure crossed her face. I had interrupted their lovely little scene, so I could not blame her entirely for being annoyed at my ill-timed entrance.

'No, I'm all right,' she said, 'thanks to Milo.'

'Yes, well done, Milo,' I told him. It was fortunate that nothing had gone terribly wrong. There had been enough disaster at Lyonsgate.

'Lucinda would have got hold of him soon enough, I think,' he said. 'Let me help you back up.'

She was disentangled from his arms, somewhat reluctantly it seemed to me, and mounted her horse. 'I don't know why that rat startled him. It wasn't even close. Romeo is highly strung, but he's usually not quite so jumpy.'

'I suppose we should go back now,' Milo said, mounting up himself and turning his horse back in the direction of the stables.

'Oh, no!' Lucinda protested. 'I'm all right. Really.'

'Yes,' Milo answered, 'but Romeo has scraped his right

foreleg on something. The groom should probably look at it.'

'Oh, no!' she said again, paling, leaning down to look at the horse's leg. 'Is it deep? My poor darling!'

'I don't think it's bad, but we should probably go back, nonetheless.'

'Yes, let's go,' she said, patting Romeo's neck and speaking in soothing tones to him.

We rode back at a careful pace. Romeo didn't seem much concerned by his injury, but Lucinda was very upset. She barely spared a glance at Milo as we dismounted, and she led him over to the groom.

'That was quite exciting,' I said, with only a touch of cynicism, as Milo and I walked back towards the house. 'No doubt you've cemented your place as her knight in shining armour.'

'It was a stupid thing to do.' Somehow I knew he was not referring to his rescue of the damsel in distress.

'What do you mean?'

'She spurred her horse. She was digging her heels into its side the entire time. Until I caught up with her, that is. Then she reined in and let me bring the horse to a stop.'

I stared at him, hovering somewhere between annoyance and amusement.

'She wanted you to rescue her.' I was bit awed by the audacity of it.

Milo was not amused. 'That's too fine a horse to risk on a stunt like that.'

'She was very upset when she found out it had been injured. At least it wasn't serious.'

'It might have been.' Milo was seldom angry, but

Lucinda had succeeded in doing the one thing that might have roused his ire: putting a horse in danger.

'You mustn't judge her too harshly,' I said, coming to her defence against my baser inclinations. 'Things must be rather dull here for a young woman with no friends. I suppose it added a bit of drama to the proceedings.'

'A murder isn't exciting enough?' he asked dryly.

'Yes, I suppose you're right. But it's really your fault, you know, for being so irresistible.'

He shot me a look, and I smiled. I felt that I should probably be very annoyed with Lucinda Lyons, but I also knew from experience that it was true: Milo was very hard to resist.

After an uneventful lunch, I donned my blue evening gown and prepared to meet Mr Winters in the conservatory. The gown was one of my favourites, which was why I had had Winnelda pack it, despite the fact that it wasn't the most practical dress for winter. While at Lyonsgate, as cold as it was, I had not yet been intrepid enough to wear it.

I thought it would work admirably for a portrait, however. It was a rich, sapphire-coloured silk with thin straps and a fitted bodice that tapered to a flowing skirt with the slightest hint of a train. I felt a bit conspicuous walking through the house in an evening gown in the middle of the day, but I encountered no one on my way.

The conservatory was, as I had expected, frigid. However, I felt as though I was becoming accustomed to the chill in the house. It almost seemed that I was adapting to it. My skin was perpetually cool to the touch, but I no longer felt the constant desire to warm my hands before the fire.

I glanced around the room. It was apparent that it had been neglected in the years that the Lyons family had lived abroad. Minimal effort had been made to maintain the plant life which had either died or grown in tangled abundance. A good many of the windows were streaked with grime, but it appeared the glass was all intact. The sun was shining brightly, which made up somewhat for the cold of the room.

I found Mr Winters there with his easel and brushes. He had set up a chair in an open space, which I assumed was where I was to sit.

He looked up as I came in. 'Come in, Mrs Ames,' he said. 'Sit down. Make yourself comfortable.'

I took a seat and he came towards me. 'Tilt your head to the side. No, no, look at me directly.'

His hands on my bare shoulders, he repositioned me to the correct angle. His long, cool fingers gently grasped my chin, turning my face towards the light.

'It's as I suspected,' he said, his hand still on my face. 'Your skin is glorious in bright light. Your colouring is exceptional. One does not often find that combination, the pale skin and eyes with such dark hair. Lovely. And your eyes are magnificent. Like cold, clear water.'

'Thank you,' I murmured, a bit afraid to move.

'What scent do you wear?' he asked, still standing very close. 'Gardenia?'

'Yes.'

'It suits you.'

'Thank you,' I said again.

I was just beginning to wonder if this had not, in fact, been a good idea when he stepped back suddenly and moved behind his easel where he stood for a long moment just looking at me.

Now that I had become accustomed to his somehow odd behaviour, I found him much less alarming than I had upon our first acquaintance. Despite his idiosyncrasies, there was something a bit soothing about his airy detachment. It was as though the realities of life had little effect on him. He lived in his own world, untouched by the troubles of mere mortals.

I studied him as he dipped a brush into paint and began to work. His unruly curls gleamed gold in the sunlight, and his eyes glimmered like there was some flame in them as well. He was incredibly striking, and I wondered idly if he had ever been painted himself. 'Have you ever done a self-portrait?'

He shook his head. 'It wouldn't work.'

'What do you mean?'

'The artwork will only be worthwhile if the artist sees something worth painting; the beauty of a thing. There is no beauty in me.'

It seemed a bit of false modesty. Surely he knew very well that he was an exceptional-looking man.

He must have read my thoughts, for he replied to them. 'I know I am considered handsome.' He said this without either self-consciousness or conceit. 'But when I look at myself, that is not what I see.'

I wondered what it was that he did see, but he did not

appear ready to divulge the information and there was no polite way to ask.

He went back to painting, and I realised that I had been mistaken to think I might have the opportunity to question him more thoroughly in these surroundings. His complete attention was absorbed by his craft, and it would be difficult to pull him away from it.

We fell into a comfortable silence as he worked. I had never observed an artist in action before, and it was intriguing for me to watch his process, the changes in his expressions as he concentrated. Eventually, I became lost in my own thoughts, soothed by the quiet and the gentle scraping of his brush against the canvas.

I didn't realise how long I had sat in the chair until I began to move, my muscles stiff from inaction. The light had begun fade, the shadows shifting. It would be time to dress for dinner soon.

I looked over at Mr Winters. He was looking out one of the windows. The pink rays of the setting sun seemed to settle a rose-coloured hue across the lawns, making everything seem bright and lovely.

'It's very beautiful,' I said. 'I imagine you look at it with different eyes, being an artist.'

'I have never been much good with landscapes,' he said, still not turning to me. 'People are different.'

'How so?'

He turned to face me then. 'I can see people much more clearly. But, I suppose in some ways there is not much difference between portraits and landscapes. The curves and lines, the inherent danger.'

'Yes, I suppose you're right,' I said thoughtfully, wondering if there was something he wasn't saying. That airy quality about him seemed to have faded. It had been replaced with a sombre sadness. He didn't look as though he was lost in another world, but was somewhere in the past.

'Is everything all right?' I asked at last.

'I wish I hadn't come back,' he said suddenly. He looked up at me, and I was surprised at the intense emotion in his eyes. 'I shouldn't have, but it was as though I couldn't stay away. She was like a magnet I was powerless to resist.'

'You loved Isobel,' I said, the realisation coming so naturally it felt as though I must have known it all along.

A smile tugged at the corner of his mouth. 'Yes. I always loved her.'

Yet another man who had fallen sway to Isobel's charms. I remembered Laurel's speculation that Isobel might have been in love with someone besides Reggie. Was it possible it had been the handsome artist who had done her portrait?

'Did she feel the same way?' I asked.

'We were lovers for a time.' He said this without embarrassment, not taking his eyes from mine. 'But she wasn't interested in anything more, anything lasting. Isobel was always one to do what she pleased with whom she pleased.'

I nodded. That had been my impression of her. I wondered if Reggie Lyons had known about her liaison with Mr Winters.

'I don't want to speak ill of her,' he said, 'but there wasn't much in her that was kind or loving.'

'I didn't know her at all well,' I said.

'Yes, I know.'

'Did you ever hear from her while she was in Kenya?'

'I had a letter. Only one. It was just the sort of thing Isobel would be inclined to send, very brief and trite, without any true feeling in it. She told me how happy she was in Africa, that there was nothing in England worth returning for. I think it was more to taunt me than anything.'

He looked up at me and smiled, and I could see no bitterness in it. I wondered if he had truly loved her so much that he had been willing to forgive her faults or if he was an excellent actor who had stabbed Isobel to repay her for all the times she had wronged him. There was passion in him. It would not be outside the realm of possibility for him to have used a knife.

Or perhaps he was nothing more than a gentle man who had had his heart broken by a heartless woman. Suddenly, I hated that I was in this situation, that I was being forced to examine people for signs of guilt, people I might have liked had circumstances been different.

I opened my mouth to say something comforting, but just like that, the reflectiveness in his face was gone, replaced with that vague, distant smile.

'I think that's enough for one afternoon, Mrs Ames. Perhaps we can continue tomorrow.'

Milo was not in my room when I finally arrived to change for dinner. It might have been just as well to wear the blue evening gown, but I was freezing and wanted something that offered a bit more warmth. I chose a dress of burgundy

241

velvet and went down to the drawing room just in time to be called in to dinner.

'How was your session with Mr Winters?' Milo asked in a low voice as we walked towards the dining room. 'Did you manage to keep your clothes on?'

'Only just,' I retorted.

I had hoped that dinner would be a fairly relaxed meal, but it was immediately apparent that tension was high. Though no one said anything, there was a feeling of uneasiness in the air.

Reggie was flushed and uncomfortable. Beatrice looked as though she was preoccupied.

I wondered if something had happened. I had been locked away in the conservatory with Mr Winters all afternoon.

I did not have long to wonder.

'That Inspector Laszlo was here again this afternoon,' Reggie said, taking a long drink from his wine glass. I noticed that his hands did not seem quite steady.

I was a bit surprised that the inspector had not asked to see me, but I was also relieved. I didn't care to have any more interaction with him than was absolutely necessary.

I glanced at my cousin and it almost seemed to me that she flushed. I wondered if she had spoken with the handsome inspector. I would have to ask her about that later.

'Did he have anything of interest to say?' Milo asked, without any apparent interest.

I wondered where Milo had taken himself off to all afternoon. I somehow suspected that he had not spent his time with Lucinda Lyons. He was still cross that she had put her horse in jeopardy. Milo seldom took things seriously, but horses were one thing he didn't trifle with.

Reggie looked at Beatrice, and she nodded almost imperceptibly.

Reggie cleared his throat, pulling at the collar of his shirt. He was immensely uncomfortable about something.

'He said . . . It seems that . . .' He broke off and Beatrice cut in, her voice crisp and cool.

'Before Isobel was stabbed to death, it seems she was also poisoned.'

CHAPTER TWENTY-TWO

'Poisoned?' Laurel cried.

Despite my surprise, I somehow had the presence of mind to glance quickly around the table, taking in the reactions of the others sitting there. Lucinda's brows had risen in surprise. Freida had paled and Mr Collins frowned. Mr Winters, as usual, exhibited very little sign of emotion. He still seemed preoccupied with the food on his plate.

'Yes,' Beatrice said. 'He was very definite about it. Thallium, they think.'

So it had not been the cyanide. This was a shock indeed. Two lethal poisons had been floating around the house, and yet Isobel had been stabbed to death. It was all so very strange.

'What does this mean?' Mr Collins demanded.

'Nothing, I suppose,' Beatrice said. 'I don't see that it makes much difference. Someone tried to kill her, and they eventually succeeded.'

'Or two people tried to kill her,' Laurel said quietly.

I looked at my cousin. She was right. Did this mean that more than one person had tried to murder Isobel Van Allen? I had certainly discovered motives enough to go around. But I did not want to believe that anyone here was a murderer, let alone that two of them might be.

What was more, poison was an act of premeditation. The stabbing might have been a crime of passion, but there was something calculated about poisoning. It seemed as though the methods indicated two separate would-be killers.

'I don't know how much more of this I can bear,' Reggie said, rubbing a hand across his face.

'It's going to be all right, Reggie,' Laurel said gently. 'I'm sure of it.'

'There's no sense in worrying ourselves sick over it, in any event,' Beatrice said. 'We've weathered such storms before, and we will do it again.'

Reggie looked at his sister, and it seemed as though he relaxed ever so slightly at the absolute conviction in her tone.

We went back to eating our food, though without much enthusiasm. I was very surprised by this latest turn of events, though perhaps I should not have been. Isobel Van Allen had been ill the night before her murder, and it had struck me that there might be something sinister in it. It must have been the poison. It seemed to me that it must have been administered at dinner. At this very table. It was enough to make one lose one's appetite.

I thought of Mr Roberts, who was still in his room, though apparently recovering nicely. Was it possible that he had had some of the poison as well? It seemed more than possible. It seemed likely. If so, had it been done deliberately, or had he been a casualty of the war against Isobel Van Allen?

'How is your horse, Lucinda?' Milo asked. I supposed he was hoping to divert the conversation a bit.

'He's very well,' she said brightly. 'The scratch wasn't deep at all. I'm so relieved.'

'I heard about the incident on your ride today,' Reggie said. 'It isn't like you to be careless.'

'I wasn't being careless. A rat ran across the field and startled Romeo. Mr Ames came to my rescue.'

The vaguest expression of annoyance crossed Beatrice's face, and I wondered if it was directed at her sister or at my husband. Perhaps she felt, as I did, that Milo had given Lucinda undue encouragement.

'In any event, I think you'd better hold off riding Romeo for a while,' Reggie said.

She looked up sharply. 'What do you mean?'

'I mean I'd rather you not take him out if you can't manage him. Take Gallahad or one of the less-spirited horses.'

'That's ridiculous. I'm perfectly capable of managing Romeo.'

'It doesn't seem so,' Reggie replied.

'That's not fair. It wasn't my fault about the rat.'

'Just the same, I paid too much for that horse to have him injured.'

'He's my horse, isn't he?' she said, her voice rising. 'You gave him to me.'

'Please don't go on so, Lindy,' Reggie said tiredly.

'But, Reggie, it's not fair.' She was growing distressed, and tears had sprung to her eyes.

'Lucinda, be quiet,' Beatrice commanded.

'You're not my mother, Beatrice,' Lucinda said hotly, her eyes flashing. 'I have only seen you a handful of times in the last seven years. I don't see why you should think that you can order me about now.'

Silence descended for a moment as Beatrice appeared to attempt to master her temper.

'You were sent away to school in Switzerland because it was what was best for you,' she said at last, her tone brittle.

'Banished, you mean,' Lucinda said. 'Banished to that wretched place, far away from everyone and everything.'

'It wasn't as though we were trying to banish you,' Reggie said. 'We just thought sending you to a different boarding school, one abroad, would be better for you, all things considered.' His eyes darted from Lucinda to Beatrice and back again. He was uneasy at the conflict that was rising between them, and I could not say I blamed him. I could feel the anger building like a storm cloud above the table.

'Alas, it appears that it was not as beneficial as we had hoped,' Beatrice said. 'You clearly haven't learnt much of proper behaviour.'

'I don't know what you mean,' she retorted.

'Don't you?' Beatrice's brows rose. 'Then you do need education. For one thing, it isn't proper etiquette to repeatedly throw yourself at the husband of a guest in your home.'

Lucinda stared at her sister, her face going white and then bright red. Then she rose from her chair and turned and fled from the room.

Almost without realising what I was doing, I excused myself from the table and went after her. I didn't know exactly what prompted me, but I felt suddenly very sorry for her.

I was not sure what I was going to say. I had not had much experience in dealing with young people. In fact, aside from my school days, when I was one myself, I had had very little contact with them. Though Lucinda Lyons was only three or four years my junior, she somehow seemed much younger.

She had gone into the drawing room, and I followed her there. She turned when she heard me come in behind her, and her face was flushed with anger, tears quivering in her eyes. 'She's wretched. They're both wretched. I hate them.'

'You mustn't mind them,' I said. 'They're all very upset at the moment. People are apt to say things they don't mean in the heat of the moment.'

'It was a cruel thing for Beatrice to say. I haven't been throwing myself at your husband. I only enjoy spending time with him because he's so kind, and things are so wretched here at Lyonsgate.'

Her voice broke and the tears began to run down her cheeks.

I felt a wave of sympathy for her. I had not much cared for the way she had been doggedly pursuing Milo, but it had been harmless enough and not exactly without encouragement from my husband. Besides, I suspected, as she had said, that she had encountered very little kindness since her return to Lyonsgate.

'You mustn't worry about that.' I smiled. 'I'm not a jealous sort of wife.'

'Yes, but perhaps Beatrice is right. Perhaps I don't know how to behave. It's not easy for me to be with people, you know. I haven't had much practice with it. I never know the right thing to say or what people are really thinking.'

'We all feel like that at times.'

She gave a rueful laugh. 'You don't expect me to believe that you ever feel that way, Mrs Ames. It must be lovely to be so calm and poised all the time, always knowing the right thing to say.'

Was that the way I appeared? I certainly tried to make a good show of it, but I often felt less than successful.

'I don't always know the right things to say,' I told her.

'You seem to. And you're so elegant and beautiful.'

'That's sweet of you.'

'It's true.'

'You're quite beautiful yourself, Lucinda.'

She sniffed, wiping a hand across her tear-stained face. 'I have always wanted to be the sort of person who always behaves properly and does the right things, but I don't suppose I ever shall.'

'That sort of thing comes with time.'

She looked at me searchingly. 'Do you really think that?'

'Yes. The more you are with people, the more you will come to understand how to interact with them.'

She sighed. 'But I don't like being with people, not really. Because people will always be cruel because of what happened here. It isn't fair. Wherever I go, people shall always say, "That's Lucinda Lyons. Do you remember what happened at Lyonsgate?"'

I hesitated. I wanted to tell her that it became easier with time not to mind what people said, but the truth of it was that cruelness always had the potential to hurt. It was more accurate, perhaps, to say that one's feelings became easier to conceal as time passed.

I offered what comfort I could. 'You'll learn eventually that it doesn't much matter what people say.'

'Yes, perhaps you're right,' she said. She drew in a deep breath. 'I'm sorry if I've said the wrong things, Mrs Ames. I didn't mean to burden you with all my troubles. It's just that I don't have very many friends. I didn't make friends easily when they sent me to a new boarding school, and Reggie and Beatrice are so much older than me that they haven't paid me much mind in the years since I've been back.'

'You may say whatever you like to me, Lucinda, and I hope that we shall be friends,' I said, and I meant it sincerely. Her life had been lonely and full of unfortunate events. It couldn't have been easy for her to make friends at school, especially after the scandal that Edwin Green's death had caused. Lucinda was right. People could be very cruel, young people especially.

She smiled. 'I should like that, Mrs Ames.'

'Call me Amory.'

She nodded. 'Thank you, Amory.'

I felt I should offer one last bit of advice. 'You mustn't think your brother and sister don't care about you,' I said.

'I suppose they're upset now, with everything that has happened. Your brother seems very distraught, and I'm sure your sister must be, too.'

In truth, I did not feel much like making excuses for Beatrice. It hadn't been a very nice thing to say to her sister, especially in the company of others. Even if Lucinda had made a very conspicuous show of throwing herself at Milo, there was no need to reprimand her for it in front of both Milo and me.

'I know that Reggie means well,' she said. 'He just doesn't always know the right way to go about it. I try to be patient with him. But Beatrice has never liked me, not really. My mother was the reason our father left her mother.'

'I see.'

This was a bit of information I hadn't heard. Perhaps that was the reason Beatrice was not especially warm towards her sister.

I reached out and patted Lucinda's hand. 'I'm certain things will get better, Lucinda. When all of this is over, perhaps your brother will take you away for a while and all of this shall seem like a distant memory.'

She smiled, and this time it looked genuine. 'Thank you, Amory. I certainly hope so.'

Reggie Lyons must have been hovering outside of the drawing room waiting for me to come out, for he approached me as soon as I left the room, a concerned frown on his face.

'Is she all right?'

'I think so,' I said. 'This is all very hard on her, of course, and she hasn't very many friends.'

He sighed. 'Things have always been difficult for Lucinda. I have never known the right way to go about talking with her. Young people are different than they were when I was young.' His gaze moved beyond me, a faraway look coming to his eyes for just a moment before he blinked.

'In any event, I'm afraid I must apologise for my sisters,' he said. He gave me a tired smile. 'It seems I am forever apologising to you, Mrs Ames.'

'Please don't apologise. I only thought I could find a way to help. Sometimes it's easier to talk to someone who isn't a family member.'

'Yes, I suppose you're right,' he said vaguely.

'I do think she would like to talk to you, however,' I said encouragingly.

He nodded. 'I shall go and talk to her now.'

It seemed almost as though he squared his shoulders before going into the drawing room. I thought it was a good sign that he cared so much for his sister. I wished Beatrice would have been as thoughtful. It would cost her nothing to be kind to her sister. After all, it was not Lucinda's fault that their father had been unfaithful to Beatrice's mother. The matter was really none of my concern, however. If there was one thing I was learning, it was that it was impossible to fix all the problems in the world, no matter how much I wished I could.

'Everything all right?' Milo asked, coming into the entrance hall and catching me frowning. It appeared that they had finished dinner, for I could hear the others approaching from the direction of the dining room.

'Yes, I think so.'

'Good. Are you coming back to the drawing room for coffee?'

I shook my head. 'I don't think so. I'm tired. I think I'll go back to my room.'

'Shall I come with you?'

'That's not necessary. Perhaps you should go in and be kind to Lucinda.'

He sighed. 'I do wish you would make up your mind.'

'It wasn't at all nice of Beatrice to embarrass her that way at the dinner table. I only thought that if you go on behaving as normal, she'll feel less awkward about it all.'

'Very well. But I go under protest.'

'Yes, I know how very trying it is for you to make yourself pleasant to women.'

He frowned at me and went into the drawing room.

'Well, that was unpleasant,' said Laurel, who had reached my side just as Milo left. 'It was kind of you to go and speak to her, especially considering that what Beatrice said was true.'

I shrugged. 'I can't blame her for enjoying Milo's company. She's lonely, and he's . . .'

'Yes, I know what he is,' she interrupted. 'Well, I'm sure it shall all pass in time. It's not as though there aren't other things to distract us.'

'Like the fact that Isobel was poisoned, for instance,' I said. 'Did you see Inspector Laszlo this afternoon?'

I had thought perhaps my question would throw her off guard, but she didn't appear at all flustered. 'Yes,' she said, 'but only for a few moments.'

'Did he say anything to you about the poison?'

She shook her head. 'That was a complete surprise. Do you really think that two people were trying to kill Isobel?'

'I wish I knew. The whole thing seems incredibly complicated. I'm sure Inspector Laszlo had his suspicions, however.'

I looked at her expectantly, and she laughed. 'Don't look at me that way. You act as though we were the best of friends. The inspector doesn't tell me anything. He's very proper, you know.'

'Yes, I'm sure that he is.'

She laughed. 'You seem to suspect me of some secret love affair, but I assure you there is nothing of interest to tell you.'

'Very well,' I said. 'But perhaps you can learn something yet this evening. See if you can talk to Reggie, will you? I'm very interested to learn more of what Inspector Laszlo had to say.'

'You aren't coming to the drawing room?'

'No, I think I'm going to make an early night of it. I'm rather worn out.'

'All right. I'll report to you in the morning, shall I?'

'Excellent. Goodnight, Laurel.'

'Goodnight, Amory.'

She went into the drawing room, and I went up the stairs and to my bedroom. Winnelda would not have expected me back so soon after dinner, so I suspected it would be a while before she came back to my room.

I was exhausted and could think of nothing I would rather do than go straight to bed, but then I caught sight of *The Dead of Winter* sitting on the table.

I felt, as I had from the beginning, that the book held the key to the entire thing. It was all well and good to hear an account of Edwin Green's death, but I needed to see how Isobel had portrayed it. I didn't have much left. It was time to finish it.

I undressed quickly and put on a nightgown and my robe. Then, once again settling into the chair by the fire, I began to read.

CHAPTER TWENTY-THREE

I read, as I had before, putting the names of the people at Lyonsgate where the pseudonyms had been. I could feel the momentum building in the story as things came rushing to a climax. Isobel had done a good job of creating tension and suspense. Even though I knew the conclusion, I found myself caught up in the drama of it all.

I came at last to the passage about the fight that had occurred between Edwin Green and Bradford Glenn the night before Edwin's body had been discovered in the snow partway between the summer house and the manor house.

The passions were building, and it was clear that they would not be denied for much longer. The storm that was brewing would not be contained, and the clouds were prepared to burst, raining down fury upon them all.

There was a tension that hovered in the air that

night, as sure as the cold that hovered in the air outside. As bitter as the wind that howled through the trees, it wound its way through their hearts, stinging everything it touched.

The water in the lake was too frozen to launch the boat as they had intended, and the cold wind had swept away much of their enthusiasm. Into the summer house they went. One of the servants had managed to start a fire, but it was a paltry weapon against the cold, and so they poured more drinks to warm themselves instead.

Beatrice sat, head held high, basking in the glow of their attentions and the heated animosity between the men who vied for her hand. She was queen of her realm and heedless of impending tragedy. She was in no hurry to make a decision between the two men. She enjoyed the power she held over them, the strength it gave her.

Already her anger at Bradford had faded, for she did not intend to lose him, not completely. She had forced him to plead, to beg at her feet for forgiveness and, with the air of a merciful queen, she had granted him pardon.

Bradford, eager to worship his gracious sovereign, had poured a drink into a glass, a bit of it sloshing over the sides in his unsteady hands, and carried it to her. Their hands brushed, and the drink spilt across her fingers. He laughed and lowered his head, his lips brushing the liquid from her knuckles.

It was only when he had managed to take his eyes

from hers that he saw Edwin Green watching him from across the room with dark eyes.

'I don't know why you look at me that way,' Bradford said, a rush of hatred welling up inside of him. 'She doesn't want you, Edwin. She never has.'

'You think I don't know what you've been doing?' Edwin cried. 'Of course, I know. And you aren't going to get away with it. I hope you understand that.'

'Why you . . .' Bradford launched himself across the room with a speed that startled them all. He struck Edwin on the jaw, and Edwin staggered back before hurling himself forward at Bradford. They began to fight, hitting, grabbing at each other. They were, neither of them, completely sober, and their blows were ineffectual. Nevertheless, they continued to rain them down upon each other, two stags fighting for their territory.

They all watched, Beatrice with the glint of approval in her eyes. It was all that she had hoped, having the two of them fight for her hand.

'Enough of this,' Isobel said at last, somehow slipping into the midst of the fray, her slender frame dwarfed by the two men who towered over her. She stood, in danger of blows from either of the enraged men, but she did not seem to realise the peril in which she had placed herself.

'There's no reason to come to blows over this. Go to your corners, gentlemen, and have a drink.'

There was a moment of silence before Bradford

turned, walking towards Beatrice and taking a seat
beside her. Edwin stared at him for a moment before
he took a seat himself.

It wasn't over between them, Bradford vowed
to himself. He had reached the end of his patience
with Edwin Green. Things would have to be settled
between them, once and for all.

I couldn't help but smile at the regal and heroic way in which Isobel Van Allen had portrayed herself. Apparently, the gentlemen had heeded her words, for they had both backed down, though there was still, according to Isobel's book, 'the stench of bitter hatred in the air.'

It was also patently obvious that Isobel Van Allen had not liked Beatrice Lyons in the least. I wondered if her unflattering portrayal of Beatrice had been out of jealousy. Perhaps Isobel had been angry that two of the men at Lyonsgate had not wanted to be with her, but had chosen Beatrice instead.

Was it possible that Isobel had been in love with either of the two men? Laurel had said that things had cooled considerably between Isobel and Reggie before that weekend, and I had wondered if she might have fallen in love with someone else. I had thought, when talking to Mr Winters, that he might have been the other man, but it seemed that he had not held sway over her heart for long.

I considered it. It seemed unlikely that she had loved Edwin Green. As mercenary as she might have been, I could not see her attempting to profit from the tragic death of a man she had loved. There was, of course, the possibility that she had done it to bring attention to Edwin's killer. Perhaps she had truly believed that Bradford had killed him and wanted to make his guilt known.

It was also possible that she might have loved Bradford Glenn and, having been scorned in favour of Beatrice, had attempted to get her revenge. If that had been her objective, she had certainly succeeded.

The next chapter was the account of the rest of the evening. It had evolved into a rather wanton affair, with all of the guests partaking in a great deal of alcohol, drugs, or some combination of the two. Isobel had not excluded herself from the revelry. Her character had consumed a great deal of alcohol and had stumbled back in a haze to her bedroom in the manor house. One by one, all of them had gone to the house until there was no one left but Bradford Glenn and Edwin Green.

At last, the moment came, and I bit my lip as my eyes moved more and more rapidly across the page.

Bradford awoke suddenly, his body stiff and sore, his head pounding, to realise that the room was empty. The others must have gone back to the house. He had fallen into a drunken stupor on the settee and hadn't heard them leave. He rose unsteadily and began to walk towards the door. He wanted to find Beatrice. He sought her, even in his drunkenness, as a sailor might seek the North Star.

That was when he saw Edwin slumped on the sofa. Edwin had had more than his share of alcohol and drugs throughout the night, and it didn't seem that he took any notice of Bradford's movements. Bradford moved closer, looking down with loathing at the still, handsome face, wondering if Edwin could feel the heat of his hatred.

Edwin shifted suddenly, and Bradford started guiltily towards the door. Yet somehow he could not bring himself to leave, not just yet. There were the hazy beginnings of a plan forming in his mind, some foreign idea that he felt he could not quite interpret. Then, as if through a fog, it came to him: he should kill Edwin.

The thought was not accompanied by the immediate sense of horror and shame such thoughts ought to have invoked. No, instead, he felt the strange stirrings of excitement, as though something he had long wanted to do was finally coming to pass. 'It would be so easy,' Bradford thought. 'So easy.'

He glanced around the room. He was still a bit unsteady, the natural movement of his muscles muddled by intoxicants, but somehow he felt that his head had never been clearer. With Edwin out of the way, he would have a clear path to Beatrice's hand. He would have her all to himself, and they could be together at last, nothing between them.

He glanced around. How would he do it? He could hit Edwin on the head with something, but even in the fog of his inebriation, he knew that would not work. He would be found out. He and Edwin were the last two here, and someone would know. Besides, he did not know if he was strong enough to deal a fatal blow, not in his current condition.

He lit a cigarette and sat on the edge of the settee, smoking and thinking. The clock ticked noisily in the background, his nerves growing tighter with each passing second, the urgency to do something building like a fire in his blood.

The wind whistled in the chimney, shrieking like the voice of an angry ghost, and it was as though that ghost spoke to him. He knew what the answer was.

He threw down his cigarette and ground it out with his toe. Then he rose and walked to the sofa where Edwin lay.

'Edwin.' He shook him with a hand on his shoulder. Nothing.

'Edwin!' he said again, loudly, shaking him harder. Still there was no movement. Perhaps it was just as well.

Edwin was unconscious, completely limp, and very heavy. Bradford pulled him up from the chair and over his shoulder. Bradford was not completely steady on his feet. He could still feel the liquor coursing through his system, slowing him down and yet giving him strength, courage.

With Edwin still draped across his shoulder, Bradford opened the door, the cold wind whipping around him. He had wondered if Edwin would wake, but he could tell now that there was no danger of that. Edwin had indulged heavily and he was already as good as dead.

The snow crunched beneath Bradford's feet,

seeping in his shoes, as he walked towards the house, his burden slung across his shoulders.

He stopped several yards from the summer house and dropped Edwin in the snow, looking down at his face for any sign of consciousness. Nothing. Edwin lay still, unmoving in the snow. He looked as though he was asleep, peacefully dreaming on a blanket of white.

Bradford looked down at him for a few moments. He felt rather like he was in a dream himself. Everything made sense, in some strange way, and yet nothing made sense at all.

It occurred to Bradford suddenly that if he wanted to make it look as though Edwin had fallen on his own, he would have to turn him. He leant down and pushed him onto his stomach, Edwin's face half buried in the snow. Perhaps he would even suffocate before he froze.

How long would it take him to die? Bradford wondered. Would there be enough time? He thought there would. The wind was blowing, and Edwin was lying on a bed of snow. Surely he would be overcome before the night was out. It would be an easy, painless way to die.

Bradford looked around, conscious now of the possibility of being seen. He looked back at the manor house, aware that lights blazed in several of the windows. It was not unusual. He knew that everyone had indulged as much as he had.

The snow had begun to increase, and Bradford

knew that it would obscure his footprints before the night was out.

He took one last look at Edwin Green lying in the snow. Then he turned and began walking towards the house without looking back.

There wasn't much in the rest of the book that was anything new. Isobel's account of the discovery of the body was surprisingly accurate, at least according to the accounts I had had from the others of that morning. Freida had gone out early and had come back screaming, having found Edwin's lifeless body in the snow.

They had all run out to where he lay, but it was too late. He had apparently been dead for several hours.

There was a chapter on the inquest and then Edwin's funeral, in which Isobel had featured prominently in her best mourning costume.

I turned to the final page.

They went their separate ways after the funeral, all of them going on to other things, to lead other lives. But for Edwin Green there would be no future. He left it there as he lay, cold and blue on the hard ground of Lyonsgate. Will his story live on? His voice whispers it into the wind. 'Who will remember me?' Who will remember the dead of winter?

CHAPTER TWENTY-FOUR

I closed the book, feeling both dissatisfied and melancholy. It was a bleak ending, and, despite Isobel's pretentions, I was still affected by the tragedy of it all. It was sad that the actions of one night had affected the lives of so many people.

I could not see, however, that it had revealed anything more than what I already knew. The question foremost in my mind had not been answered. Why had Isobel done it? Why had she written the book, and why had she implicated Bradford Glenn in Edwin Green's murder? It seemed that all of it must come back to that.

I heard a noise in Milo's room, and I assumed he must have come in from downstairs. I got up and went through the adjoining bathroom to his door.

He looked up as I entered. His valet was removing his dinner jacket, and only glanced in my direction. Parks always seemed vaguely disapproving of any interactions that took place between Milo and me in the bedroom. He thought, perhaps, that we should conduct all of our conversations in more appropriate rooms.

Milo knew this and enjoyed making Parks as uncomfortable as possible.

'You can go, Parks,' Milo said, removing his tie. 'Mrs Ames can help me undress. It's much more interesting when she does it.'

I frowned at Milo, but couldn't quite stifle a smile.

'Very good, sir,' Parks said coolly, gliding silently from the room.

'You shouldn't say such things to him,' I said when he had gone.

'I don't know who is more easily shocked, Parks or Winnelda,' Milo replied. 'It's simply too easy.'

I took a seat on Milo's bed as he continued to change from his dinner clothes.

'I've just finished the book,' I said.

'Oh? Any surprises?'

'Not really. It was all pretty much as we've heard. There's just one thing that doesn't make sense to me. I can't help but wonder why she chose to make Bradford Glenn look guilty.'

'Perhaps he was.'

I sighed. 'It can't be that easy. It's possible, of course, that she thought that he might be guilty. There was, after all, an altercation between Bradford Glenn and Edwin Green that night, presumably over the affections of Beatrice. Everyone I've talked to has admitted as much.'

'Does she say in the book how she came to suspect him?'

I shook my head. 'She only says that Bradford awoke to find himself alone with Edwin and dragged him out into the snow to die. She does mention the brightly lit windows of the house. Perhaps someone saw something out of the window. Her other scenes were accurate, from what I've been able to determine. I don't know why this one in particular should have been any different.'

'Suppose she did witness something. Why go on to write the book?' he asked. 'Out of a quest for justice? It seems unlikely.'

'Everything seems unlikely,' I said tiredly. 'Why did she do it? Why did she come back? None of it seems to make sense. And yet . . .'

There had been something in her manner at breakfast that morning. 'She asked me if I thought people must always pay for their sins. Do you think that she had come back to set the record straight?'

'Does she seem the type to travel halfway around the world to make amends for a past wrong?'

What I had seen of her did not seem to indicate that justice might have been what she was striving for. What had it been, then? Some revenge of her own? Had she known something that was worth killing her to keep secret?

'There are, it seems to me, two possibilities,' I said. 'One is that Isobel was murdered because of something she was about to reveal. Perhaps she had some new information that led her to believe that Bradford Glenn was not the killer and that someone else was. Or perhaps there was some other secret someone did not want to come to light.'

'And the other?'

'The other is that she was killed in an act of revenge for the havoc wreaked by *The Dead of Winter*. The crime itself speaks of passion. She was killed quite brutally.'

'That's discounting the poison, of course,' Milo pointed out.

I sighed. He was right. Someone had deliberately poisoned her before she was stabbed. Why could things never be simple?

'Let's collect our thoughts, shall we?' I suggested. I had always found that an orderly list was a good way in which to gather one's thoughts. I got up from the bed and went to the desk in the corner. I sat, took a sheet of Milo's stationery out of the drawer, and picked up a pen.

'Now. Where shall we begin?' I asked.

'It's difficult to decide, as she was something of a universal bête noire. You may as well begin with the Lyons family, I suppose.'

He was right. They had lost the most and had, perhaps, the most to lose if Isobel wrote another novel. Reggie Lyons had already suffered greatly as a result of Isobel Van Allen's first book. His family's reputation had been publicly destroyed, and he had been forced to leave his home for many years.

'It could have been Reggie,' I said, 'but he abhors the sight of blood.'

'Men have been known to overcome greater obstacles.'

'Yes, you're right. He has been very distraught since it happened. Perhaps he's suffering from the guilt of what he's done.'

'He might just have easily tried to poison her.'

'And when that didn't work, he flew at her in a rage.'

Milo nodded for me to continue. 'Beatrice seems like a more likely suspect than Reggie,' I said. Beatrice Lyons Kline had, as far as I could see, two reasons that she might have killed Isobel. 'She might have wanted to silence her, but she might also have wanted revenge. She seems very cool and calculating. Perhaps she has been waiting all this time to repay Isobel for what she did to the Lyons family.'

'She's capable of it,' Milo said. 'Whether or not she actually did it is another matter.'

'What about Lucinda?' I was tempted to discount the younger Lyons sister, but knew that I could not rule her out. She had not been at the scene of Edwin Green's murder, and, as a girl of sixteen, would not have had the physical strength necessary to move Edwin out into the snow. That did not, however, clear her of Isobel's death.

Milo shrugged. 'It's possible. She is a bit conniving.'

I was sceptical. Feigning a runaway horse was one thing. Murder was quite another.

'She was sent to a different boarding school abroad after what happened and seldom had the opportunity to see her siblings. Perhaps she has been harbouring bitterness against Isobel for the way her family fell apart.'

'From what I understand, they weren't much of a family to begin with,' Milo said.

'Yes, that's true. Speaking of which, how was she tonight?'

'Much the same as usual. That is to say, a bit tiresome.' This was another reason I had not wanted Milo to encourage her. I had known that it would only be a matter of time before his amusement with her waned, and her feelings were bound to be hurt. He was sometimes very careless about such things.

'Well, do try to be nice to her, Milo. She's very unsure of herself. It can't have been easy to grow up the way she did. After all, she is much younger than Reggie and Beatrice, and was sent away immediately after the scandal. Her life has been very lonely.'

'We were all sent away to school,' Milo said. 'It didn't do us any lasting harm.'

'You are much more confident in yourself than Lucinda Lyons,' I said.

'I don't know about that,' he replied. 'She seems confident enough to me.'

'Confident enough to commit a murder?' I challenged.

'Perhaps.'

'Well, in any event, while the Lyons family has its motives, it could just as easily be Mr Roberts who perpetrated a crime of passion.'

'Very possibly. She wasn't at all kind to him.'

I had seen the way that Isobel treated Desmond Roberts, heard the harsh way in which she spoke to him. She might have pushed him too far. A stabbing spoke of rage. That wouldn't explain, of course, who had poisoned her. Mr Roberts had possessed a vial of poison and a rather dubious reason for possessing it. He might have tried one and then resorted to the other.

'I don't like to think that Freida might have done it, of course,' I said.

'Of course,' Milo replied. He always liked to say that I

picked out the people I liked best and excluded them from the crime. That was simply not the case. I just felt I knew who was likely to be guilty and who was not. I was surprised he had not yet offered up Laurel as a potential suspect.

'I don't like to think it,' I went on, 'but it *is* possible Freida might have done it. She was devastated by the publication of the book. She had still been suffering for years after the loss of her fiancé and had just married Mr Collins. The fragile stability of her life had been torn apart by the scandal, but I don't think that revenge would motivate her. I find it difficult to believe that she would risk such a thing, given her love for her children, but . . .' My voice trailed off.

'The desire to protect them might prove worth the risk to her,' Milo said, and I nodded. If she was willing to do anything to keep them safe, it was possible that she had thought there were secrets worth killing Isobel to protect.

'The same might be said for Phillip Collins.' It was not hard for me to believe that he might be a killer, but what had his motive been? Were there secrets in his rather murky past that he did not want revealed? He cared for Freida. I had seen it in his eyes. Was there some secret in her past that he was guarding?

'That Collins fellow is a rotter,' Milo said without any great emotion.

'You've noticed that, have you?'

'He doesn't make any great effort to hide it, does he? I had the dubious pleasure of a long conversation with him this afternoon, and it's not an experience I would care to repeat.'

My interest was piqued. 'Oh? What did he say?'

'Nothing of consequence. He spoke extensively of his landholdings in South Africa. It wasn't so much what he said. It's his manner that's repugnant.'

'Yes, I don't think he's a nice man at all.'

'That doesn't, of course, make him a killer.'

'It would be so much easier if it did.' I sighed.

Milo smiled. 'No one said detective work was easy, darling.'

'No, I suppose not. Well, that leaves Mr Winters,' I said. 'What might his motive be?'

'Why don't you answer that? You are much more intimately acquainted with him than I am.'

'I will have you know that Mr Winters behaved like a gentleman all afternoon.'

'Well, it's a wonder he could keep his hands off of you. He waxed rhapsodic about your beauty to me for a full ten minutes in the drawing room tonight. I shall be surprised if he fails to paint you with a halo and wings.'

I laughed. 'You're quite ridiculous.'

'Not that I can blame him, of course. You're simply breathtaking. I sometimes wonder why I sit discussing murders with you when there are so many other amusing possibilities.'

'Milo, do try to concentrate,' I said with mock severity.

'If you're wondering if I think Gareth Winters has it in him to repeatedly stab someone with a knife, I would have to say no.'

I nodded. I felt much the same way. However, it was difficult to tell about Mr Winters. I had wondered more than once if his show of airy detachment was not entirely authentic. It was possible that he had fabricated the persona to keep from revealing too much of himself. Perhaps he had bared some part of himself to Isobel that he was afraid she would include in a second book.

'He told me that he loved Isobel. Do you suppose it was possible that he . . .'

'Loved her enough to kill her?' Milo supplied. 'It wouldn't be the first time such a thing has happened.'

'Murder is such a complex business.' I said. 'It could conceivably be any of them.'

It seemed likely that everyone had secrets they wanted to protect. Now I had only to discover what they were.

Unfortunately, there was no way of knowing what had happened that night, not really. Even the people who had been there didn't really know what had occurred. If Edwin Green's death had not been murder, what other secrets could Isobel have known?

I remembered suddenly that Reggie had mentioned that Isobel would sometimes use the summer house for writing. I wondered if any of her manuscripts had been left there. It was just possible that they would provide the information necessary to tie everything together.

I could think of no conceivable way to visit the summer house without appearing morbidly curious.

Milo said something, but I was too preoccupied to hear it. I looked up. 'Hmm?'

'Do you plan to sleep here tonight, or shall we retire to your room?'

'My room, I suppose,' I said, rising from the little

desk chair. 'I think it may be slightly warmer. Unless . . .'

He looked at me expectantly.

'You want to steal away to the summer house with me.'

'Absolutely not,' he answered without hesitation.

I frowned at him, but he shook his head, unmoved.

'It's not very far,' I pressed. 'We could take a moonlight stroll and if it led us there . . .'

'Are you going to your bed,' he interrupted, 'or shall I carry you there?'

Milo was seldom adamant about anything, so I had the distinct feeling he was not going to give in. Perhaps I would find a way to investigate the summer house tomorrow.

I capitulated, but he carried me to bed anyway.

CHAPTER TWENTY-FIVE

I reached the breakfast room early the next morning and found that Mr Roberts was the only one who had arrived. Though I had pestered the maids for frequent updates on his condition, this morning was the first time I had seen him since his collapse.

'Oh, good morning, Mr Roberts,' I said.

'Mrs Ames.'

He started to rise, but I held up my hand. 'Don't get up,' I said sternly. 'I don't want you to trouble yourself. How you are feeling?'

'I'm all right,' he said, though he didn't look it. He was very pale, and he looked as though he had lost weight. I glanced at his plate and saw that he had only a piece of toast with marmalade and a cup of tea. He certainly needed something more than that if he was going to regain his strength.

'You're up early,' I commented, going to fill my own plate.

'Yes, I couldn't bear to lie alone in that room any longer.'

'I imagine that it was fairly lonely. I'm glad you're feeling well enough to come downstairs.'

'Yes,' he said. 'I've had a bit to eat, and it seems to have gone down all right.'

'I'm glad to hear it.'

I poured myself a cup of coffee and went to sit down at the table across from him.

'What will you do when all of this is done?' I asked, hoping to speak of pleasanter things. 'Do you plan to go back to Africa?'

I was stirring the milk and sugar into my coffee, so it took me a moment to realise that he hadn't answered.

I looked up. He didn't meet my gaze, and, to my horror, I saw his face was streaked with tears. I felt immediately as though I should retreat, having foisted my company and insensitive questions upon him in what was obviously a difficult time for him. However, there was really no way I could gracefully extricate myself from the situation.

It was a dreadfully uncomfortable scene, but I also felt a great deal of sympathy for the young man across from me.

'I'm sorry if I've said something wrong,' I said gently.

He shook his head and wiped a hand across his face, sniffling, and he reminded me for a moment of a very young boy. My compassion warred with my reserve and won the day. I reached across the table and touched his hand. 'Is there anything that I can do for you?'

He shook his head. 'There's nothing that can be done now,' he said forlornly. 'I can never go back.'

I sat there helplessly for a moment, unsure of how to

proceed. Then I rose from my seat to approach him and pat him gently on the shoulder.

'I'm sorry, Mrs Ames,' he said, not looking up. 'I'm sorry for you to see me like this. I'll be quite all right if you want to leave me alone.'

I didn't feel as though I should leave him alone. I took a seat in the chair beside him.

'Do you want to talk?'

'Talking won't help,' he said. 'Nothing can help now.'

'Sometimes it helps a great deal.' Normally, I would have been hesitant to press someone in such a state, but I somehow sensed that he wanted to talk, that he was fairly bursting with the need to do so. Sometimes, I had learnt, one could do the most help by sitting and listening, doing nothing at all.

'You miss Isobel,' I said gently. 'Perhaps it would make you feel better to talk about her.'

He didn't respond, but I sensed that he was not unwilling.

'You met in Kenya?' I asked, thinking that recollections of happier times would be the easiest way to start.

'Yes. She was . . .' He hesitated, flushing. 'She was involved with my brother, in fact.'

'I see.' This was not exactly what I had expected, but I could not say that I was surprised. Isobel Van Allen seemed to move through young men at an alarming rate.

I didn't intend to press for details and hoped that he would provide me with none, but he continued. 'They went to the same sort of parties, enjoyed the same things. I didn't think he was serious about her, you see. My brother was quite a man with the ladies. Isobel was interesting to him because she was older, very glamorous, you know. It appealed to him.'

I nodded, silently urging him to continue.

'They had only been seeing each other for a few months when they had a row. I thought that was the end of it. They stopped seeing each other, and my brother took up with another young woman. I noticed that he had started drinking heavily, but I didn't think much of it. He had always had a strong head for drink.'

He stared down at his tea for a moment, as though seeing the story play out before him on the surface of the liquid.

'One evening I was at a party,' he went on. 'I was very drunk. Isobel was there, and we started talking. One thing led to another, and . . . well, you can imagine.'

'Yes,' I said.

'After that, we saw each other quite frequently. She would invite me to her house. She had me type things for her as a pretence, but that wasn't why I was there. I was very much in love with her, and I thought that life couldn't be better.'

He paused, and I knew that he was about to reveal that this had not been the case.

'But then one night my brother saw us together,' he said. 'He confronted me, and I admitted that Isobel and I had been seeing each other. I . . . I didn't know how he felt about her, you see. He was terribly in love with her, too . . . but he never told me. He . . . he went insane with rage. He grabbed a gun and . . . tried to kill me.'

I'm afraid my mask of poise must have slipped then, for I was quite shocked.

He continued on, staring straight ahead. His voice had dropped so low that I almost had to lean towards him to make out the words. 'He shot at me, and, when he missed, he . . . well, he shot himself.'

I drew in a sharp breath, unable to stop myself. It was such a tragic, shocking turn of events that I couldn't seem to make sense of it all.

It seemed, however, that the telling of it had come as a great relief to Mr Roberts. Perspiration glistened on his forehead, as though a fever had broken, and he spoke faster now, the words tumbling out.

'My family blamed me, of course. Rightly so. It was my fault. I didn't know he loved her, but I should never have started to see her. I didn't know that loving her would cost so much. My father disowned me, and Isobel was ruined. We had to leave the country after that.'

And so Isobel had fled Africa, another suicide in her wake. It seemed consistent with what I knew of her character that she should have romanced the younger brother of the lover she had scorned.

Perhaps it was a cruel thing to think of someone who was dead, but I could not help but feel that Isobel Van Allen had delighted in causing pain to others. She had consistently poured salt in wounds of her own making.

I was so caught up in my thoughts, that I almost missed what Desmond Roberts was saying. His next words, however, drew me quickly back to the present.

'We didn't know where to go. It was Isobel's idea to come to Lyonsgate, to write another book. She said she had always meant to come back someday, that she had unfinished business, and now that we had no money it was an ideal time. "We shall kill two birds with one stone," she said.'

This was another surprise. I had been sure that Isobel Van Allen had made enough money from the publication of her book to last a lifetime. Had she really spent it all so frivolously?

I wanted to press him on the topic, but couldn't bring myself to be so vulgar as to enquire about her finances. The best I could manage was to formulate a question about her motives.

'Then that letter she received from Bradford Glenn was not what spurred her on, and finding out who really killed Edwin Green was not her primary objective.'

He looked up at me, and shook his head. 'No. She never received any letter from Bradford Glenn before his suicide. That was all a lie.'

I stared at him, still reeling from what he had just told me. 'What do you mean?'

'She made it up. She was trying to provoke a reaction, I think. She said she wanted the truth to come out.'

'The truth about what?' I asked.

He shook his head. 'I don't know. She wouldn't tell me.'

I recalled the conversation Milo and I had overheard between Desmond Roberts and Isobel on the stairs the day before her murder. She had said that soon enough everyone would find out what she wanted to reveal. What was it that she had meant to uncover? I wondered if we would ever know.

There were footsteps in the hall and a moment later Lucinda Lyons came into the room. She stopped when she saw us. 'Oh, good morning. I'm not interrupting, am I?'

'Not at all,' I said.

'You look as though you could use some air, Mr Roberts,' she said cheerfully. 'Would you like to go for a walk with me? I don't feel hungry just yet.'

He hesitated.

'I know it's ghastly,' she said. 'Everything's so dreadful. But perhaps you would feel a bit better if you got some air.'

He looked at me, as though waiting for my input on the subject.

'I think Miss Lyons might be right. Perhaps the fresh air would do you good.'

He stood, taking in a deep breath. 'Thank you, Mrs Ames,' he said simply, before turning and following Miss Lyons from the room.

The others trickled in to the breakfast room not long afterwards. We finished breakfast, talking pleasantly of inconsequential things, but all the while my mind was churning. Once again, I had been cast in the role of confidante, and once again I had been presented with a confusing tangle of information.

Two thoughts were at the forefront of my musings. First, that there had been some hidden motive for Isobel's return. She had wanted to come back to Lyonsgate for a specific reason, something other than the desire to gather information for a second book.

The second had to do with the tragedy that had preceded their departure from Africa. It seemed to me that Desmond Roberts now had another very good motive for wanting Isobel Van Allen dead.

* * *

I had just reached the foot of the stairs when Henson, the butler, walked towards me. 'Mrs Ames, there's a telephone call for you.'

'Oh. Thank you, Henson. I'll come directly.'

I wondered who it might be. Not many people knew I was at Lyonsgate. I went into the library and picked up the receiver. 'Hello?'

'Mrs Ames, you didn't tell me that you were at Lyonsgate,' Mrs Roland said without further greeting.

'I . . .' I hesitated, unsure of what to say. She had obviously caught me.

'It was in the papers this morning, you naughty thing,' she went on, not waiting for my confirmation. 'You do know how to involve yourself in a mystery, don't you?'

'Well, I . . .'

'I have the details on the death in Kenya. Myron Roberts. Took up with Isobel and then she threw him over for his brother. Afterwards, he killed himself with a revolver.'

'Yes, I heard something about it after I spoke with you.' Another tragedy to be laid, at least in part, at Isobel's feet.

'Nasty business, that. Isobel Van Allen once again forced to leave the country. In some ways, I suppose it's lucky she died before she had no continents left where she was welcome.'

I could think of no appropriate way to respond to this statement, but, as usual, was spared the necessity as she sailed onwards.

'Now, if you want to know about what happened when Edwin Green died at Lyonsgate, there'll be no better person than Mrs Hildegard Fletcher.'

'Hildegard Fletcher?'

'Yes, she's the sister of a dear friend of mine, Emily Bridgewater. I thought that she lived nearby, but I called Emily to confirm it. Mrs Fletcher lives in the village, has for years. Emily assures me that Hildegard would be only too happy for you to drop in for tea anytime. She loves visitors. If you want to know what really happened, I suggest you go and see her. She is likely to know more about it than I could ever tell you.'

I knew this must be a very difficult admission for Mrs Roland to make, and I very much appreciated it. 'Thank you, Mrs Roland.'

'Of course, my dear. Of course. I am only too happy to help you. Let me give you her address.'

I wrote it down, thanking her again for the trouble she had gone to on my account.

'My pleasure. Of course, if you should learn anything of interest, I would be delighted for you to tell me all about it.'

Mrs Roland had a connection with the gossip columns, and I knew that anything I could tell her about Isobel Van Allen's death would be a boon. Perhaps there would be something I could share later, when I knew more. 'I will try to ring you up if I learn anything important,' I assured her.

'Thank you, my dear. I wish you the best of luck. Happy hunting!'

As I often did after speaking to Mrs Roland, I took a moment to collect my thoughts and catch my breath.

It was then that Milo wandered into the library.

'Here you are, darling,' Milo said. 'Henson said you were on the telephone. What sort of trouble is looming now?'

'I've been talking with Mrs Roland.'

'Oh dear. Better you than me.'

'I have some interesting things to tell you,' I said, 'but wait just a moment.'

I picked up the receiver once again. There was one more call that I wanted to make.

It took the operator a while to connect me to Scotland Yard, and then the switchboard operator connected me with Detective Inspector Jones.

At last I heard the familiar voice on the other end of the line. 'This is Detective Inspector Jones.'

'Good morning, Inspector. It's Mrs Ames.'

'Mrs Ames. To what do I owe the pleasure?' As usual, I could detect a faint note of something akin to suspicion beneath the pleasant tone. I was sure he realised at once that I would not be ringing him up at this time of the morning to enquire after his health.

'Have you seen the papers this morning?'

'No, I'm afraid I haven't had the time. What is it?'

'I'm afraid it's going to be rather difficult to believe,' I said.

I was fairly certain I heard him sigh. 'Someone's dead, I suppose.'

He might have been joking, but I couldn't tell from his tone of voice. He was difficult to read in person, let alone over a long-distance telephone line. I decided to answer simply. 'Yes.'

'Who?'

'Isobel Van Allen.'

There was a pause, and then he said in his deceptively neutral tone, 'You're at Lyonsgate.'

'Yes. You know about what happened.'

'Yes, of course. Isobel Van Allen is something of an infamous figure, even after all these years. My wife read *The Dead of Winter* when it was released and was quite overcome by it.'

'She was going to write another book,' I said. 'I think that's what may have led to her murder.'

'Why don't you tell me what happened.'

I related the events as they had occurred. I tried to be as clear as possible, and I found that the recitation of facts calmed my nerves. I gave him the basic information without embellishment and withheld a great deal of what I had learnt in my own enquiries. I didn't want him to know how deeply I had involved myself, although I was fairly sure that he suspected as much.

Milo sat listening, smoking a cigarette and blowing smoke disinterestedly into the air.

'And so I feel that I am so close to the truth, and yet nothing really seems to make sense,' I concluded.

'And what is it you would like me to do?' he asked calmly.

'I'm not entirely sure,' I said. 'But I thought that perhaps you might speak with this Inspector Laszlo. Perhaps you might put in a good word for us, so to speak.'

'I doubt this Inspector Laszlo will enjoy having Scotland Yard poking into his affairs. But I can make a phone call or two.'

'Thank you, Inspector. That would be lovely.'

'I don't suppose I need to tell you not to get involved in anything dangerous, Mrs Ames.'

'Naturally, I am doing my best to keep from getting too deeply involved.'

'Liar,' Milo murmured.

'Be quiet,' I said.

'I beg your pardon?'

'Oh, not you, Inspector. I was talking to Mr Ames.'

'He's there with you? Might I speak with him?'

'Of course. Thank you again, Inspector. I shall ring you up when we are back in London with a full report.'

I turned to Milo. 'He wants to talk to you.'

Milo's brow rose, but he took the telephone from me. 'How are you, Inspector? Yes. I'm afraid so. Yes . . . it seems I can't take Amory anywhere.'

I frowned at him, but he didn't look at me, listening instead to whatever Inspector Jones was telling him.

'Yes, of course,' he said at last. 'Certainly. We shall let you know. Good day, Inspector.'

'What did he say?' I asked as Milo rang off.

'It was a private conversation between two gentlemen. That's all you need to know.'

He was only trying to annoy me, and I refused to give him the satisfaction.

'Very well,' I said, sailing past him and into the hallway, 'then I shan't tell you about the very interesting conversation I had with Mr Roberts this morning.'

'Did it involve him wanting to see you in the nude?'

'Of course not.'

'Well, one never can tell here at Lyonsgate,' he said.

We reached the entrance hall and stopped at the foot of the stairs. I turned to Milo. 'I haven't time for this nonsense at the moment. Mrs Roland says her friend Mrs Fletcher might be able to provide us with information. She lives in the village. Will you take me this afternoon?'

'Of course. I've been wanting the chance to drive my car.'

'Oh, Milo, there you are!' It was Lucinda Lyons, coming down the stairs. 'I was hoping you would go riding with me this afternoon. This house is about to drive me mad. I'm sure Reggie won't mind my riding if you're with me, and I promise not to need to be rescued.'

She smiled a bit ruefully, and I supposed Beatrice's harsh comments at dinner and our subsequent conversation had discouraged Lucinda from future provocative behaviour.

'Perhaps tomorrow,' Milo replied without enthusiasm. 'I'm driving Mrs Ames to the village.'

'Oh.' She looked crestfallen for a moment, and then her face brightened. 'Perhaps I can go with you? I should love to get away from this wretched house for a while.'

'I'm afraid my car is a two-seater,' Milo said.

'Oh, I see.' She was clearly disappointed, and I felt a bit sorry for her. I could not blame her for wanting to get away from Lyonsgate, if only for the afternoon. The atmosphere seemed to become more oppressive by the hour.

Milo seemed to sense her disappointment as well. 'If you're not otherwise engaged, however, I'll teach you to play billiards after dinner,' he offered.

She smiled. Her reply was almost too quiet to hear, but I was fairly certain I had heard it right. 'I'm sure I should love anything you would care to teach me.' Apparently, she had not been completely discouraged, after all.

CHAPTER TWENTY-SIX

We drove towards the village that afternoon, Milo mercifully going a bit slower on the curving roads. There was one especially sharp curve with deep ditches along either side, and I was relieved when we passed through that area without incident.

The day was cloudy, but the occasional burst of sunlight shone through, all the more appreciated for its rarity. I felt vaguely as though I had made an escape from prison.

I leant back against the leather seat and let out a breath. 'I feel as though a great weight is lifted off me the farther we drive from the house.'

'Your colour has improved since we left.'

'It is all a bit unnerving at Lyonsgate,' I admitted. 'I'm rather on edge.'

'Perhaps it's time for the sedatives and brandy the good doctor prescribed.'

I laughed. 'I don't think that will be necessary just yet, thank you.'

We drove along in companionable silence for a few moments, and I relished the comfort I felt in Milo's presence. Things had not always been this easy between us, and the simplicity of a quiet drive along a sun-dappled road was something to be savoured. We had been through a lot together in the past year, and it had only drawn us closer.

I glanced over at him, admiring the smooth, handsome lines of his profile. I felt, as I did at odd moments, that flutter in my stomach that reminded me of when I had first fallen in love with him.

'Milo?' I asked at last, as my thoughts travelled over the events of the day.

'Hmm?'

'What did Inspector Jones say to you?'

'Still trying to extract information from unsuspecting gentlemen, I see,' he said, not taking his eyes from the road.

'I'm becoming rather good at it, I think.'

'It helps to be beautiful,' he said. 'It puts people off their guard.'

'You know that from experience, I suppose,' I replied, slightly annoyed that he should discount my skills as an investigator. 'Perhaps it's just that I have a knack for detecting.'

He glanced at me, his expression sceptical. 'Do you suppose all these men would have bared their tortured, artistic souls to you if you were a hag?'

'You're far too cynical.'

'Beauty is nothing to be ashamed of, darling. You may as well use it to your advantage.'

'Another thing you know from experience.' It was amazing the doors Milo had had opened to him – figuratively and literally – because of his good looks.

He smiled. 'I simply mean to point out that when motives are prettily packaged they are much more easily obscured.'

'Are you going to tell me what Inspector Jones said?' I demanded.

'Of course. You know I can't resist you when you frown at me that way. But I warn you: you won't like it.'

'I suspected as much.'

'He told me to do whatever was necessary to keep you out of trouble.'

'Did he indeed?' I scoffed, incensed.

'In fact, he recommended that I bring you back to London at once . . .' I opened my mouth to protest, but he didn't give me time. 'He also said that he knew you wouldn't go.'

'I'm glad my faith in his intelligence was not unfounded.'

Milo smiled. 'Now fair's fair. What did Mr Roberts tell you?'

I recounted the lurid tale of passion and death beneath the hot African sun.

'It seems Isobel incited a great many deaths,' he remarked when I had finished.

'Yes,' I replied. 'The last of which was her own.'

Mrs Hildegarde Fletcher lived in a quaint stone cottage at the end of a quiet lane in the village. She had the kind of home one would expect the village gossip to have. There was a white fence where roses would no doubt grow when the weather warmed, window boxes to hold assorted flowers, and what looked like a small kitchen garden in one corner of the tidy lawn. There were also several large windows in the house, which I felt certain would be beneficial to anyone wishing to see the comings and goings of the villagers. It was, in fact, rather an ideal setting.

I had been a bit hesitant about arriving at her house unannounced. She was, I had been led to believe, a widowed lady with a keenly developed sense of propriety. I should have thought that an unsolicited visit from a perfect stranger would be repugnant to her, but Mrs Roland had assured me that she would enjoy the company.

I had also debated the relative merits of bringing Milo with me to call. While I knew perfectly well how beneficial his charm could be, there was also the distinct possibility that he might prove a distraction.

'Perhaps you should have a drink at the tavern and come back to get me,' I said, getting out of the car before he could come around to open the door. 'I won't be long.'

Milo's brow rose. 'Trying to rid yourself of me already?'

'She is not expecting company, and I thought one might be less intrusive than two.'

'Unwanted, am I? Well, no matter,' he said. 'I shall go to the tavern as directed. I suppose there's not much mischief you can get into here.'

I closed the door without comment, and Milo smiled as he drove away.

I let myself through the fence and walked up the pathway to the door. My knock was opened punctually by a maid in a starched white apron, who told me that Mrs Fletcher would be glad to see me. It almost seemed as though she'd had warning of my coming.

I was shown into a tidy parlour that was, quite honestly, not what I expected from an elderly widow. Perhaps I had been influenced by Mrs Roland's exuberant decor. The room was exceptionally clean and almost spartan in decoration. There was a table with a serviceable white cloth and four wooden chairs without cushions, and only a few pictures hung on the walls. There were, however, bright curtains upon the window and a colourful quilt on the back of the high-backed settee.

There was a lady sitting and knitting by the fire. She rose when I entered and came to meet me at the door.

'How do you do, my dear?' she asked brightly.

She was a bit different than what I had pictured. Frankly, the name had called to mind something of a fearsome creature, but she was short and plump with a round, ruddy face. Dark eyes sparkled merrily from beneath high brows and a halo of silver hair.

'Hello, Mrs Fletcher. My name is Amory Ames.'

'Oh, yes,' she said with a wave of her hand. 'I know who you are. Your reputation precedes you.' I was not quite sure what was meant by this, but she was smiling as she said it, so I didn't think it could have been anything too dreadful.

'Sit down, won't you? Polly will bring us some tea.'

We walked to the chairs arranged before the fireplace, and I took the seat across from her. The fire was crackling merrily, and I felt immediately at home in the warm, cheerful room. The maid, Polly, came at once and brought in a tray with tea and biscuits.

When we were settled, teacups in hand, Mrs Fletcher turned her benevolent gaze upon me.

'Now, Mrs Ames, I suppose you've come to talk about Edwin Green's death.'

I was a bit surprised by this direct approach. I was not quite sure how to react to Mrs Fletcher, for she said everything in the pleasantest of voices with a cheerful expression on her face.

'Why do you suppose that?' I asked lightly.

She gave a tinkling laugh. 'Oh, Mrs Roland told me that you would likely come to call, but even if she hadn't, I keep abreast of London news, even here. You were involved in an investigation not long ago there. And before that, there was another at the seaside.'

'Yes,' I conceded. 'That's so.'

She nodded. 'Well, when I heard you were up there at Lyonsgate, I wondered if there wasn't something afoot. Not to cast aspersions on that group up there, but it isn't often that people of real quality come to these parts. The Lyonses have been gone since the tragedy, and it seemed strange to me that they should open up the manor and invite guests back so suddenly.'

She took a delicate sip of her tea before continuing.

'After I heard about what happened to Isobel Van Allen, I knew that I must be right. There was something behind the sudden gathering at Lyonsgate. It didn't take much to figure out that it must all have something to do with Edwin Green's death all those years ago. That's what started this whole mess, isn't it?'

'Yes,' I said slowly. Inwardly I was debating on how candid

I should be. I was often seen as a society wife with a head full of dinner parties and fashion. I was much more, of course, beneath the surface, but the guise was sometimes useful.

I had the feeling, however, that it would not be useful with Mrs Fletcher. It seemed that she already knew why I was here, so I could see no good reason to conceal my interest in the subject, especially if she was willing and able to share her recollections. 'Did you hear a lot of the tales of what was going on at Lyonsgate?'

'They were a wild group,' she said, but not unkindly. 'A great deal of flashy cars went careening through the village at all hours. And there were rumours of very strange parties. Not that it was entirely unusual, I suppose. My generation makes a great deal of fuss about youthful exuberance, as though we had no scandals of our own. We did, of course. Plenty of them. Perhaps we just went about it with a bit more decorum.' She smiled brightly, and I had a hard time imagining that Hildegarde Fletcher had ever had a hint of scandal in her youth. It would not be the first time appearances had been deceiving, however.

I decided to steer the conversation along those lines since we were already discussing the subject. 'I heard that there were several romantic entanglements that were occurring that weekend,' I said.

'Oh, yes, the rumour was that there were a great many romances going on at the time. It was much talked about, of course. The age difference being foremost among the quibbles. People frown upon such things.'

'Yes, I imagine they did,' I agreed. Isobel Van Allen's dalliances with younger men had long been a subject of gossip.

'None of us really knew, of course, what all went on up there. Rumours ran wild, as they always do. I didn't, at the time, think there was much harm in it.'

'Until Edwin Green died.'

'Yes.' She clicked her tongue sympathetically. 'That was a tragedy indeed. By all accounts, he was a fine young man.'

'Did you believe that he was murdered?' I was no longer making any pretences of being anything other than curious about what had happened the night he died.

'The thought didn't occur to me at the time, of course. Accidents happen when people behave recklessly. The coroner seemed quite sure of that. However, my husband turned to me as soon as he heard of it. "Hildy," he said, "something's not right." And he was correct. He usually was. Despite what the coroner thought, there were rumours that began circulating shortly afterwards that there might have been more to the situation than met the eye.'

'And then Bradford Glenn killed himself,' I said.

'Yes, that was unfortunate. He was a young man from a good family. He might have had a successful life, if not for all of this.'

'He claimed to be innocent in his suicide note, I understand.'

She looked thoughtful for a moment before replying. 'The note, to the best of my recollection read: "I am guilty of nothing but loving too deeply."'

I could not help but feel that it was a tragedy indeed that Bradford Glenn had been wrongfully accused and had felt that life was no longer worth living. I wondered what Beatrice felt about his suicide, if she harboured any reservations about turning away from him before he took his life.

'There was one other thing,' she said suddenly.

I looked up, suddenly alert. 'Yes?'

'It may have all been a rumour, but it does seem that smoke indicates fire, does it not? One night not long before Edwin Green's death, the doctor was called up there to Lyonsgate.'

'Dr Brockhurst?' I asked, recalling the name of the village physician Dr Jarvis had mentioned to me.

She nodded. 'He was the soul of discretion, Dr Brockhurst, but you know how things get around. It was whispered that one of the women was . . . in a delicate condition.'

'I see.'

I was not entirely surprised that one of the women had turned up pregnant, given that exuberant behaviour had been the norm. In fact, I rather suspected it must have been Freida. She told me that her son was nearly seven years old. That would have put his birth in the same year as the tragedy at Lyonsgate.

Perhaps that was why she had chosen to marry Mr Collins. She wouldn't be the first woman who had been forced to make a marriage she regretted because of an accidental pregnancy. Was this the secret she had been hiding?

It was certainly something to think over.

We finished our tea, and I felt that I had probably taken up enough of Mrs Fletcher's time.

I rose, thanking her for the tea. 'It was very nice of you to see me on such short notice,' I said.

'Oh, I have very little to do these days. I'm always happy

to have a bit of company. Although,' she said as she poured herself another cup, 'I was hoping you would bring your husband.'

I looked up, a bit surprised. Of course, Milo was much more well known on the gossip circuit than was I. It was, I supposed, quite natural that Mrs Fletcher should have heard of him.

'I thought perhaps it would be too much for two of us to appear uninvited.'

'Oh, I'm always happy to entertain a gentleman,' she said. 'Tell me: is he as handsome as his photographs?' She asked it bluntly, but there was that twinkle in her eye again, as though she was jesting.

'Handsomer,' I replied with a smile.

'Then you really must bring him by next time you come, my dear.'

'I shall,' I told her. I thought Milo would be interested to meet the very unique Mrs Fletcher. At the very least, he would enjoy being fawned over.

We parted ways, and I promised that I would drop in again for tea when time permitted.

As I left the house, I couldn't help but think that, as overwhelming as Mrs Roland could be at times, she was certainly a valuable resource.

CHAPTER TWENTY-SEVEN

'Did you learn anything of interest?' Milo asked, when I was back in the car.

'Yes, I think so,' I said distractedly. There had been a great deal that Mrs Fletcher had told me that had been very interesting. Some of it, of course, I had already known. I felt, however, that there was something important that she had told me, some piece of information the import of which I had not yet realised.

I went over what she had said in my mind, trying to pick out the pieces that I thought were most significant. There was something . . .

'I encountered an interesting gentleman in the pub who had some very intriguing talés to tell,' Milo said. 'Apparently, he was once an undergardener at Lyonsgate.'

This caught my attention. 'Oh?'

'Yes. I told him I was staying at Lyonsgate, which

appeared not to be a point in my favour. A few pints did wonders to warm him up, however.'

Milo might carry himself with the unmistakable air of a wealthy gentleman, but he was unfailing in his ability to set people of all classes at ease, be it with good looks, charm, or simple bribery.

'What did he say about the goings-on at Lyonsgate?'

'Much the same as what we have heard. Tales of bacchanalian revels. It appears there was no shortage of high spirits among the group there.'

I nodded. 'Mrs Fletcher said much the same thing. They were only rumours, of course, but she also said one of the women was pregnant. I think it must have been Freida Collins. Her son is about the right age. She has been hiding something. I wonder if that could be it.'

'It wouldn't matter now, surely,' Milo said. 'She wouldn't be the first woman we've known who had to rush the wedding plans.'

'No,' I said, 'and that's exactly why I wonder if there is something else . . .'

'There is, in fact.'

'What?'

'Interesting you should mention Mrs Collins. It was her husband that came up in my conversation with the undergardener.'

'Really?' I asked, suddenly excited at the prospect of some revealing clue. 'What did he say?'

'He said that, on the night of Edwin Green's death, he was up rather late, and he saw two figures coming up from the summer house. He looked away for a few moments, and when he looked back there was only one person entering the house.'

'It wasn't Bradford Glenn?'

'No, it was Phillip Collins.'

'It might have been at any time of the night. They all came up at one time or another.'

Milo shook his head. 'He said that he saw the others come up much earlier and was surprised to see a final gentleman return so much later. It seems he was rather interested in their activities. I can only imagine the goings-on at Lyonsgate provided many an interesting tale to share in the pub.'

I considered this newest piece of information. Was it possible that it was Mr Collins that Isobel Van Allen had seen that night? Had she mistaken him for Bradford Glenn and decided that he must have been responsible for Edwin Green's death?

'He never said anything?' I asked.

'Who was he going to tell? Undergardeners don't have a wide circle of influence, you know.'

'Yes, I suppose, but to think that some misunderstanding might have led to Bradford Glenn's taking his own life. It's all so terrible.'

'No one forced Bradford Glenn to commit suicide, you know,' Milo said. 'It was only a rumour, after all.' Milo was not one to waste sympathy for something he viewed as a weakness. He had never cared in the least what people thought and would therefore be unable to understand the damage that public condemnation could do to a less indomitable personality.

'Yes,' I said, 'but it's still so tragic.'

'In any event, the gentleman in the tavern gave me one other piece of information. Did you know Phillip Collins came here from South Africa ten years ago because he killed a man in a tavern brawl?'

My brows went up. 'I certainly didn't.'

'And one guess as to how he killed him.'

'With a knife,' I said.

'Exactly.'

I sat back against the seat, as the implications of this information rushed in. 'Why was he not arrested for that murder?'

'The other man had a knife as well, and witness accounts varied as to what had actually occurred. In the end, they decided not to charge him. It caused a terrific scandal, however, and that's what sent him here. I gather he took up with Isobel's lot shortly after his arrival. He entered into an investment venture with Edwin Green as the public face of it, while he wooed and won your friend Freida, forcing her to marry him when she came up pregnant. All neatly accomplished in a matter of months.'

'Reggie said Mr Collins and Mr Green quarrelled over the investments. Do you think perhaps he killed Edwin Green and then, thinking Isobel had somehow realised his guilt, killed her to cover it up?'

Milo shrugged. 'It's possible.'

It was all beginning to make sense. Freida must have known something was wrong when Edwin Green was found dead, but she had likely just found out about her pregnancy. If Mr Collins had been arrested, it would have left her in a very bad way. I didn't know if her fate could have warranted marrying a murderer, but there was no accounting for the decisions one made in extreme circumstances.

It seemed outlandish, but it was certainly possible. Poor sweet Freida. Was it possible that she had been married all this time to a man she feared in an attempt to protect her family?

'Milo,' I said, 'I think we'd better stop and have a word with Inspector Laszlo.' With perfect timing, it began to rain. It summed up perfectly how I felt about the inspector.

He glanced over at me. 'Are you certain? I thought you and the inspector were on less-than-friendly terms.'

'I'm going to have to try to look past his boorish manners,' I said. 'This is important.'

As it turned out, I did not have to worry. The sergeant at the desk looked up at me, unimpressed with my urgency.

'He's not here, madam.'

'Oh,' I said, disappointed. This I hadn't expected. I had supposed police inspectors did a good deal of sitting behind desks waiting for crimes to be committed. 'I don't suppose you know when he will be back?'

'I'm afraid not.' He looked down at a paper before him, apparently dismissing me.

'Well, do you think it would be possible to have him telephone me at Lyonsgate when he returns?' I asked.

He looked up. 'Lyonsgate is where he's gone, madam.'

That was even better.

'Excellent,' I said. 'Might I use your telephone?'

He allowed me to telephone, though he didn't look exceptionally pleased about it. I wondered if Inspector

Laszlo had been telling tales about me. Or perhaps he merely distrusted anyone who came from the vicinity of Lyonsgate.

When Laurel came on the line she sounded breathless, as though she had rushed to the phone. 'Yes, Amory, what is it? Is something wrong?'

'No. That is . . . I'm not sure. I think that perhaps I know who the killer is.'

'Oh, is that all?' she asked, her voice heavy with sarcasm. 'Well, tell me. Who is it?'

'I . . . I don't want to say just now. Is Inspector Laszlo still there?'

'Yes. Do you want to speak with him?'

'No,' I said. 'Not now. But will you tell him that I have some very important information if he will wait for me there?'

'Yes, certainly. Amory . . .'

'Yes?'

'Be careful.'

We started back towards Lyonsgate, and, in keeping with the atmosphere of the evening, it seemed as though the bottom fell out of the clouds. The rain was coming down in torrents. I supposed we were lucky it wasn't snowing. Then again, this was worse than a blizzard would have been.

Milo drove surprisingly slowly along the muddy roads, as it was difficult to see through the blinding rain. I couldn't help but feel it was more for the car's safety than for our own.

'Perhaps we had better stop until it lets up,' I said.

'It's likely going to rain all night,' he said. 'We may as well keep going. We'll be back to Lyonsgate soon enough.'

I hoped that he was right. I had a distinctly uneasy feeling that I somehow felt was not entirely to do with the rain. Perhaps it was that I felt we were very near to revealing the identity of a killer.

I thought again of poor Freida. What would she do if Phillip Collins was hanged for the murder of Isobel Van Allen? It would be another crushing blow in a life that had already been marred by tragedy. I almost couldn't bear to think of it.

Suddenly, there were lights behind us. I turned around to look. A car was coming up fairly quickly, appearing as if from nowhere out of the rain. It must have come from one of the little lanes that occasionally broke through the trees, perhaps leading to nearby houses.

The car came on quickly, as though it didn't see us, and I felt a sudden rush of apprehension. The road was very wet, and I hoped we wouldn't be hit from behind by a careless driver. Not only that, we were approaching the part of the road that was lined by the deepest of the ditches. Sliding into one at these speeds might very well prove fatal.

But no, I was being unduly alarmed. The murder had set me on edge, and now I seemed to see a threat around every corner. Still, I couldn't help but look back over my shoulder.

It seemed to me that the lights of the car behind us were growing closer.

I turned back to the road ahead of us. We were about to round the narrow curve, and the deep ditches were just on the other side.

'That car is coming up quickly,' I said.

'Yes, I noticed.' Milo increased our speed, the car shooting over the wet road, and we rounded the curve at a pace that had my heart in my throat. I clutched the edge of my seat.

The car behind us was not daunted. It matched our pace. In fact, it seemed to be gaining on us.

'Milo . . .' I began warily.

Milo looked over his shoulder and then at me. 'Darling, I think you should brace yourself.'

I looked at him. 'What do you mean?'

Milo didn't have time to respond before he swerved to the left just as the car behind us jetted past, swiping along the side of the car. It seemed then that everything began to happen very slowly, and yet there was not time enough to do anything about it. I watched the car continue on without slowing, disappearing into the rain.

It felt as though our automobile hovered for a moment on some invisible precipice and then we slid off the road into the ditch.

CHAPTER TWENTY-EIGHT

Thanks to Milo's swift reaction, we did not drop off at the deepest part of the ditch. The trench into which we slid was relatively shallow, but the impact was still jarring as we hit the bottom, coming to a stop. It seemed we sat in silence for a fraction of a moment, the rain pounding against the roof.

'Are you all right, Amory?' Milo asked, turning to look at me.

I took inventory. Everything seemed to be in working order. 'Yes, are you?'

'Certainly, but I'm afraid the same can't be said for my car.'

He pushed open the door.

'Milo, perhaps you shouldn't . . .'

He ignored me and stepped out into the rain. Because of the angle at which we had landed, I was unable to open the door on my side. In fact, I was leaning against it. Not that it mattered. I had no intention of getting out in the rain until absolutely necessary.

I wished that I had thought to bring a rain jacket. It had been cold and crisp only this morning. It hadn't occurred to me that we could be forced to drive home in a torrential downpour.

Milo circled the car, taking stock of the damage, completely ignoring the rain pelting down upon him. I caught occasional glimpses of his features in the light of the car's headlights, and it didn't look as though the news was good.

A moment later, he got back into the car.

'How bad is it?' I asked.

'It appears that the damage is minimal, but there'll be no getting it out of the ditch until morning, I'm afraid.'

I considered the implications of this piece of news. This road was practically deserted during the day. I did not think it was likely that another car would come along before morning. It was far too cold to sit in the car all night. We would be miserable, especially Milo now that he was wet to the skin. It seemed that there was only one option remaining.

'We'll have to walk,' I said. It was only a few miles back to Lyonsgate, not a walk I relished, but certainly not impossible.

'We could wait in the car,' Milo said. 'But I don't suppose anyone is bound to come along this time of night.'

'Yes, there's rarely anyone on this road, and it's getting colder. Lyonsgate can't be that far, can it? We should be able to reach it fairly quickly on foot.'

'In this rain? Your shoes won't hold up, I'm afraid.'

I looked down at my heeled leather shoes, one of my favourite pairs. I was fairly sure he was correct. Well, perhaps sacrifices would have to be made.

'It's better than spending the night in a tilted car,' I

308

said. 'We won't be able to get a moment's rest. And you're soaked clean through.'

He shrugged. 'Very well. If you're game, I am. You'll have to come out this way. Your door won't open.'

He got out of the car, then reached in to take my hand. I climbed across the seat and out of the driver's side door. His hands on my waist, he lifted me to the ground and I stepped into ankle-deep water. I leapt sideways and sank into a pool of mud. Very cold mud.

'You might have set me down on the road,' I grumbled.

'The road is wet, too. Everything is wet.'

'An astute observation.'

Milo held out his hand and I clasped it. Then we climbed up out of the ditch. In a matter of moments, I was completely soaked, my hair falling into my face, and commenced at once to shivering. I could only assume that a brisk walk would do something to warm me up.

We began trudging along, the rain showing us no pity. I had tried holding a newspaper I had found in the car over my head, but it had become limp and sodden within seconds, and I had given it up.

I stepped into another puddle and somehow a stone became lodged in my shoe. I fished out the stone, tossing it aside.

'Shall I carry you, darling?' Milo offered.

It was a tempting offer, but there was no reason why he should have to lug me across the country like a sack of grain. It wasn't his fault we had been run off the road. I thought about the driver of that car. Surely they must have seen us go into the ditch. Common courtesy would have dictated that they come back to help us.

'I wonder who was driving that car,' I said.

'A very good question. I am also curious as to why they should want to run us off the road.'

'The road was wet, and it was very dark.'

'That it was, my love, but that was not the reason the car hit us.'

I stopped and turned to look at him. 'What do you mean? Are you saying they hit us intentionally?'

He smiled. 'That is exactly what I'm saying.'

'Are you sure?'

'Quite sure.'

'But that's horrible.'

'It certainly wasn't very nice,' he agreed.

In my shock, I stood staring at him. He took my arm in his and pulled me along. 'Come, darling. You may gape at me later, when we're out of this weather.'

I quickened my steps to keep up with him. 'But who might it have been?'

'I can only assume that it was someone from Lyonsgate.'

'But, how . . .'

'There are other roads that lead to the village from Lyonsgate, I'm sure. Someone must have heard your call to Laurel and decided to stop us.'

It was possible, of course. It was likely that she had, in her haste, taken my call on the hall telephone, where anyone might have overheard her.

If so, had they really sneaked from the house and brought out a car to push us into the ditch?

'But that's dreadful!' I said.

'Well, you may tell them all about how dreadful it is if we ever get back to the house.'

Yes, but who? The likely candidate was Mr Collins. Perhaps he had overheard what I had said to Laurel and had left the house in order to silence us. He could not, however, be sure that his plan would succeed. He must have seen that we had not gone off the road in a dangerous spot and had survived his attempt unscathed. Surely he must know that we would point him out when we reached the house.

But perhaps he didn't care. After all, there was no proof against him. We could tell our theory, but I was certain that if Freida had shielded him for this long, she would continue to do so.

If only there was some way to find proof.

We walked a few more moments in silence. When I spotted a slight clearing, little more than an overgrown path through the trees, in the direction of Lyonsgate, an idea came to me.

I stopped suddenly. 'Milo, I think we should try to get to the summer house. I don't think it's very far from here.'

'The summer house?'

'Yes. Reggie told me that Isobel used to write in the summer house. And that she kept photographs and newspaper clippings about the group there. Perhaps we can find some evidence . . .'

'Darling,' Milo said, his voice betraying a hint of impatience. 'I don't think now is the time . . .'

'Now might be the only time,' I protested. 'And it's closer than the house in any event. Perhaps the rain will die down while we search.'

Luckily, it was too dark for me to see Milo's expression. I was sure it was not approving. 'Very well, darling,' he said at last. 'Lead the way.'

I trudged along the little path through the trees, my feet sliding in the mud, cold water sloshing inside my shoes. I sincerely hoped I was right about the summer house being nearby.

We reached the edge of the path through the trees and came out on the meadow. To my relief, I could make out the dark outline of the summer house situated near the lake. The water looked cold and black, and I felt a little shiver that had nothing to do with the icy water dripping on my neck.

In the distance I could see the lights of Lyonsgate. It would be a fair walk to get back to the house. I wondered how long it would be before Laurel started to worry.

By the time we reached the summer house, I was completely soaked and could no longer feel my fingers or toes. I could only imagine how my hair looked. I glanced at Milo and found that his appearance was in no way diminished by the soaking. He looked a bit more rugged than usual, perhaps, but no less attractive. I found it very irritating.

The door was, of course, locked. I tried it a second time, just to be sure, and then I stood there a moment, trying to decide what to do.

'Shall we break a window?' Milo suggested unhelpfully.

'No, we can't do that,' I said. 'Someone would notice.'

'Well, it's not as though we don't have a good reason.'

'But, perhaps . . .' I walked to one of the windows and peered inside. I wondered . . .

I put my hands against the grime-streaked glass and

pushed. My fingers slid against the wet panes, but I tried again and the window gave ever so slightly.

'It's unlocked,' I said. I pushed against the glass again and it began to rise. At last, I had opened it wide enough for entry.

'Give me a boost,' I demanded.

Milo gave a sigh, but cupped his hands for me to step into them. I put my hands on the sill and he pushed me up. I slipped through and landed on the floor in a puddle of water that had come through with me. Rising to my feet, I went to the door and unlocked it so Milo could step inside.

He closed the door behind us and we stood for a moment in the darkness, just glad to be out of the rain. It felt as though there was something a bit sad about the place, as though the ghost of Edwin Green lingered. I shivered again.

'Lucky I don't use matches,' Milo said, pulling his silver lighter from his pocket. The light flickered, and seemed very feeble in the darkness. I resisted the urge to shudder again.

'I wonder if there are any candles about the place,' I said.

I made my way to the large stone fireplace and saw in the dim light of Milo's lighter that, even better than a candle, there was a lantern resting on the mantle. Milo came to light it, and a soft glow filled the room. I felt better already.

I turned to examine the summer house. I had expected it to be more sinister in appearance, somehow. Instead, it appeared to be much like any other long-abandoned room, dusty and cobwebbed, with white covers thrown across the furniture.

'My dress is soaked,' I said. I took the hemline in my hand and wrung it out, water dripping on the wooden floors. I was half tempted to wrap myself in one of the dust covers. My teeth were chattering with cold.

Milo took off his jacket and tossed it aside. 'I hope you're satisfied now. It was your grand scheme to come to Lyonsgate instead of what might have been a perfect holiday in Italy. Now we are stranded here when we could, at this very moment, be running naked through an Italian villa.'

I raised a brow. 'That's your idea of a perfect holiday, is it?'

'Isn't it everyone's?'

'Well, we shall have to indulge your fancies at some other time. Although, I'm half tempted to take off this wretched wet dress until we go back to the house.'

'A pity Mr Winters isn't here. He could paint your alabaster skin in the lamplight.'

I gave him a dark look before looking across at the other side of the room.

There was a large piece of furniture under a dust cover by the window. It seemed to me that it might be the right shape for a desk. I went to it and pulled away the dust cover. It was indeed a desk, a solid oak piece. I wondered if that was where Isobel had done her writing. I realised that anything of value might have been removed long ago, but there was no harm in looking.

I tried to pull open the door, but it was stuck. I gave it a firmer tug and at last it came free. There was a small stack of papers inside, and I pulled them out.

'I wonder if the police went through all of these documents,' I said.

'I doubt it. They thought it was an accident. They would

have had little reason to do a thorough search of the premises.'

That was a good point, and it gave me hope that I might find something of value.

I began sifting through the papers. There were a few sketches of Isobel that seemed to me to be the predecessors of the painting Mr Winters had shown me in the picture gallery. She really had been a lovely woman.

Beneath those there were some sketches that could belong to no one but Lucinda. I remembered that she had said Mr Winters had taught her to sketch. They were done in the style of fairy-tale illustrations, in bright colours. There was one of a golden-haired damsel riding behind a knight on the back of a horse and another of a maiden in a tower. Despite the youthful subject matter of the artwork, there was merit in the sketches. Lucinda Lyons had talent.

Next, there were a few photographs. There was one of a large group in fancy dress. It appeared they had been having a Grecian-themed fete, for women and men alike were draped in revealing swaths of fabric, laurel crowns resting upon their heads. I noticed the faces of the group here at Lyonsgate, full of youthful exuberance. In addition to the familiar group, there were two gentlemen I had never had the chance to meet: Edwin Green and Bradford Glenn. There had been photographs of Edwin Green in the papers after the tragedy, but this was the first time I had seen Bradford Glenn. I recognised him at once from his character's description in *The Dead of Winter*. He was dark and very handsome, his face full of the confidence of youth. He stood beside Isobel in the photograph, his eyes shining, something of a secret in his smile. I felt again a pang of sadness that so many lives should have been devastated.

I put the photographs aside and looked at the papers underneath.

There were several pages of what appeared to be a story. I assumed it must belong to Isobel, and I began reading eagerly. I was soon disappointed. It seemed that, before the tragedy, Isobel had been writing a Gothic romance of some sort.

Despite the uselessness of the story, I found myself reading it with interest. The opening pages chronicled the start of what was clearly a tempestuous romance, but it seemed that Isobel had never finished writing it. A few pages were all there were.

I set the story aside and looked again at the sketch of Isobel. Something Mr Winters had said to me that day in the picture gallery seemed to linger in the back of my mind.

I sifted through more of the papers. Beneath a few newspaper clippings, I found an envelope with a letter inside. I read the contents, my brows rising. Then I looked through the rest of the papers, and one at the bottom caught my eye. I glanced at it again. Then I picked it up and stared at it, my blood running cold as everything clicked into place.

I turned suddenly.

'Milo,' I said. 'We need to get back to the house at once.'

CHAPTER TWENTY-NINE

We made quite a sight, I'm sure, appearing at the door of Lyonsgate out of the rain, completely soaked. Milo still managed to maintain a dashing air, for the maid stood staring at him as we dripped on the wooden floors.

'Oh, Amory!' Laurel came running out to meet us. 'What on earth? What's happened? Are you all right?'

'Yes, we're fine. Our car went into a ditch.'

'Are you sure you're all right? Come, let's go upstairs and get you out of these wet clothes!'

'Just a moment,' I said, lowering my voice. 'Where is Inspector Laszlo?'

'He's gone outside to get his car. We were going to come looking for you. I was very concerned.'

'Thank you, Laurel. It seems you were right to be worried. We were run off the road.'

Her eyes widened. 'By whom?'

'I don't know, but we think it must have been someone

from Lyonsgate. Where were you when you took my call?'

'At the hall telephone.' It was as I had suspected. The telephone was located at the base of the stairs. It was possible that anyone standing on the landing above might have heard her.

'Did you notice anyone leaving the house after Amory phoned you?' Milo asked.

She shook her head. 'I spoke to Inspector Laszlo and then went upstairs to prepare for dinner. It's not likely that we would have noticed anyone slipping out. It's likely even the servants were preoccupied, and the inspector was in Reggie's study going over some notes. It would have been easy enough for someone to leave without being detected.'

'And everyone was here for dinner?' I asked.

She nodded. 'They must have arrived back just in time to come into the dining room. Oh, how dreadfully cold-blooded.'

'Speaking of cold blood, I think I will go up and change,' I said. My clothes seemed to be growing colder by the moment. 'Where is . . . everyone else?'

'In the drawing room. We've just finished dinner.'

'Good. Keep them there, will you?'

She stepped closer, lowering her voice. 'Amory, are you going to tell me . . . ?'

'In a moment,' I said. 'In the meantime, I need you to keep everyone together, and make sure that Inspector Laszlo doesn't leave.'

She nodded.

Just then Freida Collins and Mr Winters came from the drawing room.

'Oh, dear,' Freida said, her eyes sweeping over Milo and me. 'What's happened?'

'A little trouble with my car, I'm afraid,' Milo said.

Mr Winters was observing me with his pale eyes, his head tilted slightly to one side.

'I'd like to paint you as you look now, Mrs Ames,' he said at last. 'The way your gown lays when wet . . .'

'Yes,' Milo said, moving forward and taking my arm. 'Let's just go get you out of that dress, shall we?'

'If your maid is at dinner, I'd be glad to come with you,' Freida said.

I couldn't have asked for a better opportunity to speak with her. There was one matter I wanted to clear up with her, and then everything would make sense. 'Thank you, Freida. That would be lovely.'

Laurel guided Mr Winters back into the drawing room and we went upstairs, Milo to his room and Freida and I to mine.

The room that had once seemed so cold now seemed a tropical paradise in comparison to the walk we had just had.

I went behind the screen in the corner and stripped off my wet clothes, setting aside the item I had found in the summer house. My skin was damp and icy to the touch. It would be a wonder if I didn't catch my death.

Freida went to the wardrobe and pulled it open. 'You've so many lovely gowns,' she said.

'Thank you. Choose something warm, will you?'

She brought me a gown of emerald green velvet, and it felt wonderful to pull on something dry, though I would much rather have wrapped myself in a blanket and sank into my bed.

Next, I went to the mirror and tried to put my hair in some sort of order. I knew it would likely be impossible, but I did my best.

All the while, I was turning over in my mind the best way to question Freida. Finally, I decided there was nothing to do but to go ahead with it.

'Freida,' I said, turning from the mirror. 'May I ask you something?'

'Certainly,' she said at once, but I did not miss the wariness that suddenly showed itself in her eyes.

'What really happened the night that Edwin Green died?'

'I . . . I don't know. No one knows.'

'I'm sorry,' I said. 'I know that it's difficult to do, but I feel that it's very important that you tell me the truth. Mr Collins was missing that night, wasn't he?'

She was silent for a moment, and then she let out a heavy breath, as though she had been holding it in. 'Yes,' she said. 'That's why I was out there that morning. I couldn't find Phillip. I thought perhaps he was still in the summer house. And then I found the body. Edwin's face was . . . bruised, worse than I remembered it being after his fight with Bradford.'

'And you thought Mr Collins was responsible because he and Edwin had had squabbles over their mutual investments.'

She looked up at me, unable to hide the fear in her eyes. 'Yes, but . . . I didn't know for sure.' She hadn't wanted to know, and I couldn't really blame her. 'He . . . he has had some violence in his past, you see. And he was so very secretive about that night.'

'You thought it was possible, and you've been living in fear ever since?'

'Oh, no,' she said too brightly, her face trying to convey something she obviously didn't feel. 'Things haven't been all bad.'

'Haven't they?' I was a bit surprised by my forwardness and so, it seemed, was Freida. She stared at me for a moment before tears sprang to her eyes.

I immediately regretted pressing her. I was not much good with emotional scenes, and I had been involved in all too many of them as of late. However, she recovered quickly, dashing the tears away.

'It's true. I haven't been happy. He . . . he isn't a loving man, my husband,' she said. 'I should have listened to the things that people said about him, but I didn't much care. I thought I was in love, and nothing was going to change my mind. Perhaps you understand that?'

She was referring to the fact that I had fallen in love with Milo while engaged to another man. I could understand to a certain extent. My marriage had been a hasty decision, one that I had questioned the wisdom of on many occasions. Luckily, things had improved immeasurably. Perhaps the same could happen for Freida, in time.

'I'm sorry that things have been difficult for you,' I said.

She shrugged. 'I haven't been happy since . . . well, not truly happy for a very long time. But my children make me happy. And I would do anything to protect them. Anything.'

'Including shielding their father.'

She said nothing, but the look in her eyes told me that I was right.

'I know that you want to shield him in order to protect your children . . . but he didn't do it, Freida,' I said softly.

She looked up at me, blinking as though confused. 'What do you mean?'

'Your husband didn't kill Edwin Green.'

'How . . . how do you know?' There was desperation in her voice, and something else: hope.

'Because . . .' I hesitated, knowing that what I had to tell her might bring her pain. 'Because he was with Isobel Van Allen that night.'

Her eyes widened. 'What do you mean?'

'They were having an affair.'

She frowned and then, unexpectedly, she laughed. 'An affair? Isobel and Phillip? Are you sure?'

'Fairly sure,' I told her. 'At first, I suspected that he might have been involved in Edwin's death, just as you did. Then tonight I found a note from your husband to Isobel in the summer house. It was . . . fairly evident that they were . . . involved with one another. And an undergardener saw two figures coming back from the summer house late that night. One of them was your husband. He looked back later and saw your husband going into the house alone. Isobel must have just entered the house. I think they spent the night together.'

'Then you mean . . .' a smile broke out across her face, one of pure relief, 'he didn't do it. If he was with Isobel, he didn't kill Edwin.'

'Yes,' I said.

And then, to my horror, she burst into tears.

I quickly grabbed a handkerchief and pressed it into her hand. She sobbed into it, and I patted her back, feeling helpless and a bit confused. I was not entirely sure whether she was heartbroken or overjoyed.

At last she recovered herself, wiping at her face and drawing in a shaky breath. 'I thought he might have done it. I thought . . . Oh, I'm so relieved. So very relieved.'

I was relieved, too. I had worried that the revelation of the affair might upset her, but it appeared that the proof of her husband's innocence far surpassed her feelings on that subject.

I could only wonder at the strange love of Mr Collins, who had thought it better that his wife suspect him of murder rather than unfaithfulness.

A few minutes later we went back down to the drawing room. Despite my change of clothes, I still felt chill and dishevelled. Milo, of course, had never looked better.

Laurel came at once to my side as we entered the room, and pressed a cup of coffee into my hands. 'Thank you,' I said, sipping it gratefully.

'Inspector Laszlo came back in, and I told him what had happened,' she said in a low voice. 'He went out to the garage to look at the cars.'

I nodded. Surely the water on the car would have dried by now, but there was the possibility that there might be some other sign that one of the cars at Lyonsgate had been out tonight.

'Is everything all right, Mr and Mrs Ames?' Reggie asked. 'Laurel was quite worried when you didn't return home for dinner.'

'We were, in fact, run off the road,' Milo said in a nonchalant tone, lighting his cigarette.

This announcement was greeted by the appropriate level of shock from those present.

'Oh, how dreadful!' Lucinda cried. 'I do hope you weren't hurt, Milo. Or you, either, Mrs Ames!'

'No, we weren't hurt,' I said. 'But it was rather alarming. You see, someone did it on purpose.'

This was met with silence, everyone staring at us in surprise.

'What's more,' Milo added conversationally, 'we have reason to believe that it may have been someone here.'

'Why would someone do such a thing?' Beatrice asked.

Milo smiled. 'I think that's a very good question, Mrs Kline.'

She opened her mouth to reply, but at that moment Inspector Laszlo came into the room.

There was an expression on his face and something in his posture that drew my attention at once. We all stopped and watched him, as though we knew that something important was about to happen.

It was then I looked down at the object in his gloved hand. It was a knife.

He held it up. The metal glinted in the firelight and there was something else on the blade, something which looked to be dried blood.

'Does this look familiar to anyone?' he asked. His

voice was calm, almost conversational, but his dark eyes were sharp. I wondered again if, perhaps, I had underestimated him.

'What is that?' Reggie asked, his voice strained.

'This,' Inspector Laszlo said, looking down at the knife, 'appears to be the murder weapon.'

There was a moment of silence punctuated only by a slight gasp from Lucinda and a sharp intake of breath from Reggie.

'Where did you find it?' It was Beatrice who asked the question, her voice cool and calm.

The inspector's gaze moved to her, and there was something in it that made me wary of what was to come.

'Where do you suppose I found it, Mrs Kline?'

'I'm sure I don't know.'

His brow rose. 'Don't you?'

'I've just told you I don't,' she retorted, her voice hard.

He shrugged. 'Very well. Then I will tell you where I found it. I learnt that Mr and Mrs Ames were run off the road tonight, so I went out to the garage to inspect the cars. One of the automobiles had tyres heavily caked with fresh mud. When I opened the car, I found the knife. And whose car do you suppose it was?' His dark eyes bore into Beatrice. 'It was yours, Mrs Kline.'

I looked at Beatrice. True to form, her features betrayed nothing of what she was feeling. Her gaze was cold and completely blank as she looked back at the inspector.

'I'm afraid I shall have to arrest you for the murder of Isobel Van Allen,' he said.

'Very well,' she said, her tone as expressionless as her voice had been.

'No,' Reggie Lyons said, stepping forward. 'It . . . it wasn't Beatrice. It was me.'

CHAPTER THIRTY

Inspector Laszlo's handsome face registered a brief expression of surprise. 'Is that so, Mr Lyons?'

'Yes,' Reggie said. His face was flushed and his hands were trembling. 'I . . . I stabbed Isobel. I didn't want her to write another book. She did enough to ruin our lives already.'

'How did you do it?' the inspector asked.

'I . . . I stabbed her,' he said again.

'You can't bear the sight of blood,' Laurel said, and there was a hint of anxiety in her voice. She didn't want to believe it, and she was grasping at straws.

He looked at her, the sweat beading on his forehead. 'I . . . I did it in a fit of rage. I didn't have time to think about what I was doing. I'm sorry, Laurel,' he said gruffly.

'And how did the knife get into Mrs Kline's car?' Inspector Laszlo asked, supremely unmoved by the scene between Reggie and Laurel. If anything, I thought he seemed a bit annoyed at the gentle way they had spoken to each other.

'I . . . I meant to hide it,' Reggie said. 'I thought if I put it in my car, I could get rid of it later. In my haste, I must have put it in the wrong car.'

'And you drove Mr and Mrs Ames off the road on their way back from the village?'

'I . . . Yes.'

'Why?'

Reggie swallowed, licked his lips. 'I was in a hurry. I didn't mean to.'

Inspector Laszlo did not appear to be convinced. 'I think perhaps both you and Mrs Kline had better come with me.'

Beatrice nodded almost regally, the queen on her way to the scaffold. Reggie took a jolting step towards the door.

'Wait,' I said suddenly. I had been watching the surprising scene unfold as if in a daze, but it was time to act on what I knew before things went too far. 'It wasn't Reggie. Or Mrs Kline.'

Everyone seemed a bit surprised that I had spoken, for they all turned to stare at me. I was a bit surprised myself, but I knew that I must go on now that I had started. I had discovered the final pieces of the puzzle in the summer house, and it was time for the truth to be revealed. 'Reggie Lyons didn't kill Isobel Van Allen,' I repeated. 'And neither did Mrs Kline. I'm afraid that it was someone else.'

Inspector Laszlo looked extremely annoyed, but he didn't interrupt me. I had to give him credit for that.

'You see, it seemed strange from the beginning that Isobel Van Allen had chosen to return to Lyonsgate. She was having financial difficulties, it's true, but she might have written the book from Africa or anywhere in the world. She claimed to be coming back for the truth, but I think that she was coming back to have her final revenge.'

'Revenge?' Laurel asked. 'Against whom?'

I looked across the room. 'Against Beatrice.'

For a moment the mask dropped, and she actually looked surprised.

'Isobel told me that morning at breakfast that people must pay for their sins. I wondered, at first, if she meant that she was paying the price for what had happened after she wrote *The Dead of Winter*, but I don't think that's what she meant. She spoke of having once hoped to find true love.' My eyes swept over everyone present, mentally checking off Reggie, Mr Winters, and Mr Collins. They had all been her lovers.

'She worked her way through the men in your party,' I said, 'but her sights were set on Bradford Glenn. I found pieces of a romance novel she had written in the summer house, and the description of the hero fit him exactly. However, she never finished that novel. Mr Glenn never looked her way, and I think it made her furious that her relentless pursuit of him was in vain. She was, after all, accustomed to getting what she wanted. Everyone said as much. But Bradford Glenn was the one thing that had eluded her, and she decided to make him pay. When Edwin Green died, she found the perfect way to ruin his life.'

'Then Bradford didn't kill Edwin?' Laurel asked.

'No. Isobel knew that he didn't. She and . . .' I hesitated '. . . another gentleman were seen coming from the summer house late that night. They would have come across his body on their way to the house if they had been there. I can only assume that Edwin Green was still sleeping in the summer house when they left and later tried to make it back to Lyonsgate, collapsing in the snow just as the coroner's jury had ruled.'

I glanced at Freida and saw her reach over to grasp her husband's hand. Mr Collins looked momentarily startled, but he did not pull his hand away.

'She wrote the novel to revenge herself on Bradford Glenn, for having refused her,' I went on. 'When he wrote in his suicide note that he was guilty of nothing but loving too much, it must have seemed like the final affront. She could never forget it, and she could not forgive Beatrice. And so, when things became too difficult in Kenya, she decided to come back and finish what she started. She decided to tell you all that she was writing another book. She had, after all, been making a small amount of money writing romance novels. But she wouldn't show the manuscript to you, Mr Roberts.'

He looked up, the expression on his face one of misery. I knew it must be a great blow to him to know that Isobel had been consumed with a passion for vengeance so great that even after seven years all else had fallen before it. His life, the life of his brother, had meant very little to her, and the pain was clear on his handsome features.

'No,' he said softly. 'She would never show it to me.'

'That's because she wasn't really writing it,' I said.

Everyone stared at me.

'No, she was,' Reggie broke in, his voice suddenly frantic. 'I burnt it after I stabbed her.'

'Be quiet, Mr Lyons,' Inspector Lazslo said, not taking his eyes from me. 'Go on, Mrs Ames.'

'There was something burnt in Miss Van Allen's fireplace, but I don't think it was a manuscript. I don't think she ever intended to write a book because I don't think she meant to go back to Africa alive.'

Mr Roberts moaned, burying his face in his hands.

I turned to Mr Winters. He was watching me with a dreamy expression, as though what I was saying had no impact on him. Perhaps it didn't. Perhaps he would never fully connect with reality. Maybe it was better that way.

'Mr Winters, you told me that Isobel sent you a letter from Kenya, telling you that she intended to live out her days in the country that she loved.'

'Yes,' he replied. 'She swore she would never live in England again.'

'But there was a tragedy in Kenya, and Isobel was forced to leave,' I said. 'She knew that she could never return to her beloved adopted homeland, and so she decided to come back and have her revenge, even if she destroyed herself in the process.'

'It can't be true,' Mr Roberts murmured. 'It can't be.'

I felt a wave of pity for the young man whose life was falling apart, but I knew I could not stop now. The truth had to be revealed.

'Isobel had given Mr Roberts a vial of poison. It was seen by one of the servants among his things.'

'Is that true, Mr Roberts?' Inspector Laszlo asked gruffly. 'Did Miss Van Allen give you the poison?'

Mr Roberts nodded, his head still lowered. 'She bought

it before we left Kenya. When I found out, I made her give it to me. I was afraid she meant to use it on herself.'

'I think she did,' I said. 'When the time was right and she had caused enough suffering, she intended to kill Beatrice and then herself. She had arranged already for her body to be sent back to Africa.'

Mr Roberts groaned again. 'I didn't know,' he said. 'I didn't know . . .' His voice broke and his shoulders shook with silent sobs.

Lucinda moved to sit beside him, resting her hand gently on his arm.

'Which brings us to the question of Isobel's murder,' I said. I looked over at Milo and he nodded, encouraging me to continue.

'If Edwin Green's killer was not still on the loose, who would have motive to kill Isobel?' I asked. 'It seemed that if she was not killed to keep a secret safe, she must have been killed for some other reason. Revenge seems the most obvious choice. This was not exactly illuminating. Just as she wished to have revenge, any one of you might have had reason to kill her for what she had done. She ruined all your lives, after all.'

My gaze met Laurel's. Her dark eyes were troubled and her hands were resting in her lap, clenched tightly together. I wished I had been able to confide in her before now, but I felt that much rested on the element of surprise, from Laurel and everyone else. After all, I had no proof. I could only hope that, in a moment of heightened tension, the killer would let something slip. I pressed on.

'I had thought, all along, that there might be something

to be gained from knowing the story put forth in *The Dead of Winter*, and so I read it. Two scenes in particular seemed important: the scene in which the character representing Bradford Glenn attempted to strangle the character meant to be Beatrice and the scene in which the characters representing Bradford Glenn and Edwin Green came to blows.

'In the first, Mr Glenn is so angry with Beatrice that he tries to kill her, after which he professes his love. This seemed to indicate that Beatrice had rejected him, giving him a sufficient motive to do Mr Green harm.'

I looked at Beatrice. She was watching me, her face hard and expressionless.

'Isobel wrote that she and Mr Lyons had rushed into the room and witnessed the scene, which seemed to lend it validity. Then you told me yourself, Mrs Kline, that it had happened, and I had no cause to doubt it.'

'He did try to strangle Beatrice,' Reggie said. 'Isobel and I came in to find Beatrice had been forced to hit him with the candlestick, just as she wrote.'

'Yes,' I agreed. 'But that was not quite all of the story, was it?'

Reggie and Beatrice stared at me. There was a pleading expression in his eyes, and absolutely nothing in hers.

'The other scene that caught my attention was near the end of the book. Bradford Glenn was paying court to Beatrice, fawning over her, at which point Edwin Green confronted him. Mr Green's words were something to the effect of "I know what you have been doing." These words cause Mr Glenn to fly into a rage and attack Edwin Green. Does that seem accurate?'

'That's how I remember it,' Laurel said softly. 'Edwin seemed jealous that Bradford was flirting with Beatrice, and so he provoked him into a fight.'

I nodded. 'Isobel stepped in and stopped the fight. She wanted, I think, to prove herself to Bradford by defending him, but it didn't work.'

I paused, preparing myself for what I was about to reveal. I looked again at Milo. He was smoking a cigarette by the fire, his eyes on mine. Somehow I derived assurance from the steadiness of his gaze.

I continued. 'But then I went to the summer house tonight and found several documents and photographs in the drawer of the desk, and suddenly everything seemed to make sense. I realised who had killed Isobel and why. There was a secret, and it was one that Isobel never guessed.'

I drew in a breath and let the truth rush out with it.

'You see, it wasn't Beatrice that Bradford Glenn loved at all. It was Lucinda.'

CHAPTER THIRTY-ONE

Reggie swore beneath his breath and Beatrice's already expressionless face seemed to freeze in a mask of dismay, every drop of colour leached from it.

Everyone stared at me.

'Mrs Ames,' Lucinda said with a confused smile, looking up from her seat beside Mr Roberts. 'You . . . you must be joking, surely?'

'I wish I was,' I said softly.

'It isn't true,' Reggie said, rousing himself. 'I did it. I've said as much already. Arrest me, Inspector.'

'Why don't you let Mrs Ames finish her story, Mr Lyons,' Inspector Laszlo said calmly.

'I didn't think anything of it at the time, of course,' I continued, 'but more than one person made mention to me of how kind Mr Glenn was to Lucinda. That, in itself, was not especially noteworthy. Lucinda is a very pretty and amiable young woman. It's only natural that men should be kind to her.'

'What you're saying is insulting, Mrs Ames,' Reggie Lyons said, but his voice lacked conviction.

'But then all the little pieces of the story started to come together, and I saw that it was more than that. Bradford hadn't tried to strangle Beatrice because she was in love with Edwin Green. He had done it because Beatrice was trying to separate him from her sister.'

I looked at Beatrice, and she looked back at me. I could read nothing in her gaze.

'They quarrelled about his relationship with Lucinda, and he had tried to strangle Beatrice in a blind rage,' I said. 'He felt sorry for it afterwards, of course, but his temper was quick where his secret was concerned. It was the same way with the fight in the summer house. Edwin must have suspected something was going on between Bradford and Lucinda. He said "I know what you've been doing," and it angered Bradford. He had been doing his best to make people believe he was in love with Beatrice, you see. After all, what better way for him to secure perpetual invitations to Lyonsgate, where he could be with Lucinda?'

'This is absurd!' Reggie cried.

I glanced at Lucinda. She was staring straight ahead, her jaw clenched, her face pale.

'There was another thing that drew my attention to the secret romance,' I went on. 'I spoke with a woman in the village earlier today, and she made mention of a significant age difference between a rumoured pair of lovers, saying it had caused a good deal of scandal. I thought she meant that Isobel was much older than the men with whom she chose to associate. It didn't cross my mind then that it was not the relationship between an older woman and a younger man that had caused speculation. It had been a man in his mid twenties and a child of sixteen.'

'I was not a child,' Lucinda said, rising to her feet, eyes blazing. 'I was old enough to know what love was. I loved Bradford and he loved me. We were going to be married.'

'Lindy, be quiet.' Reggie said hoarsely.

'I don't care,' she said, her voice rising shrilly. 'I don't care. I'm glad she's dead. I'm glad! I'm glad!'

'Sit down, Miss Lyons,' Inspector Laszlo said.

She glared at him for a moment and then obeyed.

'Lucinda had a good reason to believe that she and Bradford would be married,' I said. 'Because she was going to have a baby.'

Laurel gasped.

'I found this in the summer house,' I said, pulling out a sketch that I had tried desperately to keep dry on the long walk back to Lyonsgate. I held it up for all to see. It was a sketch Lucinda had done, of a young woman holding a child. The face was clearly Lucinda's, her self-portrait. Bradford Glenn was drawn behind her, looking down at both of them with an expression of love.

Reggie Lyons ran a trembling hand across his face, and Beatrice stood as rigid as a statue, her eyes on her sister. I knew that everything was crashing in around them, but I also knew that the truth must be revealed. Everyone here had lived under the shadow of the past for far too long.

'There were rumours of a pregnancy in the village, as well,' I went on, 'though I thought at first it must have been one of the other women present. It wasn't until I saw this sketch that I realised what must have happened. Reggie and Beatrice sent Lucinda away to have the child and, presumably, gave it away.'

Lucinda's jaw clenched, and I knew at that moment that I had never seen such hatred in someone's eyes.

'I think he would have married her gladly,' I said. 'But Reggie and Beatrice did not mean for that to happen. They told Bradford that he was never to see Lucinda again and took her away from Lyonsgate at once.'

'They didn't even let me say goodbye,' Lucinda said. There was petulance in her tone, but there was heartbreak, too. Despite everything, I could not help but feel sorry for her.

'And then they took my baby away,' she whispered. 'My baby with Bradford.'

'Yes,' I said gently. 'And then Isobel wrote her book, accusing him of murder. Bradford, knowing that the two of you could not be together after that, decided to end his life.'

'He might have waited,' Lucinda said forlornly. 'If only he had waited for me. I didn't care that she accused him.'

I knew that Reggie and Beatrice would have done everything in their power to keep Lucinda and Bradford apart, and Bradford must have known it, too. Perhaps he knew that it could never be, not when the stigma of murder would be for ever attached to his name. The prospect of living those long, lonely years without Lucinda, accused of a murder he had not committed, had been too much for him to bear.

'When Bradford died, I knew that I would kill Isobel one day,' Lucinda said suddenly. 'She ruined our lives, and I promised myself that I would do whatever it took to make her pay, even if that meant going to Africa and killing her there. I never imagined that she would come back to Lyonsgate. It was too easy.'

'How did you do it?' Inspector Laszlo asked.

'Lindy . . .' Reggie started.

She turned to him, shaking her head. 'It doesn't matter now, Reggie.'

His head dropped, and she looked at Inspector Laszlo. 'I tried first with rat poison from the stables,' she said calmly. 'I put it in the decanter in her room, but that only made her ill.'

It must have been what had made Mr Roberts ill as well.

'And then I went to her room to talk to her. At first, we talked about her book. She thought I was concerned about the effect on the others. She was enjoying it because she thought she had power over me. There was a knock at the door, and she didn't answer it. A little while later, Mrs Ames and Mr Roberts came to the door. Isobel sent them away.'

Mr Roberts had been correct, then. There had been something wrong when we had gone to Isobel's door. Lucinda Lyons had been inside. Had Isobel known, somehow, what was going to happen? Perhaps, in the end, she had wanted Lucinda to do it.

'After they left, I told her what she had done to me,' Lucinda said. 'She couldn't believe that Bradford had loved me. I told her then what I meant to do, but she didn't seem afraid. It made me angry that she wasn't afraid. She told me then that there was no book, that she had come back for revenge as well. Suddenly, she laughed, as though it was all some great joke. I stabbed her, stabbed her again and again.'

'Lindy, please . . .' Reggie begged.

She blinked. 'I knew that people would think she had been killed to hide some secret, so I threw her address book into the fire, hoping people would believe that it was her manuscript. Then I hid the knife in the stables. But then I heard Laurel on the phone tonight, and knew that Mr and Mrs Ames must have discovered something. I decided to take the car and run them off the road.'

She related this in a very calm way, not sparing a glance at either Milo or me.

'I thought perhaps you would check the car, and so I put the knife there when I got back. Beatrice has been horrible to me, and I wanted her to pay, too.'

'Oh, Lindy,' Reggie said brokenly.

Beatrice said nothing, her lips pressed tightly together, her face white.

Lucinda looked over at Mr Roberts. His head was still in his hands, and he was shaking it back and forth. 'I'm sorry you're hurt, Mr Roberts,' she said, 'but you're lucky to be free of her.'

He didn't answer, and Lucinda looked back up at us.

'I'm not sorry I killed her,' she said, her eyes unnaturally bright. 'She shouldn't have done it. She shouldn't have written those things about Bradford. She ruined his life, ruined all of our lives.'

Inspector Laszlo took a step forward and Reggie moved into his path.

'She didn't know what she was doing,' he said, pleading. 'I'm sorry, Mr Lyons,' he said. 'I truly am.'

Then he stepped around Reggie and moved to where Lindy sat. 'Lucinda Lyons, I am charging you with the wilful murder of Isobel Van Allen.'

We all sat in the drawing room after Inspector Laszlo took Lucinda away. Reggie and Beatrice had gone out of the room with them, and I thought it would be a while before they returned. They would, I was sure, need a few moments to make sense of what had happened. We all did.

I wondered how much they had known. They had been shielding Lucinda from the start, but had they known that it was she who had killed Isobel? It seemed they must have at least suspected as much, for they had both been willing to take the blame for her. Despite what Lucinda thought about her sister and brother, they had cared for her much more than she had ever known.

'I can't believe it's true,' Freida Collins said at last. 'I can't believe it was Lucinda.' She was sitting behind her husband, and I couldn't help but think how much younger she looked. It was as though she was lighter somehow, the weight of worry and suspicion gone. They were no longer young and carefree, but it would be easier for them now, with no secrets between them.

'So Bradford was innocent all along,' Laurel said. 'Perhaps now, at least, his name will be cleared of murder . . . but to think that he was wooing Lucinda all along. It's so terribly shocking.'

It *had* been shocking, all of it. There was a sense of unreality that I felt hovering over me, as though it was something from one of Isobel's novels. Aside from Laurel and Freida, I barely knew the people here, and yet I felt deeply affected by all that had occurred. I could only imagine how difficult the coming months would be for those who had lost so much.

'How did you know she would confess, Mrs Ames?' This question came from Mr Collins. He had never appeared more at ease than he did now. Even the lines of his face had lost some of their perpetual harshness.

'I didn't,' I admitted. 'I hoped that she would, of course. I thought that if perhaps I provoked her she might let something slip.'

'You called her a child,' Milo said. 'Nothing else could have been so perfectly designed to elicit a response.'

'I thought as much myself,' I admitted. Lucinda wanted so much to be treated as a woman. To call her a child had been too great an insult to overlook. She had, however, still been a child in many ways.

The same could, perhaps, be said of Desmond Roberts. He was still very young, and this blow had been severe. I could only hope that he would be able to move past it. He had excused himself immediately after the arrest and had walked from the room like a man half dead. I was very sorry for him.

'I do hope Mr Roberts will be all right,' I said.

'He will,' Milo assured me. 'In time.'

'She asked me to look after him,' I said, remembering that odd conversation at the door to her room right before she had been murdered. 'I think she must have cared for him, in her own strange way.'

'He'll be all right,' Milo said again. 'She would have ruined him completely.'

'Just as she nearly ruined all of us,' Mr Winters said, speaking for the first time since Lucinda had been taken away, his eerily pale eyes coming up to look at us. 'Perhaps Lucinda was correct, in a way. Perhaps we're all lucky to be free of Isobel.'

It was not until much later, when I was in my room, dressed for bed, that I became suddenly overwhelmed by all that had happened, and my eyes filled with tears. It had been so dreadful, all of it, such a horrid, useless waste of so many lives.

A moment later, I felt rather than heard Milo come up behind me.

'I'm sorry, darling,' he said. 'I know how difficult this has been.'

I didn't say anything. I felt that I was going to cry, and I didn't want to give way to emotion. I felt that if I started, I might not be able to stop.

I was not accustomed to seeking comfort from my husband, but at the moment all I wanted was to feel his arms around me. Giving in to the temptation, I turned to him and he pulled me against him. For a moment he didn't say anything at all.

'Will she hang?' I asked at last.

'I don't know.'

'It's just so sad that it had to end this way,' I said. 'It might have been different if people hadn't been so determined to hurt one another. Why must people be so cruel?'

'You must admit,' Milo said, 'that all of what happened they brought on themselves.'

It was, perhaps, something of a harsh sentiment, but there was truth in it, too.

Isobel had come to have revenge upon the woman who had won Bradford Glenn's love, but she had not known that that woman intended to have revenge upon her as well.

The two women, both their hearts set on vengeance, had destroyed each other.

CHAPTER THIRTY-TWO

'I won't be sorry to see the end of this place,' I told Laurel a few days later, as Milo and I prepared to leave. Milo's car had been safely extracted from the ditch and was, to his relief, in working order, despite a few odd dents and scratches that would need to be mended. I was looking forward to returning to London, leaving the horrors of Lyonsgate behind me.

'No,' my cousin replied. 'I don't suppose you will. This has been rather difficult for all of us. And yet, I can't help but feel that things are different somehow.'

I knew what she meant. It was as though, in some strange way, the tragedies of the past week had started the healing process. After Lucinda's arrest, the fog of oppression seemed to have lifted from Lyonsgate. There was an air of sadness, certainly. There was no way, after all, for there to be a happy ending. Nevertheless, the light of truth had cast out the shadows, and there was the possibility of peace, in time.

I had spoken briefly with Reggie Lyons, and he had been kind. He had done his best to protect Lucinda, but he understood that, in the end, she had to be held responsible for her own crimes. He had spoken with a barrister and was hopeful that her age and the circumstances would incline the courts towards mercy: life imprisonment rather than hanging. I hoped that he was right.

Beatrice I had not seen. Despite her cold exterior, I knew that she had loved her sister and was very much distraught over what had happened. I hoped that, now that it was all over, she would be able to move on with her life. Mr Kline was expected to arrive from abroad any day, and I was glad she would have him to comfort her. She and Reggie would both need all the comfort they could get in the days ahead.

As though she had followed my train of thought, Laurel went on. 'I plan to go back to London soon, but I feel that Reggie and Beatrice need a friend just now. Reggie has asked me to stay for another fortnight.'

'And . . . ?' I pressed, wondering if something more than friendship was developing between my cousin and Reggie Lyons.

She smiled. 'And I expect to see a bit more of Inspector Laszlo.'

'Indeed?' I asked, my brows rising. I had not necessarily anticipated this development, but I was not entirely surprised.

'He has telephoned me once or twice.'

'How charming of him.'

'You don't really object to him, surely,' she said. 'After all, he spoke very highly of you.'

'Did he?' I was unimpressed, but I was a bit curious to know what he had said. I had, after all, solved the murder.

'Yes, he said that he was, at first, less than pleased to receive a phone call from a Scotland Yard inspector "singing your praises" as he called it.'

Had Inspector Jones sung my praises to Inspector Laszlo? The thought pleased me.

'He said that he knew there must be something in it, however. And then, when you were run off the road, he knew that it must mean something. He thought the knife in the car seemed a bit too obvious, thought that Beatrice and Reggie must be hiding something. I think he was very impressed at how you unfolded it all and made Lucinda confess.'

'Well, he is, perhaps, not as wretched as I first thought him,' I admitted ungraciously.

Laurel laughed. 'It will serve you right if I fall madly in love with him and scandalise everyone by marrying a policeman. Then we shall both have husbands that the other dislikes.'

'I suppose I could learn to like him, in time,' I said.

She hesitated. 'I am loath to admit it – I never thought I would say such a thing – but it seems to me that Milo has changed. Not much, mind you. But there's an attentiveness in him that I have never seen before, and I notice a difference between the two of you. You're more settled, happier.'

'Yes,' I said. 'We're happier now than we've ever been.'

'I'm glad,' she said sincerely. 'But don't tell Milo I said so.'

Milo and I were in the entrance hall preparing to take our leave when Mr Winters came down the stairs. I had not seen much of him since the night Lucinda had been arrested. Where he had been keeping himself I didn't know.

'I'm glad I've caught you, Mrs Ames. I was worried you'd gone.' Today his eyes were bright and there was a focus in them that I had not often seen there. He looked as though he had wandered, at least momentarily, from his dream world into ours.

'I'm glad you came to say goodbye to me, Mr Winters,' I said. 'I was hoping I would be able to see everyone before I left.'

'I've just finished your portrait,' he announced. 'Will you come and see it?'

I was surprised. I had not, of course, had the opportunity to sit for him since that first time, and in all the excitement I had actually forgotten all about the painting.

'Of course,' I said.

'Wonderful.' He turned and started in the direction of the conservatory.

'Am I invited?' Milo asked me in a low voice. 'I'm not sure he even noticed me standing here. Perhaps I shall be intruding in the conservatory.'

'Perhaps he won't much notice if you're there or not,' I retorted, following Mr Winters.

We went to the conservatory and Mr Winters moved quickly to the easel. 'I do hope you like it,' he said, turning it towards us.

We stopped before the easel, and my breath caught in my throat. It was a flattering portrait, to be sure, but it wasn't my appearance that impressed me about the painting. It was what Mr Winters had done with the colours, the way in which the light and shadows played across the room behind me. He had conveyed a sense of sadness and hope, the exact emotions that I felt now that the mystery at Lyonsgate had been solved. There was something otherworldly about the painting, just as there was about Mr Winters himself.

'It's breathtaking,' Milo said. 'You've captured her completely.'

'It's wonderful,' I said softly. 'I love it.'

Mr Winters smiled. 'I'm so glad. It has been a long time since I've painted, you know. I think that I might take it up again. There are still people who want to be painted, I suppose.'

'Oh, yes,' I answered. 'And I shall be your devoted supporter.'

'Once people see this painting, I'm sure you'll have no shortage of subjects,' Milo said. 'Now, what do I owe you for it?'

'Oh, no,' Mr Winters said, his eyes on me. 'Mrs Ames has given me enough.'

'Thank you,' I said. 'I shall treasure it.'

'Gareth Winters is a fine artist, isn't he?' I asked Milo when we were in the car and safely on our way back to London. The sun was shining and the roads had dried. I felt light and carefree.

'Wonderful,' Milo agreed. 'He did such a fine job, in fact, that I'm thinking perhaps we should commission him to paint you in the nude after all. A companion piece.'

I glanced at him disapprovingly. 'I think one portrait is quite enough.'

'If you insist.'

'And what, now?' I asked. We would want to spend some time in London, of course, but I knew Milo would not want to stay there for long. He never much liked remaining in one place for extended periods, and I felt sure that he would be anxious to get away from the city before the month was out.

'Now, my love,' Milo said, 'I intend to take you straight to Italy.'

'I thought as much,' I replied. 'Well, you'll hear no arguments from me. I am in desperate need of a holiday after this.'

'Excellent,' he said. 'I've already secured a villa.'

'I'll have Winnelda begin packing as soon as we get home. I suspect she will be terribly excited at the prospect of a trip to the continent.'

'Winnelda is not going to Italy.'

'Oh?' I asked, surprised. 'Why not?'

'Because it annoys me when she scurries about, popping in and out of rooms unexpectedly. Parks won't be coming, either. Just you and me, alone in that Italian villa.'

I had a good idea of what he was implying, but I couldn't resist asking. 'Who do you suggest tend to our clothes while we're there?'

He gave me a wicked smile, confirming my suspicions. 'We won't be needing any.'

ACKNOWLEDGEMENTS

As ever, my sincerest thanks to all the people who have made an impact on every step of this book's journey. To my wonderful family and friends; my agent, Ann Collette; and Jennifer Letwack and the fantastic teams at Thomas Dunne and Minotaur, I offer my continued gratitude. To my new editor, Anne Brewer, my heartfelt appreciation for your expert guidance on this project and thanks also to Allison & Busby for bringing Amory and Milo to UK readers. I can't thank you all enough for everything you do!